ARM CANDY WARRIOR

THE HEIGHTS CREW
BOOK TWO

By

E. M. MOORE

Edited by Heather Long

Cover by 2nd Life Designs

Huge thanks to my beta readers: Bibi, Ashton, Lisa, Jorden, Summer, Jennifer, and Angie!

Ravana Clan Vampires Series

Chosen By Darkness

Into the Darkness

Falling For Darkness

Surrender To Darkness

Ravana Clan Legacy Series

A New Genesis

Tracking Fate

Cursed Gift

Veiled History

Fractured Vision

Chosen Destiny

Order of the Akasha Series

Stripped (Prequel)

Summoned By Magic

Tempted By Magic

Ravished By Magic

Indulged By Magic

Enraged By Magic

Her Alien Scouts Series

Kain Encounters

Kain Seduction

Rise of the Morphlings Series

Of Blood and Twisted Roots

Safe Haven Academy Series

A Sky So Dark

A Dawn So Quiet

Chronicles of Cas Series

Reawakened

Hidden

Power

Severed

Rogue

The Adams' Witch Series

Bound In Blood

Cursed In Love

Witchy Librarian Cozy Mystery Series

Wicked Witchcraft

One Wicked Sister

Wicked Cool

Wicked Wiccans

I squeeze my eyes closed. *One Kyle and An-na.*

Two Kyle and An-na.

"Babe. Oh my God, babe."

No, no, no. Three Kyle and An-na.

A heavy hand skates around my back, grips my waist, and pulls me back into a hard body. I cower away from it. *He* knew. He knew this was all going down. The rest of us were like sitting ducks.

"Shh," he whispers, trying to comfort me. My life is coming apart at the seams. It's done this once before. I had to sew the pieces back together with a shitty cob job, but this might be the time when the stitches rip out fully, unable to be tied back up in a neat little revenge-ridden bow. "Are you okay?" When I don't say anything, Johnny shouts, "Is she fucking hurt? What the fuck, Magnum? I told you to watch out for her!”

“She’s injured from the fight and the escape. Not badly though.” Magnum hisses in a breath after answering, and I peek at him to see if there’s still blood dripping down his arm from the bullet that grazed him. “We were followed. Roza’s guys were shooting at us, but she hasn’t been hit.”

He’s not lying. I’m not hurt physically, but there are a million and one ways to hurt someone.

“Thank fuck.” Johnny nuzzles me again, and I squeeze my eyes shut harder. Two different parts of my brain war with one another. The one that’s thankful he’s here trying to comfort me, and the other that wishes the hands holding me belonged to someone else. Two someone elses. Guilt forces its way into my conscience like a nail being driven in with a hammer. I didn’t want Johnny to die. Hell, I didn’t want anyone to die but Big Daddy K.

“Johnny.”

My stomach heaves. I forgot he was here. In my head, I play back Big Daddy K shooting Roza in the head. The chaos that ensued afterward. The screams. The loud crack of gunshots. Because why? Why the fuck would he do that? *I* won the fight. Goddammit. I fought for nothing. Nothing.

“Take her to your place,” Big Daddy K’s calm voice says. “We have things to discuss.” He’s acting like it’s any other day. Those words slipped from his lips just as if he was asking someone to change the channel on the TV. But this isn't TV. This is real fucking life.

Johnny pats my shoulder, squeezing me there. He lowers his voice. "Come on, babe. Let me get you settled." He moves his hands around me and starts to pull me up.

I step away from him. The fuck if I need his help. "Don't," I say.

I walk toward the still open door no one else has come through. My feet are like lead weights, and my shin hurts enough that I want to fall right back down again, but I don't let that stop me. I put as much distance between me and Johnny Rocket—the whole fucking Heights Crew—as I can.

There's still so much roaring in my ears that I don't hear anyone behind me until a hand slowly wraps around my bicep right before I hit the button for the elevator. "What are you doing, babe?"

I spin toward him. My body weighs a million pounds, measured in fear and guilt and anger, and I almost trip over my feet.

When he sees me look at him for the first time, he grimaces, eyes fluttering like he can't stand to see the look on my face.

"What am I doing?" Anger rises to the surface, burying the other emotions for the time being. "I'm leaving, Rocket."

His jaw tightens, his face like stone. "You can't go anywhere. What's left of Roza's crew will be looking for you. For any of us."

The world tilts. It's as if I've been thrown off my axis again. Even if Oscar and Brawler are okay, they'll be hunted down just like me if I were to leave this building. Roza's gang is probably staking out the place. *Whoever's left*, as Johnny put it, probably has a laser sight aimed at the exit of this place.

Leaving would be a death trap. Staying could be the same.

Rocket reaches for me, but I step out of the way again. I've reverted to a petulant child, but he doesn't deserve to touch me. He never did. Maybe I was just a fool to think he could change. That he was just a victim of his circumstances. There has to be a line somewhere, right? One that says, yes, this is how he grew up, and the other that says he knows better and he doesn't give a fuck.

"Don't pull away from me. Please," Johnny pleads. His pale blue eyes melt like ice chips. Whatever kind of fucked up heart Johnny has inside of him, it's clear my actions are bothering him.

Fucking good. "Your dad killed her. He walked right up to her and pulled the trigger." As I'm saying this, it dawns on me I shouldn't be shocked. Isn't that what he did to my parents? The only difference being my parents were innocent bystanders. They weren't trying to take away Big Daddy K's fighting ring. "What was the point in having me fight if he was just going to kill her ass, anyway?"

"*You're* the one who begged to fight," Johnny growls. The devil who waits on his shoulder takes over, spearing me with his words. There's no more concern in his eyes. It's replaced with hard steel. Stubbornness. Holier-than-thou, Godlike bullshit.

I lift my hand and slap him. The crack of my palm against his cheek rings through the hallway. It cuts through the buzzing in my ears until the sting of my palm radiates outward, acknowledging what I've done.

He slowly moves his jaw back and forth before staring at me straight in the eyes. "Again."

I slap him a second time—harder—rage fusing my thoughts together. "I fought because I thought it was going to make a difference. I thought it meant something. I didn't volunteer for the fucking fun of it, Asshole."

"Again," Johnny growls, steeling himself for another outburst.

I haul off and slap him a third time, the cracking sound ricocheting once more through the empty hall. "And you knew about it. You knew what was going to happen. You knew my life was in danger, and you told me nothing." I pull my hand back again, clenched into a fist this time, and aim right for his perfect nose.

He dodges me, parrying my punch and then pulling me toward him. He's all hard muscles at first. It's like being hugged by a mannequin made of sharp rocks. Little by little, he melts into me though. "Mag had you," he whispers into my ear. "He had you. If you think for one second I would risk you, you don't understand me at all."

Such pretty words. My heart splinters. I want these words. I want them so desperately, but I can't help but think the person saying them is a cold, hard, calculating wolf. He talks a pretty game. Sometimes he even acts like a gentleman. Heavy on the sometimes. But then there's always the devil inside him waiting to claw itself to the surface.

"I've got you, Kyla," he continues. "Nothing was ever going to happen to you. I can promise you that. I would never allow that to happen."

I swallow. His words lodge in my throat and coat my mouth in bitterness. "You can't say the same for everyone. Did *everyone* else know? Were any of them blindsided like me? What about them? Johnny—"

A throat clears behind us. "Rocket, your dad's asking for you."

I peer over his shoulder to find Magnum. His arm is properly bandaged now. He's standing in the doorway, arms crossed over his chest, his usual security pose.

Johnny pulls away until I'm at arm's length. "This is what it's like in the Heights," he says, cupping my cheek. "If you're from here, you know how things go down. It shouldn't have been a shock to anyone." He holds my gaze, and I get the distinct feeling he's telling me I should've known what was really going to happen.

The back of my neck burns. I have a problem with that, and I have a hard time believing Brawler knew what was going to happen either.

Then again, he didn't want me to fight. No one did.

Except Big Daddy K.

Johnny's cheek is a splotchy red color. I eye the crimson stains while he calls over his shoulder, "Magnum, can you take Kyla into my suite? She's had a rough day." He turns and traces his thumb just under my eyes. His striking blue gaze glints while he looks at me, and little-by-little, a soft smile curves the corners of his lips. It's a gesture I wasn't sure he'd be capable of after what happened tonight.

There are two sides to Johnny Rocket. One that can woo me. One that I can see a sense of humanity in. But then there's the other. It's like his opposite. His enemy, but they're both living in the same body. He touches his forehead to mine. "I'll be in as soon as I can. Dad and I just need to talk strategy going forward. We know what you did for us out there. Trust me. It won't be forgotten, and you're safe for now."

He walks away, taking my humanity with him. I close my eyes and try to center myself. I'm either the most naïve person alive or there's just...something about him.

Magnum moves forward. I sense his domineering presence before I even pry my eyes open. His stature rivals Johnny's, but it isn't terrifying, it's comforting.

But *why* do I think that? Magnum knew what Big

Daddy K was going to do, too. That's why he came for me right away. They'd pre-planned for Magnum to get me out of there as soon as I won.

I stare at his copper scruff. Dust coats one side with brown smears edging up his cheekbones. I wonder what I look like. A quick inspection tells me I also look a little worse for wear. My fight outfit is ripped. Pebbles are stuck in my arms, surrounded by scrapes and smudges of dirt. I probably have glass in my hair from the car and God knows what else.

"Let's get you into the suite," Mag says, gesturing toward the door on the opposite side of the hall.

His voice is pitched low, and his eyes are greedy as he watches me. I've always felt like I've been on display for him. I chalked it up to it being part of his job to watch things, but his gaze is always trained on me when I'm around.

I follow him into Johnny's suite and make my way to the black leather sofa. At first, I want to dive into it, let the cushions cocoon me, so I can close my eyes and forget any of this ever happened, but that won't do. Other things are priority. I need to know what happened to Oscar and Brawler, first and foremost.

I skew my face into a hard line. "I need to know what's being done to find the others who were there."

Magnum strokes his beard. It's like a tic at first, but then he pulls his hand away, glancing at his fingers briefly before combing his copper stubble more fully as if grooming himself. "Whoever made it will meet back here. They might have to wait awhile. Until they think it's safe."

"What about the ones who aren't in the Crew?" I keep my voice flat and only slightly interested. "Where will they go?"

"Is this about Brawler?"

Fuck. I grind my teeth together, keeping my face impassive. How much do I want to give away? Will he go running to Johnny if I tell him I'm worried about where Brawler is?

Mag swallows, his eyes never wavering away from me. His stare is something else. The way he looks at me is like he wants to rip the truth from my body.

Fuck me. I'll probably die for this.

I nod.

Magnum blows out a breath. "I imagine he'll hide somewhere. He won't go home because he wouldn't want to lead anyone to his mom. He'll go underground for a while until it's safe. You need to remember that they—we—all grew up like this, Kyla. They know what they're doing."

I nod again, not able to find the words to thank him, and I don't want to say anything to give my true feelings away either. Underneath the calm surface I'm trying to portray, I'm still reeling from the night's events. A woman got gunned down three feet from where I stood. A shootout combusted around me in a flurry of bullets and blood. I don't know where Brawler is. Or Oscar. Hell, I don't even know if I can trust my own feelings. My own self.

Magnum steps toward me. In a flash, he's the same guy who rescued me from the parking lot and brought me back here. So much has happened since then that it feels like a lifetime ago, but Magnum touched me. His hand cradled my face. The same guy who did that is now standing a foot away from me, hazel eyes staring me down. "You can trust me, you know. I'll try to find out what happened to Brawler and Oscar. For you."

My face pales. Now that the hype of the shootout isn't scorching through my veins, I realize I've given too much away. "I—"

Magnum shakes his head. "I get it. Don't say another word. It's between us."

He leaves, and I stand in the middle of Johnny's living room in shock. I reach out to make sure the couch is behind me and then sit down heavily. I thought this world would have lies, deceit, anger, and death. And it does. It has all of that. But it has more than that, too. People like Brawler come from here. People like Oscar and Magnum. They've all stepped up to help me, not understanding I'm here for a greater—if not sinister—purpose. A desire that's overwhelmed my life for so long that I don't even know what it's like to have people who care about me anymore. I live in the dark side of my self. I live in the depths of revenge and vengeance and my calm hand pulling the trigger to a bullet that will end the life of the guy who took everything from me. If anything, I thought I'd fit in here.

But maybe I don't. At least not with the people who care about me.

And maybe I fit in too well with the people I've vowed to make suffer.

2

After a long ass shower and picking countless tiny rocks out of my skin, I emerge from the scalding hot water with scrapes down my arms and stomach and my shin throbbing. I find Johnny's closet in his room and pick out a t-shirt to throw on before moving to his kitchen, so I can ice my leg. Now that my adrenaline has bottomed out, the pain is starting to flare up like I knew it would. Injuries are always worse after your body has calmed down from the excitement of the fight. I wonder what it will be like after coming down from the high of a shootout. The crash will probably suck that much more.

I don't know what time it is, but my body drags. It's telling me it's time for sleep, even though my ears are attuned to the front door, waiting for someone to come in and give me any kind of news. If I'm lucky, maybe Oscar or

Brawler will even come in themselves. That's just wishful thinking. I highly doubt any of those guys come into Johnny's suite. Especially not Brawler. He's not even a member of the Crew. *Am I?* Not because of Johnny, but because of what I did for them. That was my goal all along: *Embed myself into their group. Into their lives. Make them trust me.*

I need to call my aunt and uncle. I need to check in with them. I need to get ready for school on Monday. I need to watch the latest episode of *The Witcher*. I need to—

Damn. I'm the fucking queen of ignoring things without ignoring them. I can tell my brain not to think about Brawler or Oscar, but my body does it on its own even though I try like hell to distract myself. Eventually, I throw what's left of the ice in the kitchen sink and lie down on Johnny's sofa, knowing I won't be able to think consciously about the fate of Brawler or Oscar while I'm asleep.

I pull my knees up to my chest and pull his shirt down around my legs, using a small square pillow to lay my head on. I drift off immediately. Blissfully, I think, and dream about nothing until I'm jostled awake and lifted into the air.

My body tightens.

"Shh. You're fine. It's just me."

I instantly relax, but then I force my eyes open to see who "me" is.

Dark hair blends into the shadows. "You should've crawled into my bed."

I close my eyes again, my brain warring once more

between finding distraction in who's holding me and wanting to be held by someone else.

Johnny's hands tighten around me before he places me carefully onto his plush blankets. He moves the sheets back and straightens my legs before pulling the sheets back over me. I'm encased in silk. It's dreamy. This mattress is a thousand times better than the mattress I've been sleeping on back at the shitty apartment.

Johnny climbs in after me, moving his arm under my head to pull me close, swaddling me in his embrace. "You looked so peaceful," he whispers. "I didn't know whether I should leave you there or not, but ultimately, I'm selfish and wanted you here with me."

I try to keep quiet. My mind warring over his words and the effect they have on me, and whether I should even trust my own reactions to him. If a person you hated said the most beautiful things to you, it might put a chink in your armor. It might even continue to put dents and scrapes in the more he kept saying and doing those things. Sure, he's done some shit that has made me fill those chinks in with plaster to harden them back up, but there are other moments, too.

Like this one.

Johnny talks again, his breath caressing the tip of my nose as he speaks. "I hope you know I was absolutely certain you were going to be okay." He peers at me through feathered lashes. "That's why I didn't want to tell you. I wanted you to focus on the fight and not what would happen afterward. Hell, we didn't even know if it was going to happen. We were playing it by ear."

"What happened after I got out?" I ask, voice hoarse. I'm picturing a smattering of dead bodies with rivers of blood coursing away from them.

I sneak my eyes open, catching him staring at the ceiling. "It was chaos," he recounts, his body shuddering briefly. "I don't know when Magnum got you out exactly. I remember looking back and seeing you close to Mag, and that's when I knew you were going to be safe. Dad and I made our way to the cars with a few others from our security team before we jumped in and fled. We didn't have a tail, but we took a roundabout way here in case we were being followed."

"If they knew we'd be coming back here, how come they haven't tried to retaliate?"

Johnny pulls away, his lips a thin line. "That's the reason for doing what we did, Kyla. The only way they'll come back at us is if we didn't take out their top people. Dad got Roza. I got Evan."

"Evan?"

Johnny nods. "I owed him for laying his fucking hands on you."

I blink at him. Fighting is just that, a fight. It's not to the death. It's not so that scores can be settled outside of the competition. It stays there. The better person wins. That's it.

"Hey," Johnny says, tipping my chin up so I can look

him more squarely in the face. "Evan's one of their top three. He had to go. We just don't know if anyone got their second in command. If we didn't, we can expect retaliation. If we did, we're safe. No one's going to act unless we know for sure. We're hunkering down here, and trust me, even if they do come for us, nothing's going to happen to you. I won't let it."

Johnny thinks he can play God. A disastrous trait he learned from his father. He can take lives. He thinks he can save lives by being who he is, but that's not the way the world works. One day, his life is going to come crashing in around him. Everything he thought he knew is going to be proven a lie.

Judging by the way he's been brought up, he's not going to take it well.

He takes my face in his hands and strokes both cheeks. "Can I do anything for you? Do you need ice? Or Band-Aids?" He lifts the covers away from me, trying to check my body in the low light.

I hunker back down, pulling the sheets back over us. "I'm fine. I iced my shin before I went to bed."

"My dad wants to see you tomorrow. He wanted to see you tonight, but I told him no."

"Yeah?" I ask. Hope builds in me, but that emotion associated with this psychopath feels like a betrayal.

Johnny blinks at me. "My dad didn't want you to get

hurt either, Kyla. He likes you. I think he wants to tell you something you've been waiting to hear."

I can't imagine Big Daddy K would have anything to say that I would want to hear unless he's going to offer his dead body over to me. Not that that will ever happen.

Johnny's hand roams over my hip. "Will it hurt if I touch you?"

I stop breathing. My body locks up, and I meet Johnny's gaze dead on.

"Not sexually," he explains. "But because you're really here. Because I was worried. I was scared, Kyla. I knew nothing was going to happen to you, but at the same fucking time, I was scared to death something would. If it had, I'd never be able to forgive myself." He squeezes my hip. He nestles in closer until we're millimeters away from touching. When I breathe, my nipples brush his hard chest. "I've never wanted something more than you."

"I'm not an object, Johnny."

"It's not that at all. It's you. The idea of you." He shakes his head. "You won't get it, and I'm too fucking...fucked to explain it."

I bite my lip. Here, in his bed, with low light and an open face, Johnny is being as honest as he's ever been with me. He's raw, cut to the quick. Something is bothering him. That much is clear. Something he both does and doesn't want to talk about. Maybe it's that I mean something so much more to him than just a thing to own, something he's claimed on a whim.

I snuggle closer to him. Call me stupid. And fake, because I certainly am that, but Johnny's softer side is winning me over. Before the fight, he told me he hadn't been with anyone else since the dress shop girl. He told me he was pissed at his dad over me.

I hide my face in his shoulder and wrap my arms around him tighter. I want to believe in a softer side of Johnny. That makes me feel less sick. Less like I've infiltrated the gang and found out it's exactly where I belong because I'm just as fucked up as those guys. Maybe even moreso because I didn't grow up like them.

"You used my shampoo," Johnny groans.

I nod into him. "I didn't have any of mine."

"We'll have to fix that."

I wrap my leg around his to bring me closer and immediately still. He's hard, his cock straining against the jeans he never took off in his haste to crawl into bed with me. His body follows suit, immediately locking up. His breath leaves in a whoosh.

Because there's something wrong with me in the head, I push my hips forward, his hard cock teasing my greedy ass core. My breath hitches at the contact.

"God, don't do that."

My nipples peak, pushing against my borrowed cotton t-shirt. My breath comes in hurried, needy gasps. I don't know what's come over me. I roll my hips over him again.

"Fuck," he groans. "You're not wearing anything underneath that shirt."

I bite down on my lip to stop the whimper creeping up my throat from leaving my mouth. I am in desperate need of relief. Call it the tension of the day coming to a grinding halt right here, right now. Call it the excitement of being alive. Call it whatever the fuck you want, but right now, I'm ready to come apart.

Johnny stays where he is. Despite his heavy breathing, he doesn't move an inch even though he's as hard as a rock. He tightens his hold on my hip, clutching the end of my shirt in his fists.

I lick my lips to relieve my dry mouth. I want release like I'm desperate for air. I grind my clit against him, swirling for good measure. Pressure builds until it's unstoppable. I let out a low mewl before doing it again.

"Fuck, Kyla. You're going to—" He moves his thumb to my clit, pressing down on it.

"Yes," I breathe.

He swirls again and again until my fingers sink into the skin at his back, and my body races forward at the speed of light, my mouth open in a silent scream.

I cry out briefly before shuddering, my forehead coming to a rest on his shoulder. Fuck. What just happened? That took zero time at all. I didn't even have a moment to think clearly.

Johnny moves his hands back to my hips and traces his fingers over my bare skin. I still, wondering what he's going to do. Is he going to take it further? Is he not? I fear both these paths for different reasons. Tightening his hold, he sinks down into me for a heart-stopping second before crawling backward out of the bed. The pitch in his pants is unmistakable, as is the tortured look on his face. His chest moves up and down as he eyes me in his bed. "This isn't because of my father. This is for you." He turns on his heel, leaving me in his bed to retreat to the bathroom.

The shower starts, and I flip onto my back, staring up at the ceiling. My body has that pleasant, hazy after-sex feeling, magnified after a day like today. Maybe that's why I came so easily. All the stored-up tension in my body. All the wrongness of getting off on Johnny. Whatever it is, I stare at the ceiling and listen to Johnny in the shower. There's a loud thump like he's banged his fist against the tiles. Whatever other sounds that might have come afterward are eaten up by the running water until the water turns off.

Minutes later, he emerges from the bathroom with only a pair of boxers on. I look him over and find the same satisfied glint in his eye I'm sure is reflected back in mine. "This should go without saying, but the day I bury myself inside you, it won't be on the heels of worrying about losing you."

Despite myself, my heart pitter-patters in my chest. "Are there even any days like that inside the Crew?"

"Of course, there are." He slides back into bed, moving into the exact same position with his arm under my head and his other hand on my hip. "I'll show you."

I don't know if I want him to or not. If this is how I react to a softer Johnny on a bad day, what the hell would a good day look like?

3

In sleep, Johnny looks like an angel.

I'm not kidding. He's gorgeous enough, to be sure, but in the midst of rest, his face takes on a relaxed, peaceful look that isn't there when he's awake. Do all bad guys look like this while they sleep? Innocent. Trustworthy. Like more friend than foe.

Why do I think Big Daddy K looks the exact same asleep or awake? Like he's two seconds from putting a bullet between someone's eyes.

The sun's rays stream through the ends of the blinds like a square halo. If I ever find Big Daddy K sleeping alone in the dark, I don't care if he does look like this, he's dead. Not only for what he did to my parents, but for what he did to me, and Oscar, and Brawler, and fuck, even Johnny. He's going down for it all. No one deserves to be mixed up in this kind of bullshit.

Because I don't have any clothes here, I find a discarded pair of joggers in the closet and pull them on. Coupled with Johnny's too-big-for-me t-shirt, I won't be winning any beauty contests, but fuck if that's the reason why I'm here, anyway.

My shin aches, so I'm careful about putting too much weight on it as I walk out to the living room, and there's a tightness in my shoulder blades I need to work out from the fight. All in all, I fared pretty well from the events of last night. The scrapes on my stomach barely hurt anymore. It's just my heart that holds the worry and ache over not knowing what happened to Brawler and Oscar. If I had my gun, I'd think about sneaking next door, but then...I don't know if Brawler or Oscar are alive and I need that information. I can't leave without knowing. I can't disappear without them.

I'm curled up on the black leather couch when Magnum walks in. He stops in his tracks when he notices me there alone, and then looks around the suite, gaze stopping on the halfway open door that leads to Johnny's bedroom. "He's in there," I say.

He takes in my appearance with his eagle-like gaze. I run my hands through my hair, hoping to tame the mess it's probably in. I'm not used to seeing so many people this early in the morning. Hell, I'm pretty much used to being alone.

Magnum shuts the door with a soft click. With his eyes trained on the open door, he sneaks toward me, even though God knows he doesn't need to sneak. He's one of the most silent people I've ever met. He could creep up on a frightened animal. "Oscar checked in."

I cover my mouth after a loud intake of breath that hangs heavy in the air.

Magnum nods.

"He's okay?"

He nods again. "He'll probably show up later today. We've had eyes on the perimeter all night. We don't see anything."

I take a deeper look at Magnum next. He still has on the bandage from last night. His skin is pale, cheeks sallow with dark bags under his eyes from a full night of staying on duty rather than getting much-needed sleep. I mean he was shot for Christ's sake.

I rub my own eyes. They're not scratchy or heavy. In fact, I slept well. Too well for being in a man's bed I once thought of as an enemy. But there's a heat behind them now I want to hold back so it doesn't betray even more of the thoughts Magnum's already begun to tease out.

"It looks like you need some sleep," I say instead. "Maybe even a shower. Some food?"

I get up from the couch like I can do any of that here. I don't know where anything is, and with the bedroom door open, do I really want to make a racket trying to feed

Magnum, essentially distracting myself from the news I've just received? Johnny would be up in a heartbeat if he heard me moving around out here.

"I need all that," he says, "...but there's no time right now."

"Bullshit," I say, my voice rising above the whispered tones we've been talking in. "You'll miss shit if you stay on duty any longer. Isn't there someone else who can take over?"

My gaze darts around the apartment looking for something to focus on. Maybe a cereal box, so I can eat and force-feed Magnum at the same time. Or a cell phone to call Oscar. Or—

"Hey," Magnum says, fingers wrapping around my forearm. "It's okay."

I take a deep breath, gaze dropping to his touch. Instead of pulling away from me, he keeps his hand steady. Magnum and I are in the same boat with one another. He offered me a way to get out last night. He offered to help, and I could just as easily turn him in as he could me. What does this mean though? Are we friends? Allies? None of those seem like the right label with how he looks at me.

I close my eyes briefly before opening them again, trying to calm my beating heart. I focus on something I can help with. "How's your arm feeling today?"

"Hurts like a bitch," he says. For some reason, his response makes me smile. I figured Magnum would be a hard ass. He'd be the type to die before he let anyone know he was hurting.

"I saw some pain reliever in Johnny's bathroom. Can I get some for you?"

He nods, taking a seat on the sofa. I leave him there to retrieve the medicine and walk back into the main room. When I get there, Magnum is already unrolling the bandages from his arm. He gets to the red-stained gauze and removes it.

He really was lucky. Sure, there's a gash taken out of his arm where the bullet grazed, but it didn't pierce him. It didn't hit anything vital. I sit on the coffee table opposite him and watch as he folds the gauze a different way to a semi-clean side.

"Looks like you've had to do this before," I say, cringing a little, and wondering what he's had to do for the Crew in the past.

He looks up. "I have."

"How many times?"

He chuckles. With one hand, he holds the gauze in place while trying to wrap the bandage around him. The gauze keeps slipping, so I lean over, taking the bandages from him. He looks up at me, an appreciative look in his eyes. "Wrap it tight, but not tight enough to lose blood flow."

I nod. Sure, I've never been in a gunfight before, but I know about wounds. Physical and emotional.

While I'm wrapping his injury back up, I glance at him

to find him watching me. "You're not going to answer me, are you?"

He presses his lips together, the stubble on his chin sticking out with the movement. "Five times. And I'm not counting this one because it was just a graze."

I swallow, my mouth drying up like I've been breathing in the desert air for decades. "I think that's five too many." I get to the end of the bandage and tuck it into the top of the wrap like he had before. Then I sit back on the coffee table, watching Magnum as much as he's watching me. It's like we're having a stare-off while also trying to simultaneously feel one another out. He, of all people, has tried to help me, and I would've put him in the firmly pro Heights Crew category. I mean, he's their guard for crying out loud. He protects them. They trust him implicitly.

"You need to be careful," Magnum says, lowering his voice to an octave above silence. "Johnny—"

"Hey." Johnny emerges from his room, voice groggy. He has pants on now instead of just boxers, but his chest is still as naked as it was last night. My heart almost stops at the sight of him. Sex appeal rolls off him in waves. It's no surprise women line up to be with him. The secretary at the school. The bitch at the dress shop. He'd be alluring even if he wasn't tied to the toughest gang around. "Any news?" he asks Magnum as he comes up behind me, placing his hands on my shoulders. A shiver rolls down my spine at his touch.

When I look back at Magnum, he's in complete guard

mode. His back is ramrod straight. The bags underneath his eyes have even receded while he answers Johnny. "Drego checked in a couple of hours ago. He's safe. Uninjured. Perimeter's been clear all night. Anyone who checks in is safe to head back."

Johnny squeezes my shoulders. The movement doesn't even catch Magnum's eye as he's completely focused on Johnny Rocket right now. Maybe too focused, as if he's trying hard not to look at me. "What did I tell you, babe? My dad knows what he's doing."

I can't help the scowl that comes to my lips, but Johnny's oblivious. His dad knows what he's doing all right. The fucking coward. He'd rather shoot someone than do something upstanding like actually stick to the game plan they both agreed to.

The complete shock in Roza's eyes when he whipped the gun out on her... I'll never forget that. Not for as long as I live.

I shiver, a cold chill running up my back. It's not as if I haven't replayed what must have happened to my parents in my head, but now having seen someone get shot—close enough to almost get splattered with blood spray in the aftermath—I can't stop picturing my mom's panicked face in place of Roza's.

Did Roza have children? The cycle could start again. With all this violence, will it ever end? I doubt the Crew understands the never-ending loop they're perpetuating.

That's why I'm here. So Big Daddy K doesn't add more victims to his list. So some other kid doesn't have to uproot their life in order to take down the bad guy. I've already taken on the role, happily.

"Are you okay?" Johnny rubs my back. "Are you cold?"

I freeze, then force myself to relax. Johnny is not Big Daddy K. Right? Right.

I glance up to find Magnum staring. He watches me with his intense hazel-green eyes. Johnny squeezing my shoulder brings me back to reality. I shake my head right away. "Just...I don't know," I say honestly. "I guess I am going to need clothes at some point today though. My own clothes. Is there any way I can go back to my apartment?"

"No," a hoarse voice says. Except, it isn't Johnny who's telling me no. It's Mag. Before I can glare at him, he turns his face toward Johnny. "I don't think that's a good idea yet."

"Obviously," Johnny says as if the answer was already a given. "She's not leaving my sight for a while." He rubs his hand down my arm, then trails it back up absentmindedly. "I'll send someone to get you some clothes."

"Let's hope no one's gone through her place," Magnum adds.

My heart stops. My place. My fucking place with the hidden compartment and the only tie back to my real life. I clear my throat to hide my sudden panic and fail. I swallow several times, digging my fingernails into my thigh. "Why would anyone do that?"

"Because you're one of us now." Johnny reaches around to tip my chin toward him, so I can see his face when he says, "You've proven that."

Dread washes over me. It isn't so much what he's said. It's what it means. Being one of them is what I've wanted from the beginning. I have to get close to do what I came here to do, but what if I get too close? What if I get stuck?

What if I like it?

A musical tone sounds from the other room. Johnny stills then takes off for the bedroom, holding his pants up as he runs. The elastic band of his boxers clearly showing. Not even the sight of that can keep me chill.

"You look like you're going to be sick."

Magnum would notice, of course. It's his job. I stand and start to pace, diving my fingers through my hair. I can't let anyone get to my aunt and uncle. I'm sure it wouldn't be hard to put everything together, especially not with sadistic people like these guys. What's left of my family can't be brought into this at all. They're my only family left in this world. Fuck, fuck, *fuck*.

"Now you really look like you're going to get sick."

His voice is closer now. When I turn to make another pass through the room, he's right in front of me, a blockade of muscle and warm hazel-green eyes. There's something in his gaze that makes me remember the soft way he said I could trust him. But can I? The rational part of me says no. I can't trust any of these guys. But, I'm desperate. "What's the probability they got to my apartment?"

"I say about eighty percent," Magnum answers. "You beat their best fighter. He was third in command under Roza. They probably torched all your shit. Not that you had much, anyway."

I curl my hair around my ears, then lace my fingers around the back of my neck.

"I take it there's something in your place you want."

"I need," I say, eyeballing him so he knows how important this is to me. "I can't let anyone else get their hands on it, Magnum. It's important."

He takes a deep breath and lets it out. "What is it? I'll see if I can find it."

I shake my head. That's not fucking happening. What if this trust thing only goes so far? He is, after all, charged with keeping Big Daddy K safe, and if I threaten that, I know what he has to do. I'd be willing to sacrifice myself, but not my aunt and uncle. No one else in my family dies. "You said I can trust you, right? I need you to take me there so I can get it."

Magnums shakes his head. "Not fucking happening. We don't know who or what will be waiting for us there."

"Magnum, I'm serious. I *need* it. If you don't fucking take me, I'm going on my own."

The soft pad of footsteps sound from the other room. Johnny's coming back. Magnum's face twists into a grin. "I'd like to see you try getting away from Johnny. You're not going anywhere, Kyla. So, you either tell me what it is, or it's gone forever."

I suck in a breath. Our gazes lock on one another until Johnny reappears through his bedroom doorway. I turn away from Magnum at the sight of Johnny and take my place back on the sofa where the bodyguard found me earlier.

Hopefully, my silence speaks volumes. If he won't help, I'll just do it on my own.

4

I'm left alone again as Johnny and Magnum leave the apartment to talk to Big Daddy K. Before he goes, Johnny shows me where the food is and how to work the expensive smart TV he has even though my aunt and uncle have the same exact TV in their game room in the basement a world away. I pretend I don't know what I'm doing anyway, and Johnny loves taking care of me. Seriously. The glow on his face and the delight in his eyes is unmistakable as he shows me how to connect to Hulu and Netflix. The kiss before he leaves is strong and fueled by promises he hasn't said yet.

I'm fucking messed in the head.

While they're gone, I peek out the windows. I don't know what I'm hoping to see. A clear escape route? Arrows in the street telling me exactly where to go to avoid the bad guys—both Heights Crew and Fonz's people. What I do find are guys dressed in black, walking casually up and down the block. Maybe, just maybe, they have other people fooled, but not me. These guys have Big Daddy K written all over them for the simple fact that they look like Magnum. If I walked out of this place, they'd be all over me.

Just to ram the point home, I peek my head outside Johnny's door into the barren hallway, which isn't barren anymore. A slew of guys mill around. Big Daddy K must have brought up more security to make sure whoever's here is safe. A quick scan later and I don't recognize these guards from being here previously. A few of them might look vaguely familiar, like it's possible I know them from school or perhaps even last night.

I wonder what the casualty rate was of yesterday's shootout. Are the police asking questions? Surely, the Heights Crew can't have a shootout without the police getting involved. Somewhere, Detective Reynolds is all over this even though his hands are tied.

A whistle splits the air while I'm still looking out the hall. It's a flirty whistle meant to tell females they're looking fine even when they haven't asked anyone's goddamn opinion on the subject, and certainly not asshole men who can't restrain themselves.

The sea of black-clad bodies part and none other than Glo from the dress shop downtown comes into view. Huge-rimmed white sunglasses take up most of her face. Her lips are painted a bright pink, and of course, her fingernails match. They come out to points, looking more like weapons than fashion. "Hey Girl," she calls out when she sees me.

I step back into the room, noticing the two bags draping off each side of her. This must be Johnny's solution for not having any clothes. Glo walks in with a flourish. Next to her, I look like a hobo on the street. I haven't even bothered to brush my hair today, but mostly because I don't have the basic necessities here and I'm confined to this space.

A guard follows her in. He's not Magnum, and I'm immediately tense. She turns on her silver sparkly heels. "This is going to be all girl stuff. You'll probably get bored."

He stands off to the side, arms crossed over his chest. He watches her as she moves deeper into the apartment. I don't like this one bit. I'm not going to get ogled while I talk to Glo. "You can leave," I tell him.

His jaw hardens, but I just stare blankly back at him until he leaves the room, mumbling shit under his breath.

"So much testosterone," Glo says.

"Trust me, it's fucking everywhere," I tell her. She has no idea.

She makes a face and then looks around Johnny's digs. Her lips part slightly like she's stepped into Buckingham Palace, but Johnny certainly isn't royalty.

"Let me guess," I start. "Johnny asked you to bring by some clothes."

She drops the bags to the floor and turns. I'm barely

paying attention when she does. I'm staring at the bags of clothes like I'd rather do anything than go through the girly shit Glo has picked out for me. Or even Lynette. There probably isn't a single outfit I want to wear in there.

When a clicking noise interrupts the silence, I peer up at Glo. Her face is twisted into a mask of fury, and her bright pink nails clasp onto a small, silver handgun pointed right at my face. I gasp, and her gaze drops to the gun, stunned. I don't give her a chance to try to get another shot off. I run forward, slamming my shoulder into her side to tackle the bitch.

"You cunt!" Her scream pierces the air loud and clear as I wrestle her to the ground.

I reach for the gun. Her finger is still against the trigger. Her long ass nails capturing it there. I finally grab hold of it and rip it away from her. She cries out, her fake nail tearing off with it. A sound of fury bursts past her lips and with a sudden motion, she knocks me to the side, and the gun slips from my grip. We both scramble for it. I'm trying to push it away from her, and she's trying to grab it. She must think it was a fluke that it didn't go off the first time.

I don't want to find out if it was.

Instead of focusing on the gun, I elbow her in the face. This bitch tried to shoot me. I was five feet away from her. Even someone who hadn't shot a gun before could have hit me at that range. Thank fuck it didn't fire properly.

The door bursts open at the same time Glo pulls the end

table on top of me. The lamp crashes to the floor next to my head. She screams in defeat as the guard I sent away hauls her to her feet, pinning her arms behind her body. *She doesn't have the gun,* I realize. I breathe a sigh of relief.

More of K's guys stream into the room. Shouts rise up, and before I can even think to slide the end table off me, Magnum's doing just that, righting the table and helping me stand. In front of us, Glo sobs. Black streaks track down her face from beneath her sunglasses, which sit askew on her face from the scuffle. Her lip is split. A smear of blood mixes with her pink lipstick, ruining the whole effect she had going on. Instead of looking like a Barbie, she looks like... Well, she looks like an angry Barbie that got her ass handed to her.

"You okay?" Magnum asks.

I open my mouth to say something, but Johnny runs in, eyes wide. He sifts through the bodies in front of him, discarding them one by one until his gaze lands on me. "Fuck." He runs over, grabbing me by the cheeks so hard it almost hurts. "Are you okay? What the fuck happened?"

Behind him, his father strolls in like he's going for a Sunday drive. He's dressed in a fancy black suit, and he certainly doesn't have the disheveled look he was sporting yesterday after the shootout. There's no blood on his immaculate clothing. Not one hair is out of place. He looks as calm as can be for having a gunman in his place. Or excuse me, a gunwoman.

I'm the opposite. Now that I'm not struggling for the gun, I shake uncontrollably. She legitimately just tried to end my life. Fucking Glo. From the fucking clothing shop. The one who looks like she knows more about fashion than even what fucking day it is. Why could she possibly want to kill me?

Johnny's thumbs trace over my skin. Relief fills his crystal blue eyes when I look up at him. Maybe that's why Johnny is so alluring. He's so dark. His hair is dark. His aura. Everything except for his light blue eyes. It's alarming how attractive he is, actually.

"What the fuck happened?"

My body locks up. My mouth snaps shut. I refuse to look over because I know that voice. I simultaneously want to fall to my knees in relief and kick the person who owns that voice in the nuts. He's here, and he says that? Fucking *that*? Just like it's any other day?

"Hey," Johnny's soft voice sounds, bringing me back around. I focus on his blue-eyed gaze before I fall apart. "You're okay, right? Talk to me, babe."

I nod slowly.

"Mag," he says, calling his guard's name like what he wants is implied, and it must be because Mag has no problem coming toward me, shielding me from everyone else while Johnny walks toward Glo.

"And who is this?" Big Daddy K asks in a monotone clip. Not upbeat or depressed, but somewhere in the middle where slick meets suave. After just fighting for my life moments ago, I don't think that tone fits the situation at all. I much prefer Johnny's pissy voice.

"This is Glo," Johnny offers. With the thunderous look on his face and the growl in his voice, he's the monster that hides in the closet. He's Barbie's worst nightmare. "She works at Lynette's shop downtown."

While they discuss what happened, awareness crawls over me. I refuse to look up to find the face I know is watching me right now. I'm not playing this game. I'm already on edge. If I see Oscar now, I'm going to lose it, and I can't be fucking fragile Kyla. I have to be strong Kyla. I have to be the girl who kicked Evan's ass and watched someone get murdered in cold blood right in front of her. I have to be the girl who survived being chased and shot at in a car while driving through the Heights. I have to be the girl who just fought her attacker and won.

This is who I am now.

Glo spits in Big Daddy K's face.

It happens so fast, I don't think anyone expected it. Even with everything else going through my head, I gasp in shock. That girl has some fucking lady balls on her—and a death wish. I should know.

"You piece of shit," she barks. "My brother died last night because of you."

Johnny nods as if he's just put two and two together. "Her brother works at Dunnegan's."

"Worked," Glo growls. "Last night, he got shot in the head."

"So, you thought you'd waltz in here and take something from us?" Big Daddy K asks.

My stomach rolls at that. There's not an *us* where he's concerned. At least not truly. Not on the inside because I will hate this fucker with a fury no one will understand until the day I die.

"I was hoping for you or your shitty excuse for a son, but I decided I'd take what I could get while you cowards hid."

"Well, now you have nothing," Big Daddy K says. He reaches into his back pocket to retrieve a handkerchief. A fucking handkerchief like he's a mobster from the fifties. Then, he finally reaches up to wipe Glo's spit from his face. He does it slowly, making everyone wait as he carefully glides the cloth down his cheek, then folds the blue square in half, using a clean side to do it all over again. "Take her downstairs," he orders.

Downstairs? What the fuck is downstairs? The parking lot?

Big Daddy K turns, placing his hand on his son's shoulders. Behind him, two guards, including the one I sent away, drag Glo from the room. Big Daddy K ignores the insults she throws his way and makes his way toward me. The closer he comes, the more agitated I get. Magnum shifts his body out of the way, which makes me even more uncomfortable. It was nice to have a buffer. Eventually, Big Daddy K stops a few steps away from me, and I sigh in relief. I was just about to step back to get away from him. The more he's in my space, the more I don't like it. At least he hasn't tried to touch me. Yet.

He takes in my appearance with a small frown. I don't think it has anything to do with the fact that I was just rolling around on the floor fighting with a grief-stricken lunatic. By the way, I'm also a grief-stricken lunatic, so that's not a putdown. If you think about it, Glo and I are the same. I was just smarter about my attack. Do I think she should have tried to kill me? Fuck no. But can I blame her? Not really. The vengeance bug caught her too.

"Where was your guard when this happened?" Big Daddy K looks down at what's left of the broken lamp on the floor and accepts the gun one of his guards hands him.

"I sent him away. I thought I was going to be trying on clothes."

His jaw ticks. "Wasn't this woman checked when she entered?" he asks. He's staring at me, but I know he's not looking for me to answer, and everyone else knows it, too. The phalanx of black-dressed guards in the room hang their heads. "This, of all times," he says, voice growing harder. "We knew there would be retaliation. I don't care if you know these people or not. I don't care if you stood next to their brother yesterday in the Goddamn parking lot, that doesn't excuse you from checking each and every fucking person who comes in here." He waves his hand out. "Now leave before I decide to take my anger out on all of you."

Johnny eyes them as the group leaves. His chin is made of chiseled stone. He looks like if he could kill them all, he would.

After the mass exodus, a few linger behind. The guy I can't look at or think about, Magnum, Johnny, myself, and Big Daddy K. The latter rubs his face. Between the gaps in his hands, he lets his true feelings show. He's exhausted, and he's pissed. But once he's done rubbing his face, he smiles at me. I'm so out of my depths with his guy, I don't know what to do. "Kyla, I'm glad to see you're okay."

I swallow. I'm not thanking him. Fuck that. Though, those are the words that immediately spring to mind because if someone says they're glad you're okay, you automatically want to thank them. It's on the tip of my tongue, but I swallow it back. I don't know what he's going to do about Glo. I can't even blame her for what she did, but I doubt they carry those same feelings. If it were up to me, I'd ask her to be sent home. No harm. No foul. Maybe keep a watch on her for a few days to make sure she doesn't do anything else stupid. But the Heights Crew doesn't work like that. They're far less forgiving.

She's probably already dead.

Big Daddy K gestures toward the black leather couch behind me. I turn, make my way over to it, and have a seat. My shin is bothering me again, which means I should probably ice it. My body feels like it's been thrown in a washing machine. I don't know which way is forward anymore, all I know is I've walked through hell to be this confused and fucked up.

He sits next to me, angling his knees toward my own. I make sure I'm just out of his reach because the last thing I need is for him to put his hands on me again like we're old friends. Too many things swirl through my brain at the moment. "I didn't get a chance to talk to you properly last evening. I understand you have some questions about what happened last night."

My face flames. Not because I'm embarrassed, but because I'm fucking pissed. I told Johnny that in confidence. Or what I thought should have been in confidence. A conversation between two people, who—I don't know—fucking like each other? It certainly wasn't meant to go anywhere besides the two of us.

But because the cat is out of the bag, I lift my gaze to meet his. "Why did you kill her?"

He cocks his head slightly, like he's trying to make me out. Maybe he doesn't ever have people question him? Maybe he's just trying to figure out why I care. I don't know.

"I don't want to diminish your fight, Kyla. You fought admirably. You did what I asked you to do, and I thank you for that. What happened after was going to happen whether you won or lost. The Heights Crew is at the top of the food chain. Do you know why? Because we don't let people walk all over us. What happened yesterday was a culmination of that woman's actions. You either die a winner or a loser, Kyla, and she died a loser. Me? I'm making sure I die a winner, and that means protecting what's mine at all costs. It was my territory. Not hers. The fight was just a ruse to sucker her in so I could do what I've wanted to do for years but never had the opportunity. *You* gave me that opportunity."

Oh God, if he thanks me, I'm going to puke. He says it like I should be proud of that fact, but I'm not. If this really is all because of me, then I'm the reason why Roza Fonz died. I'm the reason why Glo's brother got shot and bled out.

"This life isn't for everybody, Kyla, but I think there's something in you. I want you to be our prizefighter in the rings. Johnny's told me you also want that, so wish granted, little fighter. You're now number one. You've earned it."

Satisfaction should be rolling through me, warming my skin. I get to fight, one of the things I loved from my old life, here, to make me feel human again in this one, but now's not the time for that. I know I've already lost before I've even begun.

But at his words, I allow myself to finally find the one person in the room I've wanted to see more than anything.

Oscar's dark eyes are already focused on me, piercing through every barrier I have in place. Funny enough, though I'm relieved he's okay, I don't know if I've ever wanted to punch someone more.

5

———

That feeling grows and grows as Johnny and Big Daddy K leave the room to deal with the situation downstairs. I can't even focus on that because I won't like the outcome, but there's also nothing I can do about it. I can't plead her case. I can't help her. She made her bed, and I'm not ruining my plans to save hers.

I stare Oscar down, and he flashes me a smirk.

I can't even with this fucker.

"I'll be just outside," Magnum says. I don't break eye contact with Oscar to look at Magnum, but he knows what's happening.

As soon as the door clicks behind him, I stand. My hands turn to fists, and Oscar looks me over. "You seem pissed."

"That's a fucking understatement, asshole."

He widens his eyes on purpose. "And here I thought you'd be all over me."

"Oh, I'm about to be all over you," I say, moving closer to him. I shove him back. "You knew what was going down."

He stumbles back a few steps, lifting his hands in the air.

"Don't deny it," I growl.

"Yes, I knew."

"And it didn't occur to you to say anything?" I seethe.

"Why? So you could worry? So you could get your ass kicked in the fight knowing you wouldn't be able to do anything about what's going down afterward? Your head wouldn't have been in the fight, it would have been on what was about to happen!"

"I thought what I was doing meant something!"

"It did," Oscar protests. He drops his hands to his sides. "Did you not just get added to the fight ring like you wanted? Do you think you would've been added if you lost?"

"Don't try to talk your fucking way out of this. Not telling me was a bullshit move, and you know it."

"Listen, I don't know what kind of power you think I have, Kyla, but newsflash, I don't have shit. I have nothing. When I get told to do something, I fucking do it. That's it. End of story."

"Oh, so you're a fucking coward? That's what you're telling me?"

He grits his teeth together, and I immediately want to

take the words back. "Walking into that parking lot last night even though I knew people were going to fucking die was a coward thing to do? Not telling you what was going to happen because I didn't want you distracted was a coward thing to do?" He cracks his knuckles. "I guess if that's being a coward, sign me the fuck up. I'll own up to it. I'll wear a fucking crown that says that shit. I'll wear it every fucking day for the rest of my life."

The fight's left me now. He's right. Sort of. In a way. What is right or wrong anymore? "Yeah, well, who knows how long that will be?" I snipe back because I can't help myself. I'm mad and I don't have a way to let it out.

Oscar's cockiness is back. "I've already outlived my shelf life because of where I am. Because I keep my mouth shut and do what I'm told. Every day after the day I returned to the Heights is a fucking blessing. That's what I know."

The short glimmer of pure hate in his eyes makes me wonder why he posed his answer that way. What happened the day he got back to the Heights? "This is insane," I say, the words dropping from my lips before I can even think about them.

"Welcome to the Heights, Princess."

His words seem all too familiar. I rub my arms to try to bring life back into them. Every part of me feels dead or lost.

"Now," he says, "can we start this again? I swear to fuck I've missed you. I couldn't come to you. I couldn't explain shit. And I knew all along you'd be wanting to castrate me."

My lips part, and I crack a smile. "Maybe."

"Fuck that. It's a definite yes. You didn't see the look in your eyes just now. That was some psycho shit right there."

"And I'm guessing you don't like psycho girls?" I ask coyly.

"Are you kidding me? They're my favorite."

He reaches his hand out to me, and I take it. He pulls me close, wrapping me in a hug. He kisses my neck, a brief touch of lips pressed against bare skin, but it helps settle me.

I pull away, not because I want to, but I don't want to get caught together either. I wipe at my eyes and then curl my hair around my ears. "Have you heard from Brawler?"

He looks to the ground and shakes his head. "The whole thing was a mess. I couldn't find you. I didn't see him. When I made contact, I couldn't even risk asking if you were fucking alive because I didn't want to raise suspicion. I tried texting you, but you must not have your phone."

I shrug. "I have no idea where that is. I think it was in the sweatshirt I took off before the fight. Hell, it might even still be in the parking lot."

Oscar shakes his head. "I was part of the cleanup crew. It's not there."

I swallow. Part of the cleanup crew? I don't even want to ask how many dead people he saw, and his demeanor doesn't make me want to ask either.

"He'll check in," Oscar says. "Not that I should want

him to, right?" He bites his lip. "Considering you like both of us."

Vulnerability doesn't suit Oscar. Not that it's a bad thing. I like it. But he looks so awkward when he peers up at me after those words hang in the air for a moment. He's miles away from the confident badass gang member right now. His words are like a forbidden heavy cloak over us. Those words shouldn't be spoken. Not in Johnny's suite. Not at all, actually. Can people even have feelings for more than one guy at a time?

Actually, yes, they can. I know for a fact because I do, and that's all the reassurance I need.

"I do like both of you," I tell him. I won't even begin to tell him about the weird vibe I have with Magnum and just the ridiculous nature of whatever feelings I have for Johnny. I haven't figured those out myself yet.

He jams his hands into his pockets. "So, still want to stay here?" he asks. "Bitches trying to kill you. Shootouts. Fights to the death."

I mentally add his name along with Brawler's to his sarcastic list of reasons why I would want to stay in the Heights, except those are my real reasons. Not to mention the reason why I came here in the first place. "Yes, I still want to be here."

"We must be the stupidest fucking people alive."

"No, we're just stuck." I'm more stuck than he knows.

He probably thinks I'm crazy, and let's face it, I am. This path was never going to be easy, but it needs to be done.

He looks over his shoulder toward the door. "They're probably wondering where I am. We don't need to be seen together like this."

I hate this. I wish I didn't have to cater to everyone. I take a deep breath. "Oscar, I need to get to my apartment. Is there any way you can take me there?"

He turns toward me, a sly look on his face. "Your apartment?"

"There's something there I need."

"I can grab it for you."

Ugh. These guys and wanting to help. Don't they know women like to do shit for themselves? "I really need to get it myself. Can you get me there?"

He blows out a breath. "I can try, but after what just happened in here with that crazy chick, I doubt you're going anywhere for a while. You know how Johnny is."

His words punch a hole in the bubble surrounding us. I'm good at pretending everything's fine. Hell, I'm even good at convincing myself that everything is fine, but in this moment, it dawns on me that I am indeed stuck. I'm worried about someone finding my cell phone. I'm worried about Brawler. About the rest of us who have to deal with this life day in and day out.

"One day, you're going to tell me what your secret is, Princess," Oscar coaxes. Instead of looking defeated, a new light burns in his eyes like I might be his greatest challenge yet. We come together like the sky meets the earth in a beautiful horizon of colors. He runs his hand over my hair, cupping the back of my head. "I'm so glad you're okay."

Fuck me. How did I end up in the craziest of worlds surrounded by guys who aren't crazy? I'm not saying they're not bad. Or that they don't have the potential to do shitty things, but deep down, I'd wager no one has determination like Oscar. Or heart like Brawler. Or—.

"Just one fix," he says, his breath teasing my lips. Our lips collide, and he spins me until my back is against the door. He presses me against it, deepening the kiss until my limbs tingle. I want more. I need more. For as much as Oscar is a badass, he's not a wild card like Johnny. I don't have to second-guess the spark between us. I'm throwing myself all in.

I curl my fingers around his lower back, yanking him toward me. He nips at my lips before diving his tongue inside my mouth where he takes complete control. He worships me, kissing me thoroughly, and I do my best to give it right back to him.

He pulls away all too soon, both of us breathing heavy. He drifts his forehead to mine and rests it there. "That was fucking...incredible."

I smile. "I guess that's why you like us crazy ones."

"Just one crazy one."

And to think he'd been messed up over Nevaeh a couple

of weeks ago. That just proves that when you know, you just know. Different people are attuned to different people. So, when you click, things just fall into place like long lost puzzle pieces. I've been trying to figure out how I'm not like these guys, but what if being like them isn't necessarily a bad thing? They're survivors, whether they know it or not. In that, we're the same. We all do what we have to do.

"I have to go," Oscar says. "If I hear anything about Brawler, I'll let you know."

I don't ask how he's going to be able to do that since I'll be stuck here with no cell, but at least Oscar has access to the tower. It's not out of line for him to be here. In fact, it's pretty much mandatory that he's here. "How deep are you in this, Oscar?"

He curls his hands into my t-shirt—well, Johnny's t-shirt. "As much as you, Princess."

I nod knowingly. At least Brawler isn't in. He could leave and never come back, and it would be okay. "You should keep up with football. You never know what might happen."

He kisses my forehead and steps away. "Talk soon," he promises, then he leaves, closing the door behind him. The air in this room is electrically charged now, pricking my skin with tiny bolts. The broken lamp on the floor holds my attention. I really did almost get shot twenty minutes ago. As far as I know, Johnny could be inflicting some sort of mortal punishment on Glo right now.

Yet, I'm not as terrified as an outsider should be. I'm not going to cower into a fucking corner and wish for my mom. That shit fucking sailed years ago.

I turn to the door closest to the main door, hoping for a closet. I'm right. Inside, I find a dustpan and a broom and start picking up the broken shards of the lamp that fell to the floor. Behind me, the door swings open. I startle, some of the lamp pieces falling to the floor again.

"What are you doing?"

I look over my shoulder and find Magnum, one hand still on the knob but staring at me as if I've lost my mind. I shrug. "Cleaning?"

He comes over, maneuvering his hand around my upper arm and gently tugging me upward. "Let someone else do that."

"Oh, is there housekeeping I don't know about?"

"Of course, there is," he snaps. The ferocity of his voice makes me take a step back. He takes the broom and dustpan from me and bends at the waist to complete what I started. "There's no way in hell you're cleaning up after the fight where you could've died."

"I didn't know who else was going to do it."

"All you have to do is say something to Johnny. He'll take care of it. If he wasn't so furious about Glo, he would've handled it already." I take a step toward him to try to take the broom back, but he moves it out of my reach. "Just relax. You had a gun pulled on you today."

I'll say one thing for gang men. They're all fucking stubborn. If he wants to clean up the mess, more power to him. I step around him and head back to the sofa, kicking the bags of clothes Glo brought aside. I bet Lynette's going to have to find a new worker. Even if they don't kill her, they won't let her work there again.

"Do you want to talk about it?" Magnum asks. He's brought the trashcan in from the kitchen, sliding the sharp blue shards into the bin before grabbing the top half of the broken lamp and tossing that inside too.

I shrug, still eyeing the clothes. She definitely had it in her. I have to give her props for that. She was just a little too dumb. She didn't think with her head, she thought with her heart. It's a good reminder that if I'm not strategic about what I'm doing here, I could end up "downstairs" just like her.

"She fired the gun, you know," I find myself saying. "I mean, she pulled the trigger, it just didn't fire."

Magnum's face tightens. He leans the broom against the couch and drops the dustpan on the floor. It clatters before everything in the room falls silent. "She shot at you?"

"I was distracted," I tell him, mistaking his tone.

"She shot at you?" he asks again.

I finally move my gaze to look at him. Usually Magnum has exactly one face. Determined. Stoic. Fierce. Even when we were being shot at, he looked like he had everything under control. Right now, he doesn't look under control at all. He looks like he's two steps away from crossing over a line. "Yeah," I say, my voice catching.

"There were bullets in that gun. I checked it myself."

"Guess I'm just lucky."

"No one here is lucky, Kyla. Not unless your name is Big Daddy K."

6

By the time Monday rolls around, I can't stand staying in Johnny's suite any longer. I was right about the clothes Glo brought, and I can't help but think she'd smile if she knew how irritating it would be for me to wear these outfits. Hell, she might have even done it on purpose in case she didn't get me. Then again, I wasn't her target—at first, anyway.

I get up early, sliding out of the bed I now share with Johnny. Nothing as interesting as what happened the other night has happened again, but as curious as it sounds, he's a good cuddler. In fact, since the shootout, he's been almost a gentleman. Glo invading his space and attempting to kill me has brought out the best in him.

After showering and putting on the least risqué outfit Glo brought me, I step out of the bathroom to find Johnny sitting on the edge of the bed, his hair mussed from sleep. He cocks his head, taking me in. "What are you doing?"

"Getting ready for school," I say, walking toward the main room. Magnum was right when he said there was housekeeping here. There's also someone who stocks their kitchens on the regular. Johnny even told me last night after turning my nose up at the fish he was going to cook that I could give him a list of foods I liked and he would make sure we had it. Living here is honestly like living in a fairy tale. It's the dream of all adults everywhere. You barely have to lift a finger.

Johnny's footsteps sound behind me. "You're not going to school."

I stop, my jaw snapping shut. I try to keep my cool when I turn because Johnny does not respond well to fighting, but what the fuck? "You can't keep me here forever, Johnny."

"Keep you? You don't like it here?"

"It's not that, but I'm going crazy," I tell him. I'd already watched two entire TV seasons because Johnny spends most of the day with his father working on "business", which leaves me in here alone. "I can't just sit still. It's not in me. I have to go out and do things."

He glowers. "That school is a farce, and you know it."

"Well, it's my...farce," I say, stumbling over what to say. "Plus, I'm eighteen, I can't just not go to school. It's like the law or something."

"Actually, you can stop any time after sixteen here. You

won't need or want for anything, Kyla. You go to school to get a job, and you won't need one of those."

One of those? I scoff. It's like the real world has no place in the Heights. "But I'll want one," I say, trying to drive the point home. "I can't just sit here all day."

A smile flits over his face. He shakes his head as it grows. "You are so unlike anyone I thought I would..." He breaks off after sighing. "I guess I just thought the girl I'd end up with would be happy just shopping, getting her nails and hair done, and whatever chicks like the Kardashians do."

I glare at him. "I am so not a Kardashian, Johnny. I'm like their polar opposite." For fuck's sake. Ew.

"I like it," he says, surprising me. His face practically glows. "And I get it, you're bored as fuck. I wouldn't want to stick around here all day either, but I don't think it's safe for you to go back to school yet. Just let me put some things in place, and I'll let you go. In the meantime, what can I do?"

If I didn't know any better, I'd say Johnny is trying. Goddamnit. Can't we just explode at each other, so I can flee from the house? I need a good excuse to get the fuck out of here. I run my hands through my hair. "For starters, I need to get out," I say. "I'll go bananas if I have to look at these walls for another day. Take me somewhere. Let me do something. I can help you," I add, thinking that whatever gets me more ingratiated to Big Daddy K works in my favor. "Also, if your dad really meant what he said about me fighting, I need to start training."

He peeks at my leg. "What about your shin? I thought it was still bothering you."

"Every so often, but I'm icing it and letting it rest. I just won't do full-on contact for another week or so, but I can punch shit. I can exercise so I don't lose muscle strength."

Johnny's gaze drops to my calves. I'm literally wearing the longest shorts that were in the bags of clothes, and they're still practically booty shorts. "You don't have to worry about that," he muses.

Flames lick my face. I try to avoid any sexual situations with Johnny because I'm still confused if I'm supposed to want him or not. Plus, it works in our favor because I'm pretty sure his father still has that rule in place about us not fucking until Johnny officially rises to second in command. It saves us both the trouble of thinking about it.

He drags his gaze up my body until it rests on my face. "Tell you what. I have to head to one of our businesses tonight to check things over. Why don't you come with me? People have been asking for you. I think you have a fan club." He strides forward. "Plus, it'll work in favor of your fights, too."

One thing I definitely enjoy about staying at Johnny's place is that he conveniently doesn't wear a shirt all the time, proving even devils can be sexy. He picks up my hand and brushes a kiss over my knuckles.

"I'd be honored to have you on my arm."

Just what I need: to be arm candy. But if it'll get me out

of here and give my fights some exposure, I'm all for it. "I'll come," I tell him. "As long as you check into me returning to school."

He pulls me in for a hug. "I'll do it today."

———

Fourteen long hours later, I'm finally inside the elevator leading down to the parking lot. Being in here reminds me of Big Daddy K telling the security guard to take Glo downstairs, and I make a mental note to ask what that means one day. Hopefully, I don't find out when I'm the one who is being hauled downstairs.

Johnny leans over, pressing a kiss to the sensitive spot below my ear. "If I haven't said it already, you look beautiful."

He has said it. He said it when he zipped up this tight ass dress. He said it again right before we left his suite. This time, it's whispered with a breathy moan that starts my heart racing. It's becoming more difficult to deny my attraction to Johnny. Especially with the way he's been acting lately, but maybe that's because I haven't been allowed out into the real world, and I'm starved for any type of interaction. And attention. Even Oscar hasn't been able to come by and see me.

I squirm out of his grip with a demure smile. He sighs. "I

know, I know." He runs his hand through his hair, temporarily messing it up before he brushes his fingers through it again until it's perfectly styled in that messy way.

"Why don't you tell me where we're going and why?"

"We're headed to Candy's."

"And Candy's is...?"

"A strip club."

I snap my jaw shut as dread pools in my belly. It's a reaction I quickly try to cover up, but it's of no use, so I just go with it. "You're taking me to a strip club."

"It's for business, Kyla," Johnny says, threading his fingers through mine as we walk to the car. "It's one of our up-and-coming ones, and we like to keep a close eye on it. Make sure everything is running smoothly. We check the books and watch surveillance from the tower, but it's not the same as going there and feeling it out."

I get in the backseat and stare straight ahead. I get what he's saying, but if he turns this into some sort of freaky business trip, I'm not going to just sit back. I don't care how pissed off he gets at me. I didn't spend all fucking weekend in his suite just to be taken out to watch some girl grind against him. Or hell, even more. I know he's not above that.

Beyond the divider, Magnum takes a seat behind the wheel. Another security guy occupies the passenger seat. I found out that the guy I told to leave the room when Glo got there was reprimanded, which I wasn't happy about. I'm the one who told him to leave after all, but Johnny didn't want to listen to me. He wants people to act for my safety, whether I give them an order to do the opposite or not.

Within five minutes, the sleek, black car comes to a halt. Johnny throws the door open and steps out. I slide along the leather seats, keeping my knees tucked together because in this dress, I could literally show everyone everything I have with very little effort. When I get to the end of the seat, I swing my legs out and Johnny reaches his hand back in. He pulls me up and into his hard chest. His eyes are such a contrast to the night, and in no time at all, I get lost in them. "Don't worry so much, Kyla. You won't have to run interference all night. We'll see if your reputation has gotten around." He gives me a quick wink. Despite how sexy I find that wink, his words clash inside me. I don't want it to be me that keeps the skanks at bay. I want it to be him. I've never considered myself a jealous person, but when he fucked Lynette's worker in one of the dressing rooms, he fucked with my head, too. He feels badly about it. Now. Not then. Then, he thought I was a Kardashian. Now, he knows better.

He turns, threading my arm through his. Magnum and our other guard flank us while Johnny tells me they started the strip club business venture last year. It's brought in really good money since its inception, and since it's been doing so good, they're keeping a keen eye on it to see if it's something they can replicate in another town.

Judging by how Big Daddy K and Johnny are taken care of, I imagine their business pursuits bring in quite a lot of money. The only thing they don't have at their disposal, that I would seriously think of getting, is a cook. Who knows, they may have already thought of that but determined it was too risky. Guys like them have to watch their backs all the time. Nothing made that clearer than Glo shoving a gun in my face.

We enter through a back door and are immediately greeted by Wild Thing being pumped through the speakers. Lasers flash in the main room, lighting up the back hallway with a sharp glow. Our security detail nods at their security detail, and we're let through without pause.

A tall, thin man in a well-appointed suit walks down the hallway toward us. He and Johnny shake hands, and then Johnny motions toward me at the same time he squeezes my arm closer to him. "This is Kyla Samson."

"Kyla," the man says, deliberately keeping his stare on my face. "Joe Dunnegan. Welcome."

"Thank you," I tell him. This place makes me uneasy. No offense, but I don't really want to sit around watching a bunch of women take their clothes off. Now, if we were in a male strip club, I'd be all about it. Especially if the theme of the night was badass fighters. Hell fucking yes. Strip it down bare.

"We'll take one of your private tables," Johnny says.

"Business or pleasure?"

"Business," Johnny says, allaying some of my concerns.

Joe turns to lead us out of the hallway. "I sent last quarter's profit-and-loss statement in earlier."

He doesn't look like a guy who would own a strip club. Then again, I don't know much about them. My knowledge comes from how they're portrayed in movies. If I met Joe on the street, I'd peg him as an investment banker. Or maybe someone who owns a sports team. He's a mid-thirties businessman who's impeccably dressed with several rings adorning his fingers. In fact, he reminds me a hell of a lot of Big Daddy K.

Instead of calling a server over, Dunnegan takes Johnny and I to a booth in the back corner. It's secluded. From here, we can see everything, but the lights aren't shining on us. When Dunnegan steps away, I ask, "So, where's this Dunnegan in the hierarchy of things?"

"My level," Johnny says. "He runs this business for my dad. He gets paid a wage, but everything funnels through to the business accounts. He's been with Dad for a long time."

"So, you trust him?" I ask.

"About as much as we can trust anybody in this business," he says, squeezing my thigh.

Now that we're seated, it's impossible to block out everything happening around us. The women delivering drinks are scantily clad. On stage, is the only place they strip as far as I can see from where we are. After watching one full routine, I have to give these ladies props. The dancing was insane. And sexy as hell. I can see why this place is packed tonight.

It might just be my limited experience with these places, but it looks as if Candy's is on the higher end of strip clubs. The girls aren't sloppy. They're skilled. They may be taking their clothes off for money, but there's a certain type of dignity to what I see them doing. Almost like an art.

A rowdy group—what looks to be a bachelor party—in the front catcalls the girl using a Victorian sofa in her dance, and a security guard promptly goes over to them to issue a warning.

Frankly, I'm impressed. I thought I was going to hate every single second of this.

A woman with a uniform that covers very little of her chest and dips low into a booty short comes over to our table to take our drink orders. She flirts with Johnny, but how could you not? He's gorgeous. Plus, what is she supposed to do? It's her job.

"What do you think?" Johnny asks when she walks away.

"It's...cleaner than I thought," I offer.

He laughs, and an alarming pair of dimples show up.

My lips part, and he immediately stops. "What?"

"You have dimples," I say. "I've never noticed them before."

"That's because you're too busy staring at my naked chest."

My mouth drops further. I can't even argue with him about that. My cheeks turn fifty shades of red. He leans forward, lips brushing my ear so he can be heard over the music. "You know what that face reminds me of? When you came with my thumb on your clit."

His fingers dig into my thigh, and my breath hitches. Did he really think it was a good idea to bring me here? "As long as my clit is the one you're thinking about," I say, pushing the boundaries far too much. "I'll blush like this for you all night long."

He nips at my ear, and I jerk away to tease him. Is it wrong that I like how sexual he is? I just want him to be sexual with only me though. I think. I mean, that's where I'm going with this right? It might seem wrong considering I'd gladly hop into three guys' beds at this point, but that's just where I stand on the subject. I'm not making a fucking apology for it.

"You make working really fucking difficult, Kyla."

I slide closer to him, maneuvering his arm around my shoulders. Our waitress brings our drinks but also places a plate of chicken wings on the table. "It's on Dunnegan. He says the best fighter in the Heights deserves some protein."

Johnny squeezes me tighter and kisses my temple. I grin from ear-to-ear. "Thanks," I tell her.

She nods and leaves, this time not giving Johnny any lingering looks. I smirk at that because how could I not?

"So," I start. Now that the wings are in front of me, I'm suddenly super hungry. They smell delicious too. "If Dunnegan is high up in the Crew, how come he wasn't at the fight?"

Johnny drops his hand to my back while I eat. "Everyone has their roles," he says. "There are others in my position, like Dunnegan, who just work the different businesses and don't really have to get their hands dirty. For me, I'm involved in everything because—"

"You're going to take it over one day?"

His shoulders stiffen, then he nods once. He's suddenly a lot more serious than he has been all night. I don't know where the good mood Johnny came in with went, but I sit and eat my wings in silence while he stares ahead. He's watching the girls on the stage, but I highly doubt he's even paying much attention to them. Besides, his gaze keeps wandering to different areas of the room. I'm sure he's watching the staff, the clientele, checking the way things are run because if anything, Johnny takes his job very seriously. He's set to take over many very profitable businesses. He's no slouch. What he does just happens to skirt the line of legality here and there. Or everywhere.

A few minutes after I finish and our waitress has come to replenish our drinks and take away my discarded wings, Johnny motions with his chin to a waitress in the corner.

She's letting a guy feel her up. It looks so private that I turn away. He shakes his head. "I have to speak to Dunnegan about her. No touching allowed here."

He eases himself out of the booth. When he moves out of sight, Magnum comes forward, sitting down next to me on the other side. I look down to find the other security we came in with following Johnny down the stairs leading to the back hallway we came in at.

"He always asks you to watch me, huh?"

"He thinks you trust me."

"I do."

He turns toward me. "Not as much as I'd like."

I lick my lips. There's nothing I can do about that. The position I'm in makes it hard to trust any-fucking-body. "What happened to Glo?" I ask. I've been too scared to ask Johnny. I don't want to hear him say the words.

Magnum's gaze skirts the room. "She wasn't going to ever get away with what she planned on doing, Kyla. She knew that when she came in."

Well, I guess that answers that question. My skin grows cold, and I hug my hands to myself.

Mag peeks at me. "For someone with so much morality, I don't know why you insist on staying here."

"Why do you think I have so much morality?"

He peers at me with hooded eyes. "The look on your face when shit goes down."

Well, that's lovely. I'll have to try to temper my initial

reactions from now on, but I'm pretty sure that's just called humanity.

Another server dressed in the same revealing outfit approaches Magnum from the side. She places her hand on his shoulder. "Hey there. Anything I can do for a big strapping guy like you?"

He shakes his head and waves her off.

She bends over, promptly putting her breasts in his face. The barely-there top only just covers her nipples.

My face burns.

He places his arm on her shoulder and moves her out of the way without looking. "I'm working," he deadpans.

"Oh, come on," she flirts. She takes his hand and moves it to her stomach, trailing it over her skin.

Magnum's jaw ticks, and I've seen about enough. "He said no," I say blandly, not liking the spike of jealousy coursing through me. Damn. I'm just a thirsty bitch all of a sudden.

The woman's eyes round as if she's just now seen me. Not that I can blame her. Magnum's an eye full. "Oh." She smirks then bites down on her lower lip suggestively. "Are you sure you wouldn't like to watch?"

She moves his hand higher until his fingers graze her breasts. I stand, pushing the table over. I pull her to me by the thin strap of her top, her breast popping out in the process. "He said no. Now, is it your job to force yourself on the customers? I think Rocket will have something to say about that."

The strip club security surrounds us in thirty seconds. Magnum stands, too, now that he's not being manhandled. The strip club security all recognize him, so they stop their aggressive approach.

Johnny angles his way through the crowd. "What's going on?" He takes in the overturned table, the spilled drinks, and the very scared looking waitress.

Magnum keeps his mouth shut. Even when Dunnegan also emerges from the ring of security around us, he still stares impassively at the situation.

It seems as if I'm going to have to speak up myself. "Your girl here wouldn't take no for an answer," I say, gesturing toward Magnum. "He's working. He's not a customer."

"I guess you'll have to add this one to your list, too," Johnny sneers. He comes over and puts an arm around my shoulders, giving Magnum a chance to duck away.

"Of course," Dunnegan says. He gestures for the waitress to follow him and then discreetly tells another waitress to fix our table so we can continue to enjoy the show.

Overall, it's handled very well. The customers who were eyeing us now return to watching the stage where everyone's focus should be. I don't know why I notice this. I shouldn't care how the strip club is run.

"You okay?" Johnny asks.

I nod, replaying the events in my head, and wondering why the hell I got all territorial over Magnum.

I dismiss it, telling myself it was because he told her no and she wouldn't listen.

Yep. That's all it was. Completely. Totally. Not because of anything else. Never.

strong grip around my middle wakes me. I'm hauled backward against a chiseled chest and abs. Not a terrible way to wake up. In fact, I'd put it down as my favorite place to wake up. "Hey, babe."

I groan, still half-asleep and not wanting to wake up to reality.

A soft chuckle makes its way through my haze of sleep. "If you want to go to school, you better get up."

My eyes dart open. I turn my head. "School?"

Johnny's lying next to me, his head propped up in the palm of his hand. "Yeah. I made arrangements for you to go back since that's what you wanted."

I turn to face him and stuff the pillow under my head to raise me up. Johnny confuses me most of all. Listen, I'm not the type to forgive and forget. I understand he's not all good, but I'm also beginning to think that he's not all bad either. This sweetness that comes out of him from time to time keeps drawing me back.

"I know you're getting bored here. Trust me, I get it. I should've realized you'd be going out of your mind waiting for me to get done at the end of the day." He runs his fingers through my hair. "This doesn't mean you can have free rein though."

My gaze narrows.

He smiles. I'm pretty sure he loves ruffling my feathers, by the way. He's always anxious for me to let my inner bitch out, like the night of the shootout when he told me to keep slapping him. "For your safety," he tells me. "That's all. But I do want you to have more freedom." He threads his fingers through mine, glancing down to watch as he rubs his thumb over my skin. "Oscar's going to watch you. If he slacks off, let me know."

I hide a grin. Oh, I'm sure Oscar is all about watching me.

"I'd rather have Magnum," Johnny grumbles. "But he's a little old to be going to school."

"How old is Magnum, anyway?"

Johnny chuckles. "You think I keep tabs on how old my dad's people are?"

Yeah, I guess he would think that was dumb. Magnum's definitely older than me though. Older than Johnny, too. He's got to be pushing mid-twenties at least, I would guess.

He can certainly fill out facial hair, anyway. I shrug, acting casual, even though ever since Magnum told me he'd help me leave, I've been curious about him. "Just wondering."

He reaches around and pats my butt. "For someone who wanted to go to school so bad yesterday, you seem to be stalling."

I lean forward to kiss him on the cheek and then scramble out of the bed to get in the shower. The weird thing is, I don't even like school all that much. Especially school at Rawley Heights, which is just a joke of epic proportions. That alone should be evidence of how freaking bored I am in Johnny's apartment all day. At least I'll have something to do there, even if it is complaining about how terrible the education system is in the Heights.

I find the second least revealing outfit Glo gave me and pull it on before running my hands through my wet hair. Johnny's in the kitchen when I walk out, sans shirt again. He throws a frozen waffle into the toaster and then spins to face me with his back against the cupboards. "If the police show up, you don't have to talk to them. Get Oscar. If anyone gives you shit, you let me know. I don't know how it was before, but Oscar will be attending every single one of your classes with you. He's not to let you out of his sight. Understand?"

Not that Oscar doesn't want to see me, but I can imagine all these rules make him want to roll his eyes. He's not the babysitting type.

"Please don't...make me regret this," he says, finally. The waffle pops up from the toaster, and he turns to place it on a plate. When he spins back around to hand my breakfast to me, he catches my gaze in his. "You know whatever I do is to make sure you're safe. I hate to say it, but if you won't follow the rules, you're going to be stuck back here again."

My neck heats. I want to tell him where to shove it. I'm my own person, and I can certainly maneuver the ins and outs of Rawley Heights on my own but telling any of this to Johnny would just get my ass sitting back here all damn day long, and that's not happening.

"Stick to Oscar like glue. Got it," I deadpan.

"I mean, don't get too close to Oscar," he says, face darkening. "I wouldn't want to have to take both of you out." The smile that plays on his lips tells me he means to joke, but it feels like a direct threat to me. Oscar and I have been up close and personal already.

I swallow. "Your jealousy is unbecoming."

He reaches over the counter to place his hand on mine. All signs of joking are gone. "You're my prize, and I intend on claiming it."

He squeezes my hand and then turns back around to throw his own frozen waffle in the toaster. I let out a breath, my heart thumping in my chest. I place my hand over my heart to try to calm it down. It isn't as if I didn't always know his feelings on this.

To Johnny, I'm already his. There's no doubt in his

mind. He walked up to me that day in the warehouse, claimed me, and that was the end of the story for him. For me, it's not. If only for reason number one: I don't intend on staying here, and even if I do like Johnny, the chances of him leaving this place are nil. He's Crew through and through.

I hurry up and eat, desperate to get out of the apartment now that I'm granted a bit of freedom. The past few days of staying with Johnny were like living in our own bubble. It was easy to get wrapped up in Johnny and the Crew when all I saw was him, but now that I'm heading out into the real world, everything I was ever hesitant about with him creeps toward the surface again.

Bottom line is: I can't get attached to Johnny Rocket because I refuse to lose someone I care for again. And with Johnny, I'm afraid that even while I have him, I never actually do. He's chained to the Crew, nothing—and no one—else.

Magnum meets me in the hallway. He's leaning against the wall by the elevators as if he's just been waiting for me to come out of the suite the whole time. It feels weird going to school without any books or learning materials, but those are in my apartment—if I even have an apartment anymore.

The days between when I've checked in with my aunt and uncle are drawing out. I need to reach out to them soon before they come looking for me. I would hope to God they would never go to such extreme measures, but crazier shit has happened. Like when Glo tried to kill me a couple of days ago. So, I guess I shouldn't say anything is beyond the realm of possibility.

When I approach Magnum, he hits the button for the elevator, but avoids my gaze. He keeps on avoiding me all the way down the elevator, and if you've ever been stuck with someone who's as badass as Magnum who won't talk to you, it's intimidating as fuck. My skin starts to crawl as I peek over at him.

The elevator doors open, and I follow Magnum to the car. He opens the door to the backseat for me, but I roll my eyes and pull open the passenger side door. There's no reason why I have to sit in the back when it's just the two of us. I'm really not a fucking princess.

I get in, and he sighs. We close the doors at the same time and then he walks around the back of the vehicle to get in the driver's seat. He starts the car, and I glance at him again. "Are you pissed at me about last night or something?"

His body locks up before he throws the car in reverse and backs out of the parking space. "I'm annoyed about a lot of things right now."

He pulls out of the underground garage, and the world gets brighter. Both of us take a sigh of relief. I didn't realize just how restricting being there can be. I get that I'm bored and that I don't like it, but when the freedom finally hits, it's like a wash of cool water against skin on a hot summer's day. It's refreshing and liberating, and you'd do anything to feel it again.

As we drive to school, my mind wanders. The last time I was in the front seat of a car with Magnum, someone was shooting at us. Today feels like miles away from that.

"Why did you do that yesterday?"

"What?"

"With the girl? Why did you dump the table?"

I rub my neck. Awareness pricks at my skin. He's sneaking glances at me now, making me uneasy. I liked it better when he was trying to ignore me. "You said no, Magnum. You deserve to be heard. Plus, Johnny would've been pissed if he came back to find that girl rubbing up on you while you were supposed to be working. He was already down there complaining about another waitress."

I glance at him from the corner of my eye. He runs his fingers through his side scruff then places his hand back on the wheel, tightening his hold until his knuckles turn white. "So, you didn't want me to get in trouble? That's why?"

"Yep," I say. Honestly, I didn't think of that right away, but it's a damn good excuse, anyway. Johnny would have flipped if he saw that girl rubbing up on Magnum when he was supposed to be watching me, and he's the type to act first and ask questions later. His fear of not having Magnum's attention on me would have overridden any sense he had.

Magnum pulls up to the school. Out the windshield, I watch as Oscar kicks away from the brick building and starts to walk toward us. Before I push the door open, Magnum places his hand on my forearm. "For future reference, I don't need your help to stay out of trouble, and I certainly don't need your help to tell girls no."

I blink at him. His eyes pierce more than normal today. It's as if his gaze and his words have struck me. "Fine," I snap. I pull my grip from him and throw the door open. My reaction says more about how I truly feel than I'm willing to let on, but sometimes ignorance is bliss.

I slam the door behind me, spin, and then immediately, Oscar's in front of me. He cocks his head to the side when he sees my face. "Did Princess wake up on the wrong side of the bed this morning?"

"Princess? Who's Princess? Never fucking heard of her."

His eyebrows rise and that sexy-as-sin smirk overtakes his face. "Oh, it's your name now. You're never getting rid of it."

I push past him like I'm eager to start my day.

"Yikes." He hurries to catch up with me. "I was informed you wanted to come to school. I mean, I barely believed it, but..." He lowers his voice. "I can't imagine being stuck with Johnny is all that pleasant for you."

I quickly check the surrounding area. Oscar knows better than anyone that ears are everywhere. People who want to move up, who would just love to throw anyone under the bus as a stepping-stone are like vultures. Something like that would make it to Johnny within a few minutes.

"Relax," Oscar says. "I whispered it."

Oscar and I walk past Security without getting checked, proving once again that if there's anyone to fear here in the school, it's the Heights Crew. Oscar probably has a weapon on him. Sure, he's not able to carry his favorite—his bat—around, but he, and everyone else in the Crew, at the very least has a small, concealable knife. I'd bet everything I own on it. Hell, I'd bet everything my aunt and uncle own on it.

"I need to get to my apartment after school today. Or during school. I don't care which, but I need to get to my apartment."

"Whoa, whoa, whoa," Oscar says, catching my arm as I continue to walk down the hallway. I stop where I am and spin toward him. He tightens his grip for a brief second until I look him in the eye. He steps forward as people walk past us, making this as much as a private conversation as it needs to be. "Listen, I get you're pissed, but we have to be very strategic about everything. You don't think Johnny has people watching your apartment? He'd want to make sure it's safe so maybe you can go back to it."

"If he was, wouldn't you know?"

He gives me a look like I'm crazy. "No, Kyla. That's not how it works. Up there, at the top, they know everything. They only tell us what we need to know to do what they ask. Right now, I've been asked to watch my boss's girlfriend. If I take you to your apartment and he finds out about it, guess what? I won't be able to be around you again. Hell, I might be out on my ass. Or worse. So, no, I'm not taking you to your fucking apartment until I think we can get away with it. Or until Johnny tells me to."

I grit my teeth. I want so badly to be mad at him, but it's not him. Not at all. It's everything that has to do with this Crew. It's stifling under their umbrella. Or maybe it's just because I'm so close to Johnny that it's like living in quicksand. I can't move forward. I can't go sideways. I'm stuck in place unless I want to drown.

I pull my arm away from Oscar and wipe my hands down my face, trying to collect myself. I'm mad at the wrong people here. I get it. "I know."

He steps closer. "Fuck. Please don't have a breakdown at school because I'll want to drag you into a closet to make you feel better, but that won't help anything."

I crack a smile, some of the tension leaving me. That actually sounds like a great idea, but I know we can't. "I'll try to behave."

"Ha. Right. You were born to get people in trouble. Now, come on. Apparently, I have to go to all of your classes instead of mine."

I shake my head. "Well, that's not going to work, will it? You have to get somewhat decent grades in your classes to still do football. I'll go to all your classes."

Oscar swallows, and he pins me with his gaze. Despite his tight-fitting shirt and impeccably shaven hair, there's a vulnerability he lets me see every time, cracking through that tough guy facade. I'm the one who sees the bags under his eyes and the worry lines on his face. "You'd do that for me?"

"Is that even a real question? You need football, Oscar. It's what's going to get you out of here."

He rubs his neck. "What about you?"

I want to laugh. Instead, the backs of my eyes heat up. This is just my pretend life. This is the one I'm going along with until I can get back to my old one. What sucks is that I want to take elements of this one and bring them with me when I leave when I don't even know if that's possible. "I'm good," I tell him. I take a deep breath and start to walk around him.

I accidentally run into a girl who apologizes profusely like I'm going to haul off and punch her in the face. I smirk because... Well, it's kind of nice to be feared. Especially when you've spent most of your life afraid. I glance up and meet a pair of deep blue eyes.

I stop, and Oscar runs into me from behind. We both stumble, but I'm too fixated on the guy standing at the end of the hall to care.

He's stopped, too. He clutches his book bag to him while we stare at one another.

Fucking shit. He's alive.

Brawler...he's here.

8

I didn't realize how much I was worried about him until right this moment. So many people told me he would be okay that I started to believe it. I just automatically assumed he was out here waiting for his chance to check in. To find me. But right now, I also recognize the weight being lifted off me, and the heat behind my eyes pooling in the corners.

"Shit," Oscar curses. "Not right here."

He pulls me into the women's room and tells all the girls in there to get the fuck out. Crew business. They all scramble from the room, apologizing to us. There's even one girl who runs from the stall, still pulling up her underwear. I watch in disbelief, but in the next moment, Brawler strides through the door, and I don't give a fuck anymore.

I go to him, throwing my arms around his wide shoulders.

Oscar sighs angrily behind us, then moves to the door, probably settling against it to make sure no one comes in while we have our reunion.

"I was worried," I manage to get out.

He holds me tighter. "I was hoping you'd come back to school. I was fucking trapped. Reaching out to you would've just drawn unwanted attention, and fuck, I knew you'd be upset."

"Not sure I got a hug when I came back," Oscar grunts.

I roll my eyes. He got more than a hug, and he fucking knows it. "At least you didn't get slapped," I tell him.

"I'm not opposed to it." Brawler looks over his shoulder, sending Oscar a dirty look. He's no doubt picturing slapping Oscar himself.

I sink my fingers into his shirt. "I was talking about Johnny."

Brawler twists to face me again. "You slapped Johnny?"

Oscar is smirking big time now. I guess it is kind of funny. "A few times."

"Good. Fucker," Brawler all but growls.

"Did you know what was going to happen?" I ask.

He shakes his head. "Of course not. It would've been nice to know, though, Dickhead."

Oscar pushes off the bathroom door. Brawler spins, putting me behind him like he's going to protect me. Oscar gets in his face. "You two don't seem to realize I can't fucking say shit. I explained to Kyla why I didn't tell her, but I don't owe you fucking anything. I don't fucking owe you a heads up if you're not even going to join the Crew. You want to know what's going down, you know how to fix that, don't you?"

I shake my head. "No, no. Brawler is *not* joining the Crew." I maneuver between the two of them and push them apart. "Fuck that. No one should join the Crew who doesn't have to."

"Then he needs to stop whining about what he doesn't know."

"Alright," I say, raising my voice. Above us, the warning bell rings. I just hope it's not the bell that signals the beginning of a fight. I can't have these two at war with one another. If we're going to all get out of this, we'll need each other.

The two stare one another down. Neither one of them apologizes, though that shouldn't be a surprise either. I turn to Brawler, my face twisting into a smile. "I'm so glad you're okay," I tell him. A warmth envelops my chest.

He smiles back, his Adam's apple moving underneath the ink on his throat. "I was so relieved when I heard people talking about not only how you beat up a grown-ass man but survived a shootout. I think you're more than just the Uppercut Princess now. You're like the Heights Princess."

I shake my head. That fucking nickname. Maybe

Oscar's right. It's never going away now. Not until I get the hell out of the Heights, anyway.

"I'm not trying to rush," Oscar says, "but let's wrap this up. We can talk at lunch."

I squeeze Brawler's hands. "Johnny put Oscar in charge of looking after me at school. That's how I was able to come back. I'm going to all his classes today."

Brawler squints, but then light fires in his eyes, like he's already put together why I'd be going to all his classes. "Okay. See you at lunch."

"Lunch," I say, like it's a promise.

Oscar and I walk out of the bathroom first. When we're just about to turn the corner toward Oscar's first class, the bathroom door swooshes open again, but I don't look back even though seeing Brawler for the first time in four days was one of the happiest moments of my life.

"Are you sure you like both of us?" Oscar teases. His arm twitches between us like he wants to throw it over my shoulder but can't. We're all working against our own natural instincts here. For a moment, I imagine telling Johnny I'm seeing Oscar and Brawler. For a split second, I even imagine what it would feel like if he was okay with it, but that would never happen.

In Johnny's eyes, I'm his. I've never been a proponent of owning someone. Even when married, you don't belong to someone. You cohabitate because you want to. Because you wouldn't want to with anyone else. Johnny didn't grow up with the same morals others do. Hell, Oscar and Brawler are different, too. The Heights is like another dimension with different rules, laws, and codes that makes it hard to navigate. But for the time being, that's what I have to do. I don't have a choice. I not only want to stay here to avenge my parents, I'm a part of this world now. I can't leave until I escape, and I'm not escaping until I put a bullet between Big Daddy K's eyes.

———

Just as I thought, none of the teachers blink an eye when I show up in all of Oscar's classes. No one gives us shit either when Oscar tells the person he sits next to in every class to vacate their seat so I can sit in it. In fact, some even ask me about my fights. They act like the shootout was UFC 238. They gloss over the fact that people died there. Or maybe it's just such a part of their world that it doesn't affect them like it should. Either way, the ones I've spoken to about it can't wait for me to fight again, most of them asking when my next fight is so they can come watch.

Oscar fields those questions. He's like a politician of the gang world. He's a smooth talker, making everything sound good even though it might be a pile of shit with sparkly accessories to dress it up.

On our way to lunch, we come across Nevaeh in the hall. She looks us over but has the brain cells to keep going without saying anything. Now, I wouldn't need to hold back if I wanted to kick her ass. I'm sure it would look good to everyone else, too. As Johnny says, 'we don't give fights away for free', but a teaser certainly couldn't hurt. Plus, I fucking owe her a few bruises.

We get to lunch and find Brawler sitting in the corner of the room by himself, telling everyone to fuck off when they try to sit with him. When we sit, the annoyances double with everyone trying to sit with us until pretty much everyone takes a seat at another table, leaving us three to ourselves.

It's difficult as fuck to sit next to two guys you're attracted to and not flirt, touch their hand, or, you know, act like you like them. I might as well wear a nun outfit while I'm at school now, and trust me, the outfit Glo brought for me to wear is a far cry away from the ample black and white fabric and headpieces nuns wear. I'm in a crop top and booty shorts, but on the upside, I do fit in with everyone else now, so there's that. If I gave a fuck about fitting in, I might feel better about coming to school now. I don't.

"So, what's happened?" Brawler asks, keeping his voice low. "Is it safe to come back?"

Oscar nods. "According to K, they got all the top dogs under Roza, so they won't be retaliating. We're clear until the next shit happens."

"Next shit?"

Oscar's lips thin. "There's always something, Princess."

I sigh, and he grins at me. He fucking knows I hate that name. He just loves to get under my skin.

Brawler pulls his bag onto the table. "I forgot to give this to you this morning." He pulls out my sweatshirt and hands me my cell phone. "I had it in my hand when shit went down, and somehow, the phone stayed in the pocket. I tried texting you and your pocket went off. That's how I knew I was stuck unless you came back to school."

"You could've showed up at the tower."

"I figured it would be suspicious."

Oscar looks away, but I want to hug Brawler. I can't believe he has my phone. Now I won't be so isolated when I'm at Johnny's place. "Thank you," I tell him. My mind automatically flicks to my other phone. If anything, that's more of a priority. "Do you know if anyone has gone through my apartment? Johnny mentioned whoever was left of Roza's people would've gone there."

Brawler picks up his fork. "Haven't seen anything, but I didn't actually look either. Are you coming back?"

Oscar's laugh cuts through the air. "Seriously? You think Johnny's going to let her out of his sight? Not after what happened with Glo he's not."

Brawler frowns, looking to me for an explanation.

I kick Oscar under the table, but I'm not going to get out of it that easy. Brawler locks his blue eyes onto mine and doesn't let up. I sigh. Brawler's not going to like this. "Glo, the girl who works for Lynette? She tried to kill me."

"What?" Brawler seethes, his voice like a buoy untethered in a storm.

"Yep," Oscar says, gloating a bit. "Johnny asked Lynette to bring some clothes by. Glo showed up instead. Her brother was a part of the Crew. He died during the shootout, and she was there to get her revenge."

Brawler's gaze flicks to me.

I sink back into my seat and don't say anything. I cast Oscar a dirty look.

"The gun misfired," Oscar throws in for good measure.

"Hey, I didn't tell you that part," I protest.

"You think Johnny didn't read me the riot act when he ordered me to watch you? You're not to leave my sight. If you have to pee, I'm pretty sure I have to pee with you."

"Well, that'll be a sight."

"I mean, I wouldn't mind seeing you with your pants down." He wags his eyebrows. "The bathroom's not my number one choice, but..."

He winks at me, and I give him a look, but a smile creeps across my face at the same time. Brawler doesn't find any of this funny though. "I can't believe she went after you."

"I don't think she technically went after me. I was just the easy target, and she wanted to make them suffer like she was suffering."

"Don't give her excuses," Oscar says, his tone finally giving the gravity of the situation away. "You're not a part of this. She shouldn't have gone after you."

I press my lips together. I disagree. I've gotten myself a part of this. "I'm just saying I understand why she would want to do what she did."

I go back to eating, but Brawler watches me with a frown. I try to avoid his eyes, but it's impossible seeing as how I'm sitting across from him and I haven't seen him in four whole worrisome days.

"I'll check in with the Crew to see if they need my help watching you again."

I shake my head. "Johnny says I'm going to be in the fights now...at your warehouse. I'm going to tell him I want to train with you."

"Like he's going to let that happen." Oscar pushes his tray away with disinterest.

"Actually...I think he will. He told me he wants to make me happy."

Both Brawler and Oscar glare at me. I'm trying to hide the odd feelings I have for Johnny, but I'm afraid they're written all over the surface.

A jovial male voice perks up behind us. "Hey, Bat. What's up?" I look around Oscar to find the asshole who manhandled me the first day in school taking a seat next to him. I glower at him, and he just nods at me.

Before the guys can even tell him to get up, I do. "Get the fuck out of here."

He laughs like I'm joking, but I'm far from fucking

playing with this asshole. This guy is a piece of trash. A bully.

I cross my arms. "Did I stutter?"

He looks between Brawler and Oscar, but they're content letting me play this one out.

I stand, leaning over Oscar to tower over him. "You think it's funny to manhandle women." The back of my neck heats remembering his rough touch. The way he wanted me to call Oscar master. I don't care if he is Heights Crew, *that* shit needs to stop. "You're a coward."

"Oh, come on," the guy says, laughter still playing over his lips, but his eyes are searching for a way out of this. "You were no one then. Give me a break. We were told to fuck with you."

"Well, good." I smirk as I move around Oscar and come up behind him. "I've been told I can do whatever the fuck I want now, so..." I grab the side of his face and smash it against the table in front of us, pinning him there. He doesn't try to stop me. His face turns a furious shade of red, and he breathes out his nose like a caged bull. I must be deranged because I find the whole thing funny. "New rule. You don't get to fucking talk in my presence. If you do, I get to kick your fucking ass. You are no longer Oscar's little bitch. You're not friends. You don't speak. If you see me coming in the hallway, walk the other fucking way. If you don't, I'm calling you out in the fights, and then the whole school can watch when I destroy your bitch ass. Do you understand?"

He groans as I press harder. "Yes," he chokes, the one word coming out strangled.

I let him up and step back, allowing him room to retreat. He does so, swiping his hands down his face and straightening his shirt. Everyone's looking at us. The cafeteria has quieted because what's happening in this corner is much more interesting than anything else. He does his walk of shame away from our table, and I take a seat where I belong.

Oscar grins. "Why did that just turn me the fuck on?"

Brawler flicks his gaze toward the guy walking away. "You just ruined his life."

My breath leaves me. I stick my chin in the air. The guy's an asshole. He doesn't deserve the Crew.

But at the same time, Brawler's right. I have a hell of a lot more power than I think I do. If I told Johnny that guy—or anyone for that matter—fucked with me, he'd have them killed. Disposed of. Taken away without a second thought.

Power is awesome, but it's also scary as fuck.

I'll have to remember that next time I want to get revenge on someone who's just a fucking scumbag and not a murderer.

9

I spend the last period of the day texting Johnny, telling him Brawler's at school and that he had my phone. He writes back that getting me a new phone was on his to-do list, so he's glad I have my old one back.

The fact that he would even be thinking about my cell phone amidst everything else is just extraordinary. In any other dimension, Johnny would've been the nicest guy. Behavior is learned, right? Not inherent. I've never been a science or psych type of person, but that's what I think. Imagine if decent human beings had brought up Johnny. He'd probably be a disciple of Mother Theresa.

When I ask Johnny if Brawler and I can train after school, his response is slow. I imagine him fighting against his own initial reactions. Like he's trying to do better for me. But the reality is, he might just be in another meeting and can't write me back right away. Either way, when the response does come, he says yes.

I slip my phone to Oscar whose eyebrows rise into his hairline. He turns toward me, not giving a fuck that the teacher in front of the class is lecturing about something pertaining to biology. To be fair, the teacher doesn't care either because he's just reading from the textbook, which we could all do ourselves, anyway. Leaning toward me, Oscar whispers, "I didn't know he was capable of it, but if I didn't know any better, I'd say he's in love with you, Princess."

I press my lips together and grab my phone back. His words ricochet through my head. Is someone like Johnny even capable of love? Like, real love. Not what someone like him might think love is, but bone-deep, Earth-shattering, raw-to-the-core love.

I don't know if I'll ever find out.

School ends. On a scale of one to ten, I'd give it a seven for getting me out of the tower instead of hanging out by myself all day. While walking down the hallway, Oscar and I run into Brawler. "I hear I'm taking you training?" he questions. "And if you get hurt on my watch, I'm dead."

I shrug. "Is it wrong if I say, 'sounds reasonable to me'?" I laugh nervously because Johnny doesn't make idle threats.

Brawler steps up to me, clearly not finding Johnny's remarks humorous at all. "I'm not going to let anything happen to you because *I* don't want anything to happen to you. Not because he ordered it."

I can't wait to kiss him. I can't wait to throw my arms around him and lose myself in him. He must see it in my face because his jaw tenses. Once, Brawler told me that a lesser man wouldn't walk away if I gave him that look. What will it mean if he doesn't walk away? I mean, right now, we would get ourselves killed, but I'm talking about when there aren't a bunch of prying eyes.

"I've got practice," Oscar says, glancing away from the moment Brawler and I are sharing.

I turn toward him, standing there awkwardly. I can't really give him a hug, so instead, I say, "Have a good practice." It's lame as fuck, but he doesn't mind.

He looks at me, a wistful smile on his face. "I guess we'll do this all again tomorrow?"

"Most definitely," I say, already eager to get out of the tower again. Thankfully, today went so smoothly there's no reason why Johnny won't let me come back.

Oscar gives us a mock salute and then walks toward the boys' locker rooms. Brawler and I take off in the opposite direction, exiting out the main doors of the school. I should've known a sleek black car would already be out there waiting for us. Brawler opens the rear door, and I slide in. I look up just long enough to see Magnum sitting behind the wheel and then look away. When Brawler gets in, Magnum turns. He and Brawler shake hands through the divider before Magnum moves his gaze to me. "I told you he'd be okay."

I don't look at him for very long. I don't even acknowledge he's said anything because what does he want me to say? He scolded me earlier like a child and now he wants to make nice? I shake my head. I just can't deal with that right now.

"Where are we headed?" Magnum asks.

"There's a gym on the edge of town." I look to Brawler who leans forward, telling Magnum where to go.

As soon as he does, Magnum hits the button to raise the divider. Soon, Brawler and I are in the back of the car...alone. For the first time in too long. We turn toward one another. I reach out, feathering my fingers over his skin. I trace the angel wings on his neck like I'm touching the most sacred parts of him. "I bet these angels kept you safe."

He cups my face. "I don't know how anyone got out of there."

"Magnum dragged me out," I tell him. "Literally."

He swallows when I reach for him, my thumb skimming over his pulse point before moving around his neck. His pulse thunders a mile a minute, and his expression darkens. "We've got to get out of here, Kyla." True emotion coats his words. "If we stay, we're going to end up dead. *You're* going to end up dead."

His stare is so forceful, it makes me gasp for breath. I hate hurting him, but I can't do what he's asking. Not now. "I can't leave."

"We need to try." He grabs my hands in his. "We could do it. I'll keep you safe. I promise."

"I can't leave *yet*," I clarify. I'm all in with Brawler. I have been. If trusting him is the wrong move, then I'll die by that sword.

"Does it have something to do with this?" He pulls out a small cell phone from his pocket.

I cover it like I don't want to see the sight of it. "Where'd you get that?"

"You know where I got it," he says. "I didn't look through your stuff. Your place was trashed. I went in to salvage what I could and found this. Whoever trashed it must have missed it."

"Was there a—?"

"A picture?" He opens the small front pocket of his book bag, allowing me to peek inside. I cover my mouth, trying to hold everything inside. "I thought maybe it was important to you."

"Those are my parents."

I press down on his book bag, enclosing the picture once again in the zippered pocket. I can't bear to see their faces right now. The two most important things I own, and Brawler has them. I push the bag back over to him along with the phone. I can't think of a better person to keep these things safe.

I sit back in the seat and take a deep breath. Turning my head to the side, I eye an unsure Brawler. He's put his book bag down on the floor and is fully facing me now. "I can't tell you why," I start. "But can you keep those two things with you? I can't take them back to Johnny's apartment. He can't know about them."

"Of course, but whoever's contact you have in that phone, I'd call them if I were you. They've called and texted a bunch."

My pulse ratchets up. "You read them?"

He shakes his head. "I turned it on to see if it belonged to the person who ransacked your place. That's all."

Relief floods me when Brawler doesn't ask any more questions. "I'll call them at the gym. If you'll cover for me."

He nods, then reaches over to place his hand on my shoulder, squeezing me gently. Despite what his tattoos and badass muscles portray to the world, he's got such a good heart. Naturally. I've been surrounded by all walks of life, and I just might have found the person with the biggest heart in the slums of Rawley Heights.

When the car pulls to a stop, Brawler and I get out. He slips my small cell into his pocket. Instead of waiting in the car, Magnum follows us. My heart rate picks up. Having Magnum join us just means more eyes. I only hope I can get a moment to myself to call my aunt and check in with her. Then, I can give the phone back to Brawler where he can keep it safe for me.

We stride in. One of the trainers we had before straightens. He'd been giving instructions to a lightning quick teenager jabbing the air in front of him, but now he's focused on us. He hits the other trainer in the chest a couple of times to draw his attention. "No shit," the guy says, all smiles.

"Don't tell me Uppercut Princess wants to train in our gym."

I roll my eyes into the back of my head. "I will if everyone stops using that name."

"I like it," Mag says, shrugging.

I glare at the back of his copper head. The trainers shake hands with Magnum, Brawler, and I. "Jax," by the way, the first trainer says. He's the more serious one. Cropped, jet black hair glistens with sweat. He's a few inches shorter than the other trainer, but no less fierce. Tattoos adorn each knuckle.

"Kyla," I tell him.

He nods, and it's possible I actually have a shot of him calling me Kyla instead of Princess. Like a mutual respect kind of thing. I like him instantly.

The other trainer, Finn, I'm not so sure I have a shot. He's more playful, and even though they're brothers, the two trainers couldn't be more opposite. Finn has lighter hair, pulled back into a short ponytail. He has some height on his brother, and a bit more weight to him too. They're both good looking. Obviously. I mean, I don't need to explain how hot I think fighters are anymore, do I? I have a type. Maybe Oscar, the star quarterback, or Johnny, the gang leader's son, don't play into that type, but that's okay. I'm an equal opportunity hottie lover.

Magnum takes over. I just stare while he explains to Finn and Jax that I'll be fighting in the underground fights and that I need a place to train.

"Well, officially," Finn says. "We don't condone underground fighting." A giant grin splits his face. "But unofficially, we're all for it."

Jax gives him a look. Yep, he's definitely the more serious brother. He doesn't look like he's quite so sure about this. He opens his mouth, and I'm almost positive he's about to tell me to get lost when he says, "Tell me you have something more appropriate to train in."

He stares me up and down, looking at my clothes with distaste, and I grin. "Trust me, I wouldn't wear these clothes if I didn't have to." He gives me a strange look, but I don't bother explaining. The story is just way too involved. "You got a shop in here?"

A smile swallows Finn's face. "Did someone just ask about our shop?" He raises his eyebrows at his brother in quick succession. "Someone's going to eat those words about selling attire being a gigantic waste of money."

Jax blows out a breath, and I try to contain a smile. Brothers are fun.

"Right this way," Finn says, hiking his thumb over his shoulder. He brings us to the corner of the gym. There's mostly guys' stuff, but there are a few sports bras, and I honestly couldn't care less if I wear guy's sweats or women's. I'll just have to get a smaller size in the men's cut.

Magnum reaches into his back pocket and takes out a black wallet. Of course. The color is unsurprising. He opens it and extracts a credit card. "You're not paying for it," I say, placing my hand over his to stop him.

Magnum turns to look at me and then points to the name on the card. Rocket Enterprises. Ah, well, okay. I guess that's acceptable. "I've been instructed to make sure you have everything you want." He hands the card over to Finn. "Put the training fees on there as well."

Finn looks positively giddy as I grab clothes from the racks. "I'll try these on."

"Whatever you want, Princess."

I scowl at him, which only makes him more light-hearted. What is with guys loving to piss girls off? It makes me want to punch something.

I walk by Brawler, and underneath all the clothes I've just piled on, he slips the small, nondescript phone into my palm before I head to the changing rooms. Before I even start to change, I quickly scroll through the texts on my phone. As usual, they start out casual and then turn more frantic when I don't answer. I don't even bother checking any of the voicemails she's left other than the last one. "I need you to call me. Okay. Bye."

She's pissed. Rightfully so. It's been too long since I've checked in.

I dial her number, counting the rings and hoping she'll pick up instead of leaving a voicemail. If I have to leave a voicemail, I'll just have to call her again tomorrow, so she can grill me about what I'm doing and why I can't return her calls right away. "Hello?" she says, breathless.

"Hey," I say, tongue sticking to the roof of my mouth.

The phone crackles for a moment because of the heavy sigh she releases right into the speaker. "You're okay."

"Yeah," I tell her. "I'm okay."

"Do you remember when I told you I was okay with you going to high school somewhere else that I also said one of the stipulations was that you checked in with us regularly? That hasn't changed." She groans. "I knew I shouldn't have let you do this."

"I'm okay," I say. "Really. I just got caught up doing things, and the phone was...not working, so I couldn't call you back on it." Well, that sounded lame as fuck.

"I'm worried about you," she says, her voice breaking. "I think you should come back."

"I—I can't," I say. "Everything's fine here, really. You know I can take care of myself."

"I just..." She breathes out. "I think Anna would've hated that I let you do this. I—"

"It's one year," I tell her. It's the same exact reasoning I used on her to get her to agree to this in the first place. "I'll be off to college next year anyway, so it's fine."

"But I don't know anything that's going on. How are

your grades? Are you safe? Are you eating? Are you dating? These are things I need to know because I worry."

"My grades are fine," I tell her. She has no reason to think otherwise because I was always good at school. Even at the private prep school with all the bitches and jerkoffs. "I'm eating. I'll send pictures to prove it to you. I've found some friends. That's why I haven't called you back as much. I've been...hanging out with them." I've just redefined 'hanging out', but she doesn't need to know my version of hanging out means almost getting shot.

"Friends?" She perks up at that. My aunt and uncle always tried to get me to be friends with their country club friends' kids, and I rebelled. They just weren't my people.

"Yep," I say, happy to be on a different topic. "Honest to goodness friends."

She doesn't say anything for several long moments, but she finally breaks the silence. "I just worry, you know."

"I know," I tell her. Not for the first time, I think about how different my aunt and mom are. I don't know how my mom would've acted when I was older, of course, but she let me be my own person when I was younger. She encouraged me to try different things and spread my wings. My aunt is a little steadier. She likes her big house and huge paycheck. She enjoys the cushioned life, which is why I always felt bad for crashing it and ruining everything for her. I was never part of her plan until there wasn't a choice. "I'm actually at the gym now. I'll call you in a couple of days, okay?"

"Fine. But a couple," she says, voice stern.

"Agreed," I tell her. "Tell everyone hi."

"Love you," she says.

I lick my suddenly chapped lips. I've said 'I love you' to people. I know what it's supposed to feel like, but saying I love you to someone you owe a lot to never feels good. At least not to me. "Love you, too," I choke out.

*N*ear the end of our training session, Johnny strolls in. He's wearing a suit, much like he wore yesterday when we went to Candy's. Because I'm distracted, Finn almost gets a punch in on me, but I parry it at the last possible moment.

It's a good thing, too, because I'm sure Johnny wouldn't take well to Finn hitting his girl, even though it would have been my fault entirely and not Finn's.

"Jeez," Finn jokes, cracking a smile that beams like the sun. "I thought I had you there for a minute."

"Good luck," I tease, smiling back at him with my mouthpiece in, which I know from experience looks more like baring my teeth than an actual smile. In the underground fights, we don't wear mouthpieces, but training is a different story. There's no sense in trying to hurt one another while we're preparing for the actual fight.

I excuse myself from Finn and slip out of the boxing ring. I take my gloves off and remove my headgear. My sweat-dampened hair is plastered to my head. I'm sure I look like something the cat dragged in.

"Look at you." Johnny's ice-blue eyes glisten like diamonds as he looks me up and down. "I don't think I've seen you this happy in a while."

"What can I say? I just like to hit stuff."

"Stuff." Finn snorts. "Me, I'm stuff."

Johnny eyes him, and I step in to introduce them right away, explaining that Finn and Jax own the place...where I'm training...so there's no reason to want to kill them. I didn't realize these two owned the gym when Brawler and I were here before, but some of the things they've said today, including fighting over who has to clean the toilets next, makes me think they definitely own the place. Two brothers who went into business together, and from what I can tell, have been bickering ever since.

After shaking both their hands, Johnny addresses Brawler. "Glad to see you're good."

My big man nods. He's not happy with Johnny, the Crew, or Oscar for that matter. He thinks everyone should've been told about the possibility of things escalating after the fight. To him, it hit a little too close to home, driving the point in that the Crew doesn't care about anyone but the Crew, innocents be damned.

For a tense-filled moment, I glance between the two, wondering if anything is going to be said that will piss the other off. Luckily, Jax continues to train with Brawler, thereby keeping him preoccupied. Maybe Jax sensed the tension and stepped in before it got worse. Jax and Finn aren't being obvious or saying anything, but they know who Johnny is. Everyone does.

Johnny slides his arm around me, pulling me closer to him. "I missed you," he whispers, dropping a kiss to my temple.

I peer down at my sweat-soaked training gear. "Even like this?"

He drags his gaze down me slowly, lighting up every inch of my skin. "Definitely like this." His breath feathers over my cheek. "I came by to see if you wanted to hang out with me tonight. I've got some Crew business, but I thought we could make it a date night too."

"Is it Candy's again?" Not that I wouldn't mind going back, but the way we left things there wasn't exactly hunky-dory.

He laughs and shakes his head. "No, I think Dunnegan will be happy if he doesn't see me for a long time. I had to tell him to straighten up his staff requirements after the problem you had and the other girl who was clearly inebriated. The

Crew can't look bad like that." His gaze darkens, and I can tell he's retreated from the conversation for the moment. I'm sure the conversation he had with his father today about the strip club didn't go over well. The Crew is all about appearances, and sloppy employees just aren't acceptable. Except, in their world, staff isn't just written up for infractions. Depending on the severity, they could be fired, or much, much worse.

Brawler's standing entirely too close to me right now to be having this conversation. Even if he was a hundred yards away, it would be too close. The hatred I know he stokes inside him for the Crew makes guilt wrench my stomach. The tips of my ears burn as I guide Johnny farther away from him. "So, where to tonight?"

Johnny grins at me, pressing his fingers into the palm of my hand. "The track."

After stopping briefly at Johnny's suite so I can wash the fight training off me and dress more appropriately, Johnny and I drive to the edge of the next town where apparently there's a race track. Fields and small houses surround the bleachered structure, and honestly, I can't imagine why the Crew would be interested in this place. From what I've seen, they like to keep their businesses in the Heights.

"I see that look on your face. You're probably wondering what our interest in this is."

The roar of dozens of engines pierces the inside of the car. Now I understand why Johnny made sure we brought earplugs. "Yeah, a little," I say, shouting over the screaming engines.

He grins, looking less Johnny Rocket and more like just plain Johnny. He hands me a pair of the earplugs. "We thought since the fight business has been lucrative for us, we might branch out to other sports."

"But racing?" I can't help but cringe. I'm biased, sure, but racing sounds so damn boring compared to fighting. Is there blood involved? What about pure, unadulterated rage?

Johnny shrugs. "We're just looking into it." The Crew entity itself is always looking for ways to make money. Honestly, if they weren't criminals, they'd be damn good businessmen.

Like usual, Magnum parks the car and the three of us head toward the entrance of the track. Magnum's presence is more unnerving than it's ever been. When his gaze is on me, my skin pricks, and it's always on me, so I'm in a constant state of nerves. For someone who wants me to stay out of his business, he seems to take a keen interest in me.

Johnny shows our tickets to the woman scanning them, and then she directs us to one of the boxes that stands high above the actual track. We climb three tiers of seats before we end up in an enclosed, square room, much like the one rising above the fights in the underground warehouse. This one isn't as fancy though, nor as secluded. Other spectators are already here enjoying the races below, heads together discussing race-type things. Like tires and gas and engines and a bunch of other words that may as well be a foreign language to me.

A man looks up from his perch in the corner. His aging, gray hair around the temples adds a softer edge to a sharp face. The man does a double take when he sees Johnny and then moves toward us. "Sir," the older gentleman says, shaking Johnny's hand.

"Mr. Richmond, I take it?"

The guy nods in the affirmative. "Let me know if you have any questions."

He gives me a pleasant smile and returns to his seat. I watch him go, brows pulling together in confusion. It's not that he knows Johnny. I'm getting used to that by now. Johnny Rocket may as well be a celebrity for everyone who knows of him whether they've even met or not. I'm not getting that same sense in this instance. "Who's that?"

"The owner," Johnny clarifies. "My father contacted him to let him know we were going to come look at the place. There's a rumor going around that he wants to sell."

"So, you're thinking it could be like the fight ring? Bets? Attendance? That kind of thing?"

"It's a possibility." He glances around the room, lips

pulling together. He's not very impressed with what he sees. "I think we might need to add some sex."

I drown the urge to roll my eyes. "Like a racing strip club?"

His boom of laughter crinkles his eyes. "No, babe. I was just thinking maybe we could add some staff who were halfway decent looking."

I shake my head at him.

"Oh, come on. You know sex sells. Why do you think everyone is dying for you to fight?"

I turn away from the cars lapping the track to face him. My hackles are up because if he's insinuating people want to watch me only for my physique rather than my fighting skills, we're going to have problems. I blink. "I'm a good fighter."

"Well, yeah, that. Of course," he quickly backtracks. "But you have other appeal too." He runs his finger under the tiny strap of my top. Apparently, when I was at school today, Lynette dropped off a stack of clothes for me and apologized profusely about Glo. I only wish I could have been there to see if I could get a feel for whether Glo was still around or not. And when I say around, I mean breathing. Johnny locks gazes with me. "All the guys want to fuck you, and the girls want to be you."

I don't think that's true. That's his jealousy rearing its ugly head. "How will you ever stand letting me do it then?" I tease. Pushing his boundaries is fun.

His eyes flare. "Because I know who you're coming home with at the end of the night, and any guy who touches you has a death wish. I think I've made my intentions clear."

My body heats in response. I can't help it if I find his possessiveness a turn-on. It's a science-y thing, not a conscious thought. If I thought too much about it, my body would blaze with feminist outrage, but can't a girl just want to feel possessed every now and then? Johnny would rip apart anyone who ever tried to hurt me. If they even just thought about it, he'd be there, setting the world on fire because of me. No, *for* me. The thought is oddly tantalizing.

"Can I get you guys anything?"

Johnny and I stay with our gazes locked before I tear my eyes away from his and blink at the woman who's punctured my little bubble. She smiles, looking a tad awkward. I see now what Johnny meant about adding a little sex appeal to this place. The uniform seems to just be a pair of overalls with plaid shirts underneath. Not that I'm a proponent of women having to show off for marketing purposes, but a little more of that wouldn't hurt the place. Maybe like a Hooters for the race track. That is, if Johnny and his father decide racing is even worth it.

Johnny orders us some appetizers and drinks and then asks for a table. When we're sat in the middle of the room surrounded by giant TV screens, he leans in close. "If you're looking into purchasing a business, you have to scope the current place out. Is the food good? How do the clientele act? What kind of people are they? This will all go into our decision whether we purchase the place or not. We've asked for their financial statements, and that will help, but it's not quite that easy. If we get our food and it sucks, for example, we'll know why they don't do a lot of kitchen business. If there are fights in the stands, we know we'll have to up security if we buy the place so the regular crowd will know that won't fly anymore."

I catch the gleam in his eyes, and my stomach flips. "You like this, don't you?" I'm slowly piecing together the puzzle that is Johnny Rocket, and I like what I see. Well, most of it anyway. He's redeemable.

"Regardless of what some people think, I've earned my spot in the Crew." He leans back, a shadow crossing over his face. "I'm young, so I don't always get the respect I deserve. I'll have to be better than my father to gain their respect, and I will."

I scoff inwardly. He's already a better man than his father with little effort. The bacteria on the underside of my shoe is superior to Big Daddy K. Fuck. I need to change the subject before my face betrays everything. "You know, we haven't really talked much about ourselves. Your mom...is she around?"

Johnny's face shuts down. It doesn't darken or harden, it just loses all emotion whatsoever except a vacantness that I can tell has been perfected over the years. "My mother left when I was a kid."

"Your mother...left?" The leaving part more than anything is the most shocking piece of information out of his entire sentence. *She got out? Holy shit.* How *did she do that?*

It opens up so many questions in my head, including how and why, and whether Big Daddy K let her out or if she escaped. At the same time, though, I feel for the guy in front of me. As stoic as he's trying to be, any time a parent leaves, whether purposefully or tragically, it sucks. His gaze darts to me and then moves away immediately. "It was a long time ago, Kyla. You can stop looking at me like I'm going to come apart."

I sit up straighter in my seat, avoiding his gaze. I flick my stare toward the TV screens, but racing *is* boring as fuck, like I imagined. When the waitress brings our food, I'm happy for the change in context. Bringing up Johnny's mom seems to have soured the night for him. He eats a mouthful of each dish we ordered and finishes his drink, but he doesn't do it out of pleasure. He really is all business.

Me? I'm so hungry from training that I have no problem polishing off the different appetizers. They're not over-the-top delicious, but they're not terrible either. I mean, it's fried food. It's kind of hard to fuck up. Shortly after I practically lick the plates clean, Johnny asks for the check. The waitress tells us the owner covered it, so Johnny helps me stand. Placing my arm through his, we walk toward the older gentleman to thank him for our food. Johnny tells him they'll keep in touch, but I can't tell if he means it. He's just on edge all the way around, which has more to do with the question I asked him than whether he thinks the track is a viable business decision.

All semblance of normal conversation is gone. It's disappeared into the ether. Probably hiding wherever Johnny put his good mood because it certainly isn't on him anymore.

Magnum follows us out of the box seating, and I bite the inside of my cheek. Here I am with two guys in shitty moods. I also left another at the gym, pissy because of who I was leaving with. I just can't win today.

I catch a guy's eye as we head toward the exit. He leans against the ticket booth flirting with the girl inside when he gives me a stare down that lasts far longer than necessary. He wobbles on his feet. "Hey there, sweetheart. Don't you look like a peach?"

I ignore him and continue on, but Johnny pulls my arm out from around his. He moves so lightning fast, I look back to find his fist already connecting with the guy's face. The girl inside the booth gives a short scream as Johnny tackles him, the collar of the guy's shirt clenched in his hands as he leans over him. "Maybe you missed the fact that her arm was in mine." He punches him square in the jaw, and the guy's head whiplashes back, hitting the dirt behind him. A trickle of blood runs from his nose, and he groans.

Johnny's shoulders heave as he gulps in air. At first, neither Magnum nor I go for him. I'm not worried that the guy is going to try to hit him back. At this point, I'd be more worried that Johnny would lose his shit and just murder his ass. Instead, I watch as Johnny tries to collect his thoughts. He has one knee on the guy's abdomen and one in the dirt. The girl in the booth has her hands over her mouth as she looks down at the scene. We're probably too far away from the Heights for these two to know who he is, but that doesn't mean they don't understand when they've come across someone who gives zero fucks. Finally, I walk forward and place my hand on Johnny's shoulder, squeezing him for good measure. He barely registers that I'm there. The internal war with himself still waging.

He peeks over at me. "Mine."

I don't like that word…necessarily. The way he's saying it now gives me goosebumps from head-to-toe. I don't know if it's my body warning me off him or telling me that I really freaking like it when he says that. At least in this scenario.

I lick my lips. I can't tell him the guy didn't notice I was with him because he obviously did and was just drunk. Or didn't care. I bet he wishes he cared now. "He's not worth it," I say instead, nose twitching over the smell of bitter alcohol. The guy probably won't even remember how he ended up with a shiner a couple of hours from now.

I grab Johnny by the upper arm and drag him up. His suit is dusty now, and he's got the shakes from adrenaline coursing through him.

Magnum doesn't say a word through the whole thing.

Hell, he doesn't even blink as Johnny and I make our way toward the car.

Though we're right next to each other, a divide splits Johnny and I now. On the surface, that outburst was about me, but I'd bet everything I have it wasn't. It was about something much, much deeper.

Magnum holds the car door open for us, and I scoot in first with Johnny following right after. Magnum closes the door and while he's walking around to the front seat, Johnny glances down at his knuckles and says, "Don't bring up my mother again."

If that's what he's worried about, he could've saved himself the trouble of warning me off because I won't be making that mistake again. At least not to him.

We stay on opposite sides of the car, but I want to go to him. Not because I think the sudden urge to fight was about his mother, but because he just showed he has the capacity to feel deeply after all. It wasn't something I was sure he was capable of, but now I know.

I slide over the seat and place my head on his shoulder. Even asshole bad boys need comforting every once in a while.

When the car comes to a stop, Johnny gets out so abruptly I almost drop to the leather seat. I glare at his back, moving after him as he stalks toward the elevators. We wait in tense silence as the elevator moves down to collect us. Magnum doesn't follow us. Briefly, I glance over my shoulder and find him still in the car. The interior light is on, and he's watching us, unmoving and unwavering. The back of my neck pricks, but then the elevator dings and we step inside.

In the confined space, it's easy to tell just how heated Johnny is. For a moment, in the car, I thought he was better. I was wrong. His fists clench and unclench. He avoids looking at me, even though it feels as if I'm the only thing he wants to focus on at the same time.

I refuse to apologize for bringing his mother up. Isn't

talking about the past what people do when they're in a relationship? Even a forced one?

Though, that's just me being petty. I don't think I'm being forced anymore. I hate that he's upset. I want to make it better, which just makes me all that much more frustrated and lost. The elevator dings with each floor we move up, and with it, it's like the countdown to a volcano erupting.

Johnny takes his phone out of his pocket when we reach their floor. He glares at the screen. "My dad needs to see me."

Fuck that. I'm not sitting in his apartment thinking about how fucking furious he is right now. He claims he wants me so bad, then we can talk this out. "No."

Johnny's gaze moves to meet mine. His pupils dilate. "No?"

The elevator door opens. The two guards waiting outside immediately turn toward us, but it's just another added layer of tension hovering over us. I shake my head. "Not before we talk this through."

Johnny licks his lips. His pale blue eyes darken like a sudden storm surge. He grips my upper arm, practically dragging me past the two members of security, and we enter his suite with a flurry and a slammed door.

I slap his hand away from me. I know now. Johnny is better than this monster he turns into when he's pissed. He's better than this life. He has real feelings. He just needs to listen to them. He needs to trust other people who aren't his father and have nothing to do with this life. "Don't touch me if you're going to touch me like that," I fume. "You either touch me like I'm your girlfriend, or you don't at all." Johnny's eyes flare, but I don't stop there. "You go from telling me I'm beautiful one minute to scolding me the next. You trust me with shit, and then you shut me out." I swallow, watching Johnny's fists ball. He doesn't scare me, but this talk does. "You hold me in bed like you don't want to let me go, then dig your nails into my arm like a caveman, making sure I do your bidding. Which guy are you, Johnny? Can we talk calmly, rationally? Or do I have to worry every time you get upset you're going to be..." I gesture toward him. "...this guy."

His jaw hardens. He stretches his fingers out like he's trying to ward off some of the tension. Or gathering it back up. It's hard to tell with him.

"You make me this way," he growls.

I shake my head. "Sounds like something an abuser would say. It's my fault, right? It's my—"

Johnny moves so fast, I flinch. I wait for the crack of his hand upside my head or another bite of his nails into my skin, squeezing me like he has before. None of that comes. Instead, his fingertips graze my cheek. "It's you because I've never felt this way," he says on a breath. "I've never wanted to keep someone safe before. From me. My life. My past. I didn't know how hard it was going to be. How terrified I'd feel every second of the day when you're not here, *right here* where I can keep you safe."

My eyelids flutter open. The guy staring at me now wrenches my heart from me, making it pump for him despite all my attempts otherwise. "There you are," I whisper, recognizing the guy I know is in there. He may be deeply hidden most of the time, but he's there.

Johnny closes his eyes and takes a deep breath. "I don't want to talk about my mom, but that's not your fault. I don't know how I'm going to keep you safe when I'm not around, but that's not your fault either. I don't know what to do with all these emotions, but again..." He slides his hands down over my shoulders and squeezes. "That's not your fault."

Our mirrored gazes draw us to one another. Recognizing that the same fucked up shit that's in me is also in someone else is a silent call. I want to see what happens when we come together. It could be oh so perfect or burn entire cities to the ground. There is no middle ground with Johnny and me.

At this point, I don't care. I'm sick of that voice in my head saying this isn't a good idea. I'm sick of always second-guessing why these feelings come up when I'm around him. I should tell him he's got to fucking stop giving me whiplash. Should make sure he knows he can't touch me like that anymore, but instead, I wrap my arms around his neck and seal my lips to his. This kiss is scorching hot from the first moment. I meld into him as he moves his hands to my hips, pulling me closer. We devour each other, the tangle of our tongues and press of our lips ending in small sighs and moans captured by yet more kissing.

Liquid heat slithers straight to my core until I'm throbbing with need. I press against him, the tight ass dress shimmying up my thighs. The fabric comes to rest on the curve of my ass while Johnny roams his hands freely over my newly exposed skin, pulling me tighter against him like he can't get enough.

I'm salivating for him. My panties soak through. In one second, my breath gets knocked right out of me, while in the next, I drag in a whole lungful to sustain me. I rest my hands on his chest and then roam upward, taking his suit coat with me until it's over his shoulders, down his forearms, and drops to the floor. He's not wearing a tie, so I pull his button-down shirt out of his pants before resting my buzzing fingers at his fly. Brushing my fingers against his tight skin seals my decision. I unzip and unbutton his suit pants until they're resting low on his hips.

He breaks the kiss, gaze searching mine. Dropping his hands to my shoulders, he moves the spaghetti straps of my dress down until the top pools outward giving him an ample view. Even my lungfuls of air don't help. The dress tightens over my breasts with each breath, then slips lower when I release it.

Lowering his gaze, he focuses on my chest and each minute movement. "I've been wanting to see these," he purrs, the top finally dipping past my nipples. If he was thrumming with energy before, he's high off it now. He dips his head, flicking his tongue over my left nipple.

I moan and hike my leg up like I want to climb him. My dress rips, slowly giving way until my leg is securely around his hip. Johnny's mouth quirks, but then he pulls my leg higher, ripping the dress even further as he lifts me into the air. I cross my ankles over his ass as he takes another mouthful of my breasts now that they're in his face. He doesn't mind. He feasts on them like they're his last meal. I drop my head back, reveling in the sensations he ignites in me while begging him to drop me lower so I can seek the hardness I need.

"I've been jerking off every fucking day to you," Johnny growls. He nips at my nipple, and I shudder.

He backs up and turns before slowly lowering me to the couch. I arch into him, drawing his head back to my breast. He quickly flicks his tongue across my nipple several times until I grind against him. His stupid pants are in my way, so I use my feet to push them lower. When I can't quite get the grip on them I need, I use my hands, pushing them down, before grabbing his ass and forcing him to my core.

"Fuck me," Johnny shivers. He presses down until we're fucking grinding like we're actually having sex, except we're not. I cup Johnny through his boxers, and he jerks. "Fuuuck."

He's bigger than a handful. Much bigger. Hard. Straining. I slip my hands under the waistband of his boxers and run my palm down his hard ridges. Pre-cum brushes over my wrist. He pushes into my grip, then slides back, his hot mouth encasing my breast again.

Leaning on one hand for support, he reaches up to pull my dress out of the way and move my panties down. I kick them off once they're past my knees, and Johnny and I lock gazes. I run my fingers along the top of his boxers and then slide them over his hips, finally freeing his dick. I stroke him toward me. He's so close, I can almost feel him. I lift my hips, searching for him. The silky skin of his head brushes over my entrance, and I lose all thought. My fingers sink into the skin of his ass, pulling him toward me like a crazed druggie looking for her next fix.

Johnny pulls back. I'm so shocked that I peek up at him. His whole demeanor has changed. The air in the room shifting already, going from *fuck me now* to *I need a breather*. "Johnny, don't stop."

He drops his head to my chest. His hot breath coats my already wet nipples.

"We can't," he breathes out.

Frustration rears its ugly head, but I try to think clearly. I place my palms on his cheeks and make him look at me. "I want you," I say. "I'm with you. Not your dad or the Crew or some stupid rule." I lick my swollen lips. Surely, he can't want to stop now. He was just eating me up. "I want you inside me. I'm dying for it."

He slides his palm down his length, angling his head toward my entrance. He presses into my clit, and I gasp. He circles the head of his cock there until my core clenches. I grip his ass again, waiting until the teasing relents and he pushes inside, but instead, he sighs. This time, his expel of air is angrier. "Fuck." He releases his dick and swirls his thumb over my clit, making rapid circles.

I blink at him. Don't get me wrong, it feels fucking amazing, but he's not going to fuck me, and I'm—I'm... Christ, I don't know. "Johnny?"

"I'm going to make you come." His brow pulls together as he focuses on my clit. He flicks his tongue over my nipple again, but it doesn't have the same effect. I push his hand out of the way and try to sit up.

"What are you doing?"

"It's okay," I tell him, trying to pull my dress back up so my tits aren't in his face. I press my knees together and attempt to squirm my way out from underneath him.

The throb between my legs tells me my body hates me right now, but Big Daddy K is not going to rule my bedroom. I'm drawing the fucking line there.

Johnny sits back and presses a hand to my thigh. "Stop trying to get away from me."

My face flushes. I just threw myself at him, and he... turned me down? I try not to think about how he was all too willing to stick his cock inside the girl at the dress shop. I know this has nothing to do with that. This has everything to do with his loyalty to his Crew. His dad laid the law down. He follows it. He doesn't think beyond that.

"I fucking want you," he growls, pinning me in place.

I can't find anything to say to him. I can't tell him I don't give a fuck about the Crew or that I'm not following the Crew's stupid rules and never have been. He might see through me. The only thing that's changed in this scenario is me. I should've known he would've put a stop to it. "It was dumb," I say. "Forget it."

"It's not," he bites out. "I'm going to spend my life between these legs," he says, caressing his fingers down my thighs and back up again. "Just not yet."

Instead of placating me, his words piss me off. It's my shit, and I should have the say in what happens. "Is your father always going to be in our bedroom?"

His face reddens. He grapples with his anger, maybe, hopefully, because of the conversation we just had. Now I just have to see which side wins. "I told you I'd make you come. Didn't I the other night? I'll do that," he says seductively, trailing his fingers toward my core again. "I'll bury my face in your pussy. I'll do whatever you want. Just not this."

"That's a shame," I say, anger and embarrassment mixing inside of me for a tumultuous cocktail of emotions. "Because all I want is your cock inside me."

His shoulders sag forward. He's a sight to see. I'm sure we both are, staring at one another half-naked. He moves forward again, dropping his head to my shoulder. His hot breath caresses my skin there. "Everything you say is perfect." He presses his lips briefly to my collarbone. "You make it so damn difficult to be a good little soldier."

I close my eyes, taking in his words. This is the second time he's insinuated things about his dad. That maybe he doesn't look up to him as much as I thought he did. Or as much as everyone else thinks he does. I want him to keep talking about it, but I don't want to pry either. Johnny always takes giant leaps backward when I do that. He's not used to anyone caring about anything that isn't surface level. Like he said, being a good soldier boy is the only thing anyone cares about.

The sexy moment is gone, I quickly realize. He's not going to fuck me, and honestly, I don't want him to now, anyway. I shift to my side, facing him, and he mirrors me. Vulnerability skates across his face. Crinkles deepen the corners of his eyes, and a bone-deep tiredness sags off him. I press my hand to his chest, and he looks up at me. He frets over his lip. "I've never had someone I actually thought twice about before. I don't know what it is about you, but you make me question everything."

"You can talk to me about stuff, you know?" I say, starting out small. I don't need to push his boundaries too far right now. "I think that's how this works."

I gesture between me and him, and he huffs. "I wouldn't know. This life is all I know, and for some fucking reason, it feels like you're pulling me out of it instead of me guiding you into it."

"I..." I blow out a breath. I have no idea what to say to that. Everything I say could be wrong.

Johnny drags a hand through his dark hair. "For the first time, I don't fucking understand something my dad's told me to do. I don't know why he fucking cares if we fuck or not. Other than that, he's just...fuck. I don't know."

His mind works. Different emotions cross his face like he's coming to the right conclusions, but as soon as they're about to break through the surface, he takes a step back.

"He won't know if we do," I say, hoping I don't sound like I'm begging. This just feels important. It's not about wanting sex with Johnny, even though I really do. It's about Johnny proving to himself that he doesn't have to listen to everything his dad says. The Crew does not own him.

"But *I'll* know," Johnny says, locking eyes with me. "I don't lie to him. Period."

I search his gaze and find a stark contrast from the guy who second-guesses to the one who doesn't lie. He means those five words more than anything. And I can't blame him, really. His father is all he knows. He's been his only parent for the majority of his life. Of course, he trusts him absolutely. It'll take more than me throwing myself at him to get him to break that pact.

A knock comes on the door. Johnny sighs and shouts over his shoulder, "Give us a minute!" When he looks back at me, instead of scowling about the intrusion, he says, "That's probably Mag sent here by my father."

"I guess you better get dressed then."

He lowers his gaze. "It's you I'm worried about." He pulls my spaghetti straps back up, while I carefully stow away my breasts again. He finds my panties by our feet, and instead of giving them back to me, he pockets them, winking. "To remind me of what I could have had."

He stands, then reaches out to help me up. He pulls me to my feet, and I arrange my dress, so I look like I did before things got hot and heavy between us. The ripped seams give me a little more room in this dress, anyway. Johnny does the same, leaving his suit jacket off, but tucking his button-down shirt back in and buttoning and zipping his pants into place.

"Alright, come in," he finally calls out.

Magnum walks into the room. He focuses on Johnny, but I'm not naïve enough to think he doesn't understand what he just interrupted. "Your dad's brought Dunnegan in. They've been waiting for you."

Johnny picks up my hand and kisses it, his lips lingering as he locks gazes with me. "I don't know how long I'll be."

Well, that's my life now, isn't it?

Johnny walks from the room, but Mag lingers. In a regular voice, he asks, "Is there anything I can do?" I give him a look, but when we both hear the door across the hall click shut, Mag closes the door, securing us together in Johnny's suite. He lowers his voice even though there are now two doors separating us from them. "I was a dick earlier. I'm sorry." He looks me up and down, and I swear he can tell I'm not wearing any underwear. He nods to himself. "You can't let Big Daddy K know you—" He gestures toward me. Or maybe a little toward my pussy. It's hard to tell. He drops his gaze, but then immediately moves it back up. "—You fucked. You'll be out before you know it. No fighting. No Johnny. Or Oscar and Brawler for that matter."

"We didn't," I say, automatically, only because I'm so shocked that's what he's brought up after apologizing for his behavior earlier. "Not that it's any of your business."

"It's the whole Crew's business, Kyla. You don't think everyone knows what the deal is with you two? That's how Big Daddy keeps everyone on the straight and narrow. Trust me, there are more than a few people who'd love to see Johnny get taken down, so be careful who sees what. You're a target for everyone. Johnny haters. Johnny lovers. Johnny's enemies."

"So, you're saying I'm screwed?"

"I'm saying you should have listened to me when I said I could get you out."

His threat lingers in the air, but it doesn't faze me. I'm the one who put myself in this position, and I wouldn't have done it if I was going to run away scared. I don't have time for that.

Like yesterday, Oscar meets me at the front of the school. The crowd parts for him as he makes his way to the sleek black car. Magnum and I haven't spoken the entire trip here. There's so much he already knows that I'm scared to say anything more that he can use against me. He picks up on the littlest things, so I've done nothing but stare out the window the whole drive. Now, I'm preoccupied again as Oscar Drego swaggers his way across the sidewalk. He tilts his head to the side as if he's asking what the hell I'm still doing in the car, and I realize I could be getting out, but I was too distracted. By him. And his cocksure attitude.

I push the door open, but before I get out, Mag asks, "I'll pick you up after? Take you guys to the gym?"

"Yeah," I say distractedly. I even remembered to bring

gym clothes today. It's practically the only thing in my backpack besides a notebook and a pen. Johnny was right when he called school in the Heights a farce.

I go to get out, but Magnum speaks again. His voice is low, making me strain to hear. I even turn toward him to watch his lips move. "Remember what I said about people watching." He drags his gaze to Oscar and then back to me. "Just be careful."

"I will." My throat is suddenly dry because I know I didn't even handle myself well already this morning. As soon as I saw Oscar, all rational thought went out the window, and I practically drooled all over myself.

Oscar leans into the car, flashing a smile at me. "What's up, Mag? Princess and I are ready for another intellectually stimulating day at Rawley Heights High."

"I bet," Mag says. "I'm sure nothing's changed."

Oscar moves back so I can get out. We keep an appropriate distance between us as we head to the front entrance. Sneaking a glance over my shoulder, I ask, "Mag went to school here?"

"Born and raised. You can't tell?"

I shake my head. Honestly, he looks a little squeaky clean for the Heights. It must be his security persona because I can't see him walking the halls of this school, acting like most of the guys my age.

"Trust me. You do not want to fuck with him. Why do

you think he's top security dog? They don't just hand that position to anybody."

I cast a glance over my shoulder once more to find Magnum still where we left him. He's pitched forward in his seat, watching us as we make our way past security. His face is blank, serious. He moves his gaze to mine, and it doesn't waver until Oscar and I are ushered past the metal detectors and into the shitty school.

As soon as we get past that, trouble waits for us. Today, there aren't just other students walking the halls, I also see the guy who has the nerve to call himself our principal. Oscar and I skirt around him while he has his back to us, but just as we're about to escape unnoticed, the figure he's talking to comes into view.

"Son of a bitch," Oscar curses under his breath.

My sentiments exactly. Detective Reynolds is chatting up the principal. Oscar and I both try to duck our heads, but it's too late. He's already seen us. "Oscar Drego and Miss Samson. Just who I wanted to see."

"Save it," Oscar says. He's perfected that bored as fuck voice like he looks down at anyone attempting to talk to him. "We're not talking to you."

"No?" the detective asks. A glint lights his eyes. "Actually, you, we're taking downtown. It's Miss Samson we're talking to."

Oscar laughs. The sound is so incredulous and laced with humor that a sliver of apprehension races up my spine.

I peek over at Oscar. Dark, indignant eyes latch onto the detective's. "What is it this time?"

Detective Reynolds smooths out his tie. Watching him and Oscar respond to one another is like watching a battle of who can look the least affected. "Someone pulled away from a convenience store early this morning without paying for gas. Thief matches your description."

Oscar shakes his head. He turns toward me while the sea of students go out and around us. They act like they're not listening, but they are. This is juicy gossip to them. "Detective Reynolds just wants a way to get to you."

"Detective," the principal finally says. "You can't just come in here and—"

Reynolds raises a hand. "We know you're in the Heights Crew's pockets. Shut it."

A uniformed cop strides into the school. He reaches around his back and brings out a pair of cuffs that glimmer under the fluorescent lights. "Turn, Drego," Detective Reynolds instructs. "You know the drill."

I look on, helplessly. Oscar turns, placing his hands behind his back. He gives me a wink, but I can tell he's pissed. How many times has this happened to him? How many *unfounded* times? *Go*, he mouths. His gaze quickly portrays panic now that he's not putting on a show for everyone. *Now.*

I take another look of him being handcuffed; my feet rooted in place. I grew up to respect police, and honestly, I am on the wrong side here. But not Oscar. Oscar's on the right side. Using this bullshit about him stealing gas just to get me alone is wrong.

Oscar gives me another pleading look, so this time, I do spin on my heel and merge with the crowd.

"Hey, hey!" Detective Reynolds calls out behind me.

The crowd swallows me up, and as a unit, we all start running. The barricade of bodies impresses me. Even more so because they did this without being asked. "Hide," someone urges.

"Fucking pigs," another grunts.

To me, running makes it seem like I'm guilty of something. It's the exact opposite of what I was brought up to do. I should be listening to Detective Reynolds demands for me to stop, but I can't. Over it all, Oscar's laugh synchronizes with our feet like he's our escape trumpet, urging us on.

Before we turn the corner, a louder disturbance erupts behind us. I turn in time to see Magnum Superman punch Detective Reynolds, knocking him to the ground. The angsty crowd cheers, and I raise my eyebrows in kudos. Nice fucking shot. Damn.

Mag looks over the heads of all the students until he spots me. He steps over Detective Reynolds, who he knocked out cold, and strides toward me. The crowd once again parts, leaving me now that the threat is gone.

I want to pout. I'm being taken from school again, and who knows if Johnny will let me come back after this.

Magnum puts his hand on my shoulder and rushes me toward a set of side doors. Just before we disappear down that hall, I glance over my shoulder to find Oscar shrugging, his hard mask back over his face. I peek at Mag to ask if we're going to help him out, but Mag only shakes his head like he knows what's about to come out of my mouth, and he's already telling me no. The policeman who handcuffed Oscar speaks into his radio while the principal stares at Detective Reynolds' slumped form on the floor.

Magnum and I step outside and jog back toward the car. He parked it like he was in a rush. The front passenger tire is up on the sidewalk and the driver's side door is open. He ushers me inside and then runs around the side of the car to get in himself. "You punched a cop," I say, as soon as he slides in.

He doesn't react to my statement. Instead, he says, "I saw the bastard parked around the corner like I wasn't going to notice. I came back as soon as I could."

"I'm pretty sure you're going to be in so much trouble."

Magnum runs his hand over his scruff as he peels out of the parking lot. He doesn't look as distressed as I am. Hell, he doesn't look perturbed at all. I shift back in the seat and blow out a breath.

"There goes going to school."

Magnum sighs, too. "We can't keep it from him. He probably already knows." He gives me a sideways glance as if he wishes we could keep this one to ourselves. "Let's swing by your apartment. Didn't you say you needed something?"

I shake my head. "Brawler already got it. Thanks though."

My phone rings. I pull it out, already knowing who it will be. Except, it's not who I thought it was. I answer it, and his panicked voice rings through the speaker. "Are you okay?"

"Yeah," I say, angling my body away from Magnum to make the call as private as possible. "Mag came in."

"I know. The whole school is talking about it. They've already taken Oscar away."

"It's bullshit," I say.

"Yeah, well, that's what fucking happens when you get mixed up in the Crew."

I pinch the bridge of my nose. I wholeheartedly agree with him, but also, the whole Oscar fits the description of someone stealing gas was just an excuse to get him out of the way, so they could get to me. I rub my neck. That means they know too much about who's watching me.

My phone beeps. I pull it away to see who's trying to call through and see Johnny's name. I put the phone back to my ear. "I have to let you go. Johnny's calling."

"Text me if you can get away," Brawler orders.

"Yeah," I choke out. I let out a breath before answering Johnny's call. "Hey."

"I'm going to kill that detective. I'm going to chop him

up into tiny parts, starting with his hands so he can never touch you."

"I'm fine," I grumble. I consider myself a strong person but being in situations like what just happened is like having your hands handcuffed behind your back. You're stuck. There's nothing you can do.

I just want to punch something. Or someone.

"I'm going to take care of it," Johnny says.

I nod absently. As we drive, the blocks are ticking away. Before I know it, I'll be back at Johnny's suite for the rest of the day, and who knows for how long after that.

"Can you put me on speaker?"

"Sure." I take the phone away from my ear. "Johnny wants to be on speaker," I tell Mag, then hit the button so we can both hear Johnny.

"Take Kyla back to school. It's clear. Give her a weapon. I'm sure you have at least one extra on you. Kyla, if anyone tries to touch you, use whatever Mag gives you. I don't care if it's a teacher, policeman, or another student, use the weapon first, ask questions later. We'll clean it up if something happens."

I blink, taken aback by this whole conversation. I expected him to tell Magnum to hurry his ass up back to the tower. "What?"

At the same time, Mag says, "Turning around now."

"Wait," I say, still trying to wrap my head around this. "You're letting me go back to school?"

"Take me off speaker."

I hurry to press the button and then bring the cell back to my ear. "Really?" I ask.

"You're not a Kardashian. I get you loud and clear, Kyla. I listen. It might take a while to get it through my thick skull, but I want the best for you. Do I think staying in my suite is the safest place for you? Yes. Of course. I get you can't do that, though. That's one of the reasons why I like you so much."

My cheeks burn. Johnny has said a lot of things to me. He's called me beautiful. He's told me I'm his. I'm not so sure he's ever said he likes me though. Not the actual words.

"You still there?" he asks when I don't respond.

"Yeah." I struggle with the emotions bubbling to the surface. "Thank you."

"I mean it though. I don't care what you have to do. Stay safe. At all costs. You understand?"

"Yes," I tell him, my voice clear and concise, so he knows I mean business as well.

"I'll call Brawler. They won't release Oscar for a few hours."

I chew on the inside of my cheek. "You're going to help him, right? Oscar? He didn't do anything."

"I'll call the Crew's lawyers. They're just being dicks. I'll see what they can do, but he might just have to ride it out for a while. We've all been there."

All *been there?* Yeah, not me. I couldn't make it in prison.

"Can you cut your training short tonight? I've got something to discuss with you. You left before I was even up this morning."

I angle away from Mag again. This time when I glance outside, familiar landmarks of the ride to school rush by. We're only a few blocks away now. "I didn't want to disturb you."

"So, you're not avoiding me?"

I grin at the worry in his voice. "If I say no, does that mean you're going to make me come back to the suite?"

He laughs. The sound free and contagious. "No, I didn't tell you to go back to school just because I thought you were mad at me."

"Good," I tell him.

"See you tonight, babe."

"Tonight," I promise. "I'll be there."

"You better be." He hangs up the phone at the same time Mag turns into the school parking lot. He parks the car outside the front entrance again, only this time, there aren't droves of bodies also making their way into the school.

Mag pulls a knife out of his pocket and hands it to me. I take it, making sure I can open and close it on my own. "Can Johnny really clean anything up?" Not that I'm going to go stabbing a bunch of people. I only have murderous thoughts about one person, but it's information to stow away for later.

"He'd turn the world upside down for you."

My heart flutters. Stupid, deranged blood-pumping muscle. Those words should not bring me the warmth of joy that they do.

"You actually like him, don't you?"

My heart thumps one exaggeratingly long thump, like the final toll of a bell. "I do," I tell him, then I push the door open and stride back into Rawley Heights High, the knife secure in the waistband of my pants.

13

Mid-period, I stroll into Brawler's classroom and tell the person sitting next to him to find another seat. Actually, I don't have to say anything to the guy at all. I stand there, and he moves. The whole time, Brawler tries to not look at me.

The teacher lectures for only ten minutes more before letting the class do their homework for tomorrow in class today. Students leave the room, so I stand and make my way out, too, hoping Brawler will follow. I head toward my locker. Before I even turn the corner, footsteps thud behind me. I'm almost to my locker when Brawler takes my hand, pulling me into an empty classroom. He keeps the lights off and carefully shuts the door behind us. "Shh," he says. He steers me around several lab tables and opens a door in the back of the classroom. We step inside, and when he closes the door, he turns the light on, illuminating the tiny room. I look around, only to find an old desk on one side and rows of cabinets on the other. The room is long, but narrow, spanning the length of the classroom.

"I had lab in that room last year. This is where they keep all the slides and specimens." He turns me around and scans the length of me. "You're sure you're fine?"

I nod. The concerned look in his eyes mixes with his badass tattoos until I'm putty in his hands.

He pulls me to him, pressing my head against his chest. I wrap my arms around his waist, savoring the moment. Brawler is—well, I can't believe I'm saying this—but Brawler is safe. Nice. He doesn't belong here anymore than I do. If you look at the two of them—Brawler and Johnny—Brawler is the one who looks like he's the gangster's son while Johnny is the nice kid from down the hall whose Mom bakes treats for the new neighbors. They couldn't be more opposite, which is why I don't understand why I have the same feelings for both of them.

"I wish you weren't staying with Johnny. Then I could at least see you like before. Or know that you're okay. I don't know what the fuck goes on over there, and it kills me."

"Other than being bored out of my mind, I'm fine there. Johnny's good to me."

His jaw ticks. "When someone's not trying to kill you, you mean?"

"That wasn't his fault." Brawler gives me a strange look, so I quickly change the subject. "I miss you too, by the way."

His gaze softens. He moves his hand up tentatively to cover my cheek, but then his body tenses, as if he's trying to hold back. "I was so scared after the fight. I thought you were going to end up just like my sister. An innocent caught in the crossfire."

I squeeze my eyes shut at his words. I'm no innocent. If anything, Brawler's the innocent one in this duo.

"I was scared, too," I confess. "I didn't know how you were. Or Oscar. Or—"

"What's keeping you here, Kyla?" Brawler asks, interrupting. "You have to tell me. I need a reason why you and I can't just fucking leave this place right now."

"Other than the fact that Johnny will hunt us down and kill us?"

"At this point, I would do it. We'd hide. Who's to say they would find us? Or if they did, that I couldn't end this?"

I flinch. I don't want Brawler and Johnny fighting. Not at all. But I also know there's some deep-seated hatred in Brawler, and I can't blame him. I'm that way too.

I wrap my hands around his and squeeze, dropping our interlaced fingers in front of us. I just stare at him for a while, not knowing what to say. I never pictured I'd come to the Heights and meet anyone I'd consider a friend let alone someone more than that. Someone I'd trust. Someone I'd care for like this. I didn't have a plan in place for this scenario.

"You still don't trust me."

"No," I say automatically. "I do. I just know that when I tell you why I'm here…" I shake my head without finishing the sentence. I honestly can't guess what his reaction will be. My circumstance, my life, it seems so extraordinary. Who would do what I've done?

Yeah, so maybe I'm scared to tell him, too. What if he thinks I'm a complete fucking nut job and drops me? I need Brawler. He's the only sane person keeping me tethered to the normal life I'll have in the future.

My heart rate kicks into high gear. I'm about to tell Brawler what's going on. Doubt and anxiety crash together. What if he tells someone? What if he decides he doesn't want to get mixed up in my shit? "I don't know if I can tell you," I say honestly. The corners of my eyes fill with hot tears. I will myself not to cry. I'm fucking stronger than that. I'm braver than that. But I have something to lose now. Before, in my old life, I didn't have anything that mattered to me. Something I wasn't willing to give up. Now, I do. I don't want to give Brawler up, and I don't want to change my course of action either.

I take a few deep breaths, trying to settle the chaos firing in my body. I start to shake, and Brawler looks on helplessly. He picks me up and sets me on the desk, then moves closer, forcing my knees wide, so he can step inside and place his hands on either side of me. He stoops to eye-level. "I'm one-hundred percent in this, Kyla. Tell me."

I wipe my hands down my thighs and then squeeze the area above my knees. "You know how you lost your brother and sister?"

He nods.

"I'm going to take a couple leaps of faith here," I tell him, biting my lip. I'm silently pleading he'll understand what I'm about to say. "You lost your brother and sister, and you hate the Heights Crew because of it. It makes me wonder if at any time you might have thought about taking your hatred one step further. Like, what would you do if you ended up in a room alone with the person who shot your brother? Or the person who shot your sister?"

"I don't know who shot them," Brawler says. His gaze searches mine, and I can tell he's already trying to put the pieces together just from the tiniest bit I just shared with him.

"Say you did," I start again. "What would you do?"

He blinks.

"First reaction," I say, because if I know Brawler as well as I think I do, I think he'd talk himself out of it.

"First reaction is I'd kill them," he says flatly.

I nod.

His gaze narrows.

I breathe in deep. "When I was twelve, my parents were murdered. They were shot," I say, trying to calm my beating heart. I can think about my parents all I want inside my head, but the moment I start to talk about them aloud, it starts to break me. Like talking about it makes it real.

Brawler's shoulders pull back. I wonder if he knows where I'm going with this yet.

"They bled out in the alley. They were out on their weekly date. They always had date nights on Fridays. The neighbor lady was watching me when the police showed up to tell us what happened."

"Kyla, I'm so sorry."

It's funny how I've acclimated to this new name. I am Kyla now, the fusion of two people who meant the most to me in this whole world. I don't even think of me as that little girl anymore. I can't.

"Like your sister's death, it was a senseless murder. It didn't need to happen. My parents weren't some criminals, they were just in the wrong place at the wrong time."

Brawler lifts his hand to tuck a strand of hair around my ear. "Why did you ask me what I would do if I knew who killed my brother and sister?"

Here we go. I'm so close to the truth I might as well say it now. There's no going back. "Because I know who killed them, and I'm going to make them pay."

Brawler stands to his full height and turns, his hands diving into his hair. "Fuck, Kyla." But he's not mad, he's sad. "What the fuck is wrong with this world?" he asks, looking up at the ceiling of the cramped room we're in, but he's not asking the ceiling, he's asking whoever's above that. The angels, maybe? Like the ones on his neck. One dark. One light.

I gasp. I'm the dark angel. It's just dawned on me now. A harbinger of death, and I don't care. I only hope that once I do this, I can turn light again. I hope I won't be too far gone.

"Who is it?" Brawler asks. "The person who killed your parents? I'm guessing he's in the Crew."

I remember when I found out who it was. The policeman, explaining to my aunt and uncle that they knew who did it, but that there was nothing they could do about it. No evidence. No witnesses. It was a gang hit after all. Like Johnny said, they can clean up almost anything.

My stomach rolls. In that moment, I'm the embodiment of Brawler's tattoo. Half bad. Half good. I know what I'm doing is wrong, but that's not going to stop me, anyway. It only makes me more determined.

"Who is it?" Brawler asks again.

I picture myself on the day I found out, hiding around the staircase as my aunt and uncle talked to the homicide detective in charge of my parents' case. He was explaining to them they were going to shut the case down. I remember my aunt's sobs. Even now, I don't know how she heard what he said through all her pain. *We know who did it, but our hands are tied. The DA won't prosecute.*

"Who?" My uncle asked. "Who did it? You can at least give us that much."

"Kingston Marx."

I meet Brawler's stare with one of my own. "Kingston Marx." The inflections, the tone, everything I use to say that name is just how I heard it the first time all those years ago.

The color drains from Brawler's face. "Kyla..."

I steel my shoulders. "Big Daddy K killed my parents as an initiation to take his spot atop the Heights Crew. I guess that's what those vile, fucked up, murderous fucking assholes do. Prove their allegiance. Prove they're badass enough. Prove—"

"—they're less than human," Brawler says, finishing for me.

I nod, swiping at my eyes.

Brawler approaches me. It might just be me, but he seems skittish now. Like maybe I have completely ruined this whole thing, but honestly, I'm glad someone else in the world knows my parents' story. Knows *my* story. "You can't kill Big Daddy K," he says. I open my mouth to tell him some indignant phrase like 'Fucking watch me', but he continues, "It's just not possible. Even if you did, what then? It's a death wish."

"Thanks for trying to mansplain this to me. You don't think I've thought about everything? You've known about this for a whole half a minute, I've had six years. I know what I'm doing."

"Okay, okay," he relents. His voice is soft, but then his

face turns hard the longer the silence grows between us. "That doesn't mean I have to fucking like it."

I jump off the desk. "You don't have to, and I don't care. I'm doing it. When I'm done, I'm leaving the Heights behind me. You just said you wanted to run away with me, can you wait? I have to do this, but then we can go. I'm starting a new life. One that's not dictated by what someone did to me, but by what I want to do. You can do it, too, Brawler. You can leave the Heights with me, and we can both start over."

"Together. With Oscar?"

His gaze slices through me, but who I want to come with me is the least of my worries. "If he'll come."

Brawler swallows. "Does he know any of this?"

"Are you kidding? He's in the Crew."

"Who else knows?"

"Just us."

"And the people on the other end of your cell phone?"

"My aunt and uncle," I say, sticking my chin in the air. "They have no idea what I'm doing, and it's going to stay that way. They took me in after my parents died."

Brawler does a few laps around the room. Every once in a while, he glances over at me. He's not mad, per se, but it's evident he's having some sort of war with himself. "You're so fucking stubborn," he says finally.

I shrug. Not the first time and not the last time I'll hear those words directed at me.

He moves in front of me. "I'm in," he says. "On every-thing. I'll keep your secret. I'll help you stay. I'll even pull the goddamn trigger."

"No. That's me." Once again, I get a quick hit of satis-faction by imagining Big Daddy K's brains being splattered all over the place. Vengeance will be mine and mine only. "It's important that I do it."

Brawler threads his fingers through my hair and then pulls me to his chest again. "Our relationship just got a whole lot crazier."

I smile into his chest. It isn't often that Brawler jokes. Why he chose this specific time, I'm not sure.

He kisses the top of my head. "I mean it, Kyla. I'm in. I get it. You can trust me with anything."

Guilt bubbles up. "My name's not really Kyla."

His lips curve against my scalp. "Of course, it's not."

"But I like Kyla better," I say quickly. Half my mom and half my dad. It reminds me every day of what I'm doing here.

He pulls away, trailing his finger over my bottom lip. "It suits you."

He hasn't even heard the reason behind my name yet. He will. I angle my face upward and slide my hands around Brawler's neck to pull him to me, sealing this moment of breaking down barriers between us with a kiss.

He knows who I am. He knows why I'm here. Right now, he knows me better than anyone.

14

ow that Brawler knows everything about me, it's harder to pretend. At the gym, I keep sneaking glances at him. Jax even catches me on the chin for it. He pulled it at the last minute so it didn't hurt as much as it could have, but still. I'm a wreck today.

"Where's your focus, Kyla?" Jax asks, irritation lacing his voice. "Aren't you fighting this weekend?"

I grit my teeth. I am fighting this weekend, thank fuck. It gives me something else to focus on instead of my real-fake boyfriend, the gangster's son, and my fake-real boyfriends, the fighter and the quarterback.

Whoa. Did I just think of them as all my boyfriends? Jax must've hit me harder than I thought.

Jax's glove brushes my forehead. "Come on. I don't have time to waste on someone whose head isn't in the game.

Let's go." He punches his gloves together in front of him and bounces on his toes.

Heat creeps up my cheeks while Finn looks over warily, raising an eyebrow at his brother. Sure, Johnny paid enough to get us private lessons, so there's actually no one else in the gym while we're here, but Jax is right. I'm out of focus. Distracted. Stressed. Did I mention fucking horny? All revved up with nowhere to put it. That's what happens when you have three boyfriends and two of them you can't touch in public, and the other, you literally can't touch because his dad's an overbearing asshat, not to mention a douchebag murderer.

Jax throws another punch at me, and this time, I dodge out of the way just in time. He grins, his neon green mouthpiece peeking through his parted lips. "That's it. Come on."

We circle one another. I get in a few good jabs, making sure to get in and get out. Jax has longer arms than me. I can't stay in his zone or he'll take me out fast. I have to get in where I can get him, then pop right back out before he has a chance to retaliate. It's like a fun game where the reward is not getting hit and the punishment is getting knocked upside the head.

Sweat trickles between my breasts. The headgear is almost suffocating, perspiration dampening the shorter hairs at my neck. I flex my fingers inside the gloves as I look for another opening. I'm fighting a girl this weekend. I haven't heard much about her other than that she's above

Cherry in the female pecking order. To be honest, and this will sound fucking cocky as shit, but I'm not worried. I haven't had much time to think about my last fight because of what happened afterward, but I beat Evan. That was the most nervous I've ever been before a fight, and I won.

Jax lands a punch straight in the middle of my face, and I stagger back.

"Come on, Princess!"

I roar in frustration, grabbing my headgear off and throwing it to the ring. Jax smirks, but Finn ducks underneath the ropes to enter the ring. "Hey, hey." He slides his brother an incredulous look.

"If you don't like that name, stop acting like one."

"Jesus, Jax. What do you think 'hey, hey' means?" Finn throws at him.

Brawler enters the ring next, coming up behind me. He's so close that it immediately relaxes me. "You okay?"

"I'm just frustrated at myself."

Jax arches a brow at his brother as if to say, "I told you so." He takes his gloves off and then his headgear, high-lighting his dark hair and knuckle tattoos once more. "I can tell you're thinking too much."

Brawler places his hand on my shoulder. I immediately stiffen, but that isn't weird, right? Brawler is...what? My fight organizer? He can touch me, can't he? I mean, I'm allowed to have friends, aren't I?

Brawler slips his hand off as soon as he feels my reaction.

"I know you know this, Kyla," Jax says, using my real name again. He only used Princess before to get a rise out of me. Asshole. At least it worked. "But your head has to be in the present. We can't spar if you're not in it."

I nod, knowingly. He's one hundred percent right.

Finn quirks a smile. "I volunteer as a good listener." He winks at me and pops his eyebrows up his forehead suggestively.

"Kyla has enough fanboys." Magnum's voice sounds just behind us. He's moved closer. The sound of me throwing my headgear down probably caught his attention.

Finn mouths 'fanboy' to his brother as if he's all broken up about being called that. Me? My back stiffens. Magnum says I can trust him, but that sounded a hell of a lot like a jibe. Maybe he disapproves of the whole Brawler and Oscar thing.

I follow Jax's lead and take off my gloves. Finn had a pair of neon pink ones here waiting for me today, and I'm kind of in love with them. He also stocked up on more clothes in the apparel section, getting cuter sports bras and more women's gear in. Earlier, he asked if he could take a picture of me decked out in my fighting gear, so he could put it up in the gym. He thinks it will attract customers or something like that.

I think he's delusional, but I agreed anyway. That is, I

agreed until Magnum spoke over top of me and told me I'd have to check with Johnny. Then, Finn rambled on about doing a legit photo shoot in the gym with lighting, makeup, and a real photographer. The Heights Crew guys are a lot like celebrities in the Heights. Everyone knows who they are. They're celebrities for the real world, dealing in organized crime rather than starring in fictional tales about organized crime. Maybe he thinks that's what I'm going to be, but I still think he's crazy.

Finn throws me a fresh hand towel, and I use it to wipe the sweat from my face and hands. He gestures toward it with a mocking smile. "What do you think, bro? Sell that on eBay?"

My mouth drops. He goes to take it back from me, and I move it out of his reach.

"Oh, come on," Finn says, laughing now.

"No one wants this shit." I grip my sweat towel tighter in my hands, trying to figure out if he's joking or not.

He takes a slug of water. "You obviously haven't heard anyone talking about you lately. Everyone who steps in here is buzzing about The Princess. I wouldn't be surprised if you have to get a bigger venue to hold your fights. You'll be turning people away."

I turn to glance at Brawler. His neck pulses, moving the ink displayed there up and down. It's fascinating watching it, as if the angel is alive. But what the hell? Sweat towels? He's certifiable.

"It's been brought up," Brawler says. "We'll see how the first fight goes."

My gaze narrows at him. No one's told me about this. He gives me a small shrug, and I shake my head. At school, people have been acting like I'm some sort of movie star, but I thought that was mostly because of Johnny and being involved with the Heights Crew. Everyone who's in the Crew gets treated with respect, and if they don't, the offending parties get the shit kicked out of them. That's just how things are.

"Okay," Finn says. "I'm getting the sense the towel is a no-go, but still think about the poster. Kyla: Uppercut Princess. One badass bitch."

I press my lips together. I don't feel like a badass bitch today. I flick my gaze to Jax. Boredom has set in on his face, and it's obvious Finn's the dreamer in this business partnership of theirs. I suck up my pride and walk toward Jax, holding my hand out for him to shake. "Thanks for the training session. I'll be more focused tomorrow."

He grips his large hand in mine, giving it a squeeze that's just the right amount of pressure. I have no doubt he's stronger than that, but if he used his full strength to shake my hand, he'd probably break it.

Magnum moves the ropes apart, so I can duck under the top one and swing my leg over the bottom. He takes my sweat towel from me, eyeing Finn warily. It almost makes me laugh. Almost. Finn may have been serious on that one, although he'd be sorely disappointed when the thing didn't sell.

I throw a t-shirt on and wave goodbye while heading to the gym exit. Magnum strides ahead of me, making me wait while he checks the perimeter outside. I glance over my shoulder to find Finn and Jax staring after us, and I just know that all this extra security is playing into Finn's head about how I'm supposedly this famous fighter. I wonder if they even know about the shootout. I'm sure they've put two and two together by now that I'm Johnny Rocket's girlfriend, but the part about being in danger? That's uncertain.

"I've got the rear," Brawler says, coming up behind me. My back pricks at being so close to him, but I shoot him a look over my shoulder, anyway. He's wearing a smile that ghosts over his face. He's got the rear, alright. I only wish we could do something about it.

"Alright, let's head out," Mag says. His gaze darts around the area until he opens the back door of the car for us.

I slide in, Brawler folding his larger body in after me. As soon as he's inside, he checks the partition. Noticing it's up, he cups my cheek. "Are you okay?"

"Just couldn't keep my head in it," I say, embarrassed all over again. I acted like a newbie in there, for fuck's sake.

Brawler pulls me onto his lap in one swift move. My heart lodges in my throat. His hands sneak under my t-shirt, settling on my sweat-dampened torso. He leans forward, licking a drop that's running down my neck. "There's something about you all sweaty and half-naked."

I could say the same thing for him. He's one of the reasons I was distracted tonight. I only wish he'd taken his form-fitting tank off, so I could ogle what he has going on under there. "Maybe I should have signed my sweat towel for you."

"You've already left more of an imprint on me than that." He nudges his hips higher, and his growing desire lengthens. His head drops to my shoulder as he releases a long breath. "We need alone time together soon. More than just ten minutes in the car with a guard a couple of feet away from us."

I hear him loud and clear. Actually, I feel him long and hard. "You don't think I can get you off in ten minutes?" I quirk an eyebrow at him and start to slip backward over his knees, so I can drop down in front of him. Thankfully, my shin isn't hurting anymore, or I'd never be able to do this.

He takes my chin in his hands, forcing me to look at him. "I'm willing to fall for the bad guy's girlfriend. I'm willing to help her take someone out. I don't need you on your knees in front of me, racing the clock. I need you in my bed, wrapped up in my sheets, being as loud as you want to be."

My breath leaves me. The scene he described sounds divine. "You're just making me want to suck you off even more."

He urges me forward, pressing his lips to mine. Already,

the car is slowing. Brawler intensifies the kiss for a brief moment before pulling away. Sure, it's evident Magnum knows what's going on between Brawler, Oscar, and me, but I don't need to throw it in his face either. I slip off his lap and scoot over until there's a foot between us.

"See you tomorrow," Brawler promises.

He pushes the car door open, but Magnum lowers the divider between the front and the back. "Johnny says you can check your apartment to see if there's anything you want to bring back." I know his guys have already salvaged what they could, but I'm not letting this opportunity pass me up. "You'll watch her, right?" Magnum asks, eyeing Brawler with an intensity that says there's a double meaning in his words. Johnny probably told him to escort me up there, but he's giving us this time. Alone. "Don't be too long."

I want to smile, but instead, I nod at Magnum and then get out of the car after Brawler. It feels like forever since I've been in front of this apartment building. Though I hadn't stayed here long, the memories I have are fond. Of Brawler mostly.

As we walk into the building, I want to take his hand. I want to wrap my fingers around his like we would if we were any two people other than who we are. Instead, I walk side-by-side with him and then single file as we march up the stairs to our floor. As soon as we turn the corner, I pick my door out. Here, I was free, even if living a lie held me back. Freedom lay in not having to pretend for my aunt and uncle. It was not having a foot in this life and a foot in theirs. Now, I'm back to being restrained again, but in a whole different way. So, yeah, this stupid, shitty apartment means a lot to me.

The apartment was busted into, so it has a new lock on it. We have to call the super to come and open it for us. I stop as soon as he swings the door open. The new furniture is slashed to shit. The cutlery in the kitchen is all over the floor. Cupboard doors are hanging awkwardly on their hinges. A rank smell wafts from the refrigerator like it was left open for a long period of time even though the door is shut now.

"We think a member of Fonz's crew came here and trashed it. Then, our lovely neighbors probably scoured the place as soon as they saw it was broken into."

"It's a shame Fonz's Crew ruined the furniture. I'm sure someone here could have used that."

"They took the TV though."

I laugh. "Well, good. At least someone got something."

Though I'm joking, a weight settles in my stomach. This was a complete and total invasion of privacy. At least Brawler was able to get the picture and the phone. I head toward the bedroom. It's more of the same. The bed is stripped bare, like someone desperately needed a new sheet set. My bedside tables are knocked over, the drawers broken on the floor. My super-secret hideaway shelf is lying on the floor just under where I had it hung.

Brawler kneels next to it. "The hinge was open just barely, but there were sheets and clothes over it when I got here. Someone had a field day ripping everything apart. They didn't even notice what they had."

I run my hands through my hair and then get on the floor, peering underneath the bed and picking other trash up from the floor, searching for the gun I had in there.

"Was there something else?"

"A gun."

Brawler heaves a sigh. "I didn't see a gun."

We both tear the place apart a third time, looking for the gun I had stashed, the one I'd planned on using to take out Big Daddy K. "Fuck," I groan in frustration.

"It's gone," Brawler says, standing to his feet. "There's no way of knowing who got it, but I don't think it was Fonz's men. It must have been the vultures afterward."

At least there's that. "I'll have to get another one." I stare at the bed. They'd told me the place was trashed, so I don't know why I thought I'd get up here and Brawler and I could have a moment to ourselves without the real world pressing down on us.

"You'll never get it through security at the tower."

"Unless they give it to me," I tell him, forming a plan in my mind. In the car, Mag's knife lies in the bottom of my bag. Johnny *is* willing to give me weapons. Now I just have to convince him I need a gun for self-protection. If that doesn't work, I'll get Brawler to hold on to it for me.

"Is there anything in here you want?" Brawler asks. He places his hand on my neck, gently massaging me there.

"There's really nothing here that's mine anyway," I tell him, realizing I've been living in a place that isn't really mine, yet I have very real memories attached to it. "I bought everything second-hand. The clothes, the furniture, the kitchen stuff." I glance over at him. "You have the only two things that are mine."

He cups my face, making me face him. "How much time do you think we have?"

I don't know, but I don't care either. I'll survive Johnny's wrath, but for right now, I'm sinking back into the girl who had the apartment. The girl who was almost free. And that girl? She wants Brawler more than she can stand.

15

Brawler takes my hand, holding me tight as we exit my apartment and move down the hall. He stops at the last door and unlocks it, using a key. Thankfully, no one else is in the hallway to see us together or notice we're entering Brawler's apartment alone.

Brawler clicks the door shut behind us softly. "My mom should be taking her afternoon nap, depression medication induced." He locks the door, flicking across three interior locks. I turn to find an apartment that's laid out the same as mine, except there are bedrooms on both sides of the main room. Brawler takes me to the one on the left, pulling me inside and practically collapsing against me once we're on the other side, flicking yet another lock just behind my hips before dropping his hand to cup my ass. I'm interested to see what his bedroom looks like, but his touch distracts me. I'm so damn easily distracted these days.

"What's your real name?" he asks, teasing my ear with his teeth.

I wrap my arms around him, pulling him closer. "I'll tell you, but I want to be Kyla. Even after all of this, I still want to be Kyla to you. To everyone that matters. It's been a long time since I've been that other person."

He pulls away, running his hands through my wild hair. I'm sure it looks a mess after drying from the training session. "I promise. I just want to know everything about you."

I smile a little. "Jo. Short for Joanne, but everyone called me Jo."

His lips quirk. He doesn't tell me I look like a Jo, or that I don't look like a Jo. He just takes in the information, internalizing it.

"What's your name? Your *real* name?" I qualify because everyone—and I mean everyone—calls him Brawler. Even the teachers at school, though I doubt that's the name on his birth certificate.

"Marcus, but I used to make people call me Mack until I got the nickname Brawler."

I stare into his face, his halo of blond hair contrasting the ink on his neck and arms. I don't know if I'll ever use his real name, but knowing it makes another barrier slip away between us. It's like we're two normal people right now, not holding back any deep, dark secrets.

He nips at my ear again, running his hands up my back until I'm forced to raise my hands above my head so he can lift my t-shirt away from me. His hands dip into the waistband of my joggers next, then he moves them over my ass. I lift my legs, so he can take them all the way off. He leans back, gaze moving over my sports bra and panties. Hell, I'm not even wearing sexy panties. I learned a long time ago that having underwear ride up your ass while training is a terrible idea, but Brawler looks at me as if I'm a Victoria's Secret model, anyway.

I slip my hands down the back of his joggers, cupping a handful of his ass. All thoughts of needing to get back downstairs or what will await me back at the tower, are gone. This is just about Brawler and me.

Brawler kicks off his shoes while I lower his joggers. His muscle tank is next until he's standing there with pitched boxers. He leads me to the bed, and for the first time, I can see more of his room. His comforter is a solid dark blue. A dark shade of gray coats the walls. He has a Rocky poster on one wall, and Muhammad Ali on the other.

He captures my mouth again before I have more time to look around. He moves me to the mattress, and when I sink into his comforter, the smell of fresh sheets greet me. He hovers over me, and for the first time, I get a good picture of his muscled chest and torso. There are more tattoos there. A fiery sun over his pec that's done in black ink, thick, broad lines shaping the circle and rays. I run my hands over it while he watches me. "What's this one about?"

The lines are faded, not as bold or as dark as his neck tattoo. It's older. "That one's about waking up every day, feeling like it's a fresh start. Maybe the sun is shining. The wind is blowing. And you take a breath of that fresh air... only to realize it's just the same old day, laced in darkness." He blinks. "I got it after my sister died."

His brother died the same day, but when we discuss anything to do with that day, it's about his sister and her innocent life. Not his brother.

I don't know what to say to that, so I push up onto my forearms and kiss the center of his sun. He shivers. "I'm going to have to get one to represent you now."

"Me?" I lick my lips. "That's kind of, I don't know, permanent."

"You're kind of permanent." He kisses a trail down my neck, warmth spreading through my chest. "The sun is the old me. Since you got here, it's been different. I've been different."

"You mean like I might be your ray of sunshine?"

He maneuvers his hands to my back, unclasping my sports bra. "I mean like you might make everything worth it."

Even after everything I've told Brawler, he can still look at me the way he is now. He can still think such nice things of me. Maybe I can come out the other side of this a normal person. He gives me hope.

He helps me out of my bra, tossing it over the side of the bed, taking me all in. He doesn't immediately go for my breasts. Not like Johnny. His touch skirts around them, trailing over my needy flesh. Fire erupts in his wake like a lava flow chasing after his fingers no matter where they touch. After he's mesmerized every freckle on my torso, he tugs on my panties. I lift my ass to help him and then they make their way over the side of the bed too.

He trails his fingertips over my lower abdomen, skirting my mound before he cups my hip. "When it occurred to me that you might've died in the shootout, I promised myself that if we ever got to do this, I'd take my time. I'd worship you like you deserve."

He lowers his head, kissing a trail straight down the center of my breasts to my belly button and then back up again, first taking my left nipple in his mouth while he kneads the other, and then the right. I arch into him, craving more of his touch. I liked the intensity of the moment with Johnny, but what girl doesn't want to be worshipped either?

I take my fingers and hook them around his boxer briefs before pulling them down. He pauses his attention on my nipples to kick out of his boxers before lowering himself again. "Open your legs for me, beautiful."

I push my knees to the side so he can settle comfortably between them. He hovers just out of reach, so I tip his chin up so I can kiss his lips, while wandering my fingers through the hard dips of his abs and then lower until I brush his cock. He jerks toward me at first contact and moans into my mouth. I stroke him, my palm running down his hard length and back up again at the pace of our kissing. My core throbs. Brawler lowers his hands, brushing his thumb over my clit. I buck into him, needy for more. He places a finger at my entrance, teasing me first.

"Wet for me."

"Mm-hmm," I sigh.

He pushes his finger inside, and I break the kiss. All thoughts obliterate as I focus on his finger and match my strokes to his. The slow burn of us easing into this has only intensified every spark of desire coursing through me.

"Brawler," I warn, trying to tell him that if we're going to do this, we have to do it now because I'm not going to last long.

He pulls his finger away, kissing me on the lips before reaching over to the stand by his bed and opening the small drawer there. He fishes out a condom wrapper, and I wait as he rips it open and guides it down his length. I watch in awe at just how long it takes for him to unroll the condom over himself. Brawler's big.

I don't have too much time to think about it though because he hooks his hand around my thigh and pulls me close to him, lining us up. He pauses a moment, waiting until our gazes connect, before he pushes the head of his cock inside. My toes curl as he strokes all the way in, only stopping when he's fully seated.

I smile. It's the most ridiculous thing to do in that moment, and I instantly regret it. Before I can hide in shame, though, he smiles back. "Fuck," he says, chuckling. "You feel too good." He moves out and pushes back in, reaching a little further this time until both of us react, a moan from him and a short cry from me.

After that, all bets are off.

The bed creaks underneath us. I hope to God his mother is still sleeping because it's obvious what's going on in here. Every time he pushes inside me, he grinds over my clit, and I suck in a breath at the explosion of pleasure. My hands roam over his firm, tight muscles as he drives us both higher and higher.

Trembles overtake my body, and I dig my heels into the bed, matching him stroke for stroke until my fingers sink into his skin as soon as my orgasm hits. "Yes, yes."

Wave after wave of pleasure rocks into me. Brawler's whole body tightens, then he strokes inside me one last time, his arms quaking as he holds himself up. After a moment, he drops his forehead to mine, silencing us both as we share an intense stare. In that moment, everything that needs to be said between us is said with our eyes.

Brawler will be following me when I leave the Heights. That much I'm sure of.

We dress slowly. I liked being in the Brawler bubble, but

now that reality has set back in, I know I have to leave soon. Brawler hands me my t-shirt, and when I pull it over my head, he grasps the material in his fists and pulls, bringing me closer to him. He kisses me, a tender press of his lips against mine until footsteps sound on the other side of the door.

He pulls away. "Shit."

A knock sounds. "Marcus, are you in there?"

The voice is gravelly. I can tell it's a female, but it's also a lower tone than I would've imagined coming from his mother. Or any female for that matter.

"Yeah, Mom."

I raise my eyebrows at him, and he lifts his shoulders. *Dear God, I hope we didn't wake her up.*

He straightens the fresh shirt he pulled on while I take my hair out of its ponytail, run my fingers through the dark strands, and then put it back up again. He takes my hand, and we walk out together. His mom looks over her shoulder. She's wearing a nightdress. She can't be that much older than what my own mom would be, but looks aren't just measured in years, and I can tell the years have not been kind to Brawler's mom.

My heart sinks.

Her eyes widen when she sees me next to him. Her gaze drops to our entwined hands, but I'm not afraid of her telling anyone. She looks like she doesn't get out of the apartment much at all. "Oh, hello."

I slip my hand from Brawler's and move toward her. "I'm Kyla," I tell her. "Nice to meet you."

She gives me a limp shake and then retracts her hand, rubbing it down her disheveled nightgown. Crimson colors her cheeks, and I glance away at her embarrassment. "I didn't know Marcus had anyone over. A girl...friend? A girlfriend?"

I look over at Brawler. His gaze softens when he looks at her. For the first time, he's not a badass fighter, he's someone's son. A caregiver. "Kyla and I really haven't talked about it yet. Thanks for bringing it up."

I laugh, and his mom hobbles over to the sofa before falling backward into it.

"She's the neighbor I was telling you about. The one you made the cookies for."

"Oh, yes. How were they?"

"Really good," I say, almost choking on the words and hoping she doesn't spot the lie. "Thank you. It's always nice to be welcomed somewhere."

A small smile flits across her lips, but it looks almost staged, as if someone wrote it on a script that she had to smile at this point, so that's what she's doing.

Brawler puts his arm around my shoulders. "Kyla has to go now, Mom."

"Yeah? Well, I'm glad I got to meet you."

"Me too," I tell her, before Brawler leads me toward the door.

"I'm going to walk Kyla out. I'll be right back up."

She bobs her head, and Brawler ushers me out the open door. We're silent as we move toward the stairs at the end of the hallway. Before I can think of anything to say, Brawler speaks up, "She's changed a lot since my sister died. She didn't used to be like that."

"I'm sorry," I tell him because what am I supposed to say? I can't lie. I'm not going to tell him it was really great to meet his mom because he'd see through that shit. She was half a person, like going through the motions of everyday life. It was awful.

"Did you really eat those cookies?"

"Fuck no."

He barks out a laugh, the area around his eyes crinkling adorably. Right before we hit the front entrance, he pulls back on my hand before letting it slip through his fingers. We face each other. With others milling around the lobby, there's nothing we can do or say to one another right now. Instead, I smile and nod as the sapphire blues in his eyes focus on me.

Brawler and I just shared something special. If I could do anything differently, it's that I wouldn't have to hide it.

But because we want to stay alive, we have to.

16

<hr>

When I get in the car, I expect Magnum to give me shit about being careful, but he doesn't. Brawler walks back toward the apartment building, and Magnum takes over like this is a trade-off of highly valuable belongings between dealers.

"Find anything you wanted to keep?" he asks as he puts the car in Drive.

I shake my head. "Everything was pretty much destroyed."

"The thing you wanted though?"

"Safe," I tell him. *Thankfully.* If anyone found out who I was, I'd end up dead, for sure.

I bite down on my lip, my heart coming to a startling halt. When Johnny finds out why I'm here, *he's* going to be devastated. Furious. Confused.

Betrayed.

Just like me. Just like I felt when I heard the news about what someone did to me.

"You okay?" Magnum asks. "You're pale all of a sudden."

"Fine," I croak. "Great." *Fan-fucking-tastic. I have feelings for a guy who I'm intent on ruining. You know, the usual shit when it comes to the Heights.*

"You can talk to me," Magnum urges, shifting in the driver seat. He looks over his shoulder, sharing his attention between the road and me. His acute hazel brown eyes read me. If anything, Magnum is damn good at his job. Too fucking good for my liking.

"Why do you care?" I ask, head swimming. "You work for Big Daddy K and Johnny, and yet, you wanted to get me out of here. You let me spend time with Oscar and Brawler even though you know Johnny would be pissed," I say, remembering he'd done this even before the shootout with Oscar. He let me go to his football game by myself. My brow furrows as I wait for his reaction.

His copper scruff can't keep the tightening of his jaw hidden away from me. "Everyone needs a friend. Moreso when you're thrust into a situation you can't handle."

"I can handle this," I scoff, hackles rising down my spine.

"You can handle being in a shootout? You can handle

having a gun being pulled on you?" He shakes his head. "We weren't designed to handle those things."

"Sounds like you're in the wrong profession."

He glowers at me. "Trust me, I'm in the right fucking profession."

I don't know why every time I talk to Magnum lately, we end up arguing like enemies. It feels like we're on two separate sides even though he keeps telling me I can trust him. If that's the case, he can answer a few questions for me, can't he? "How'd you get into the Crew? Oscar told me you went to school in the Heights. I'm assuming that's where it started."

Magnum settles back in the seat. Even though he's practically my valet with some bodyguarding duties, he's a badass one. His all black outfit with arm muscles poking out from underneath his sleeves would tell anyone not to fuck with him. The copper scruff adds to his aura of badassery. "I've been running with the Crew since school, yeah. I'm a lifer. What can I say?"

His bored tone aggravates me. "Can we stop playing games? Why haven't you told Johnny about Brawler and Oscar?"

Magnum hits the breaks and swerves the car to the side of the road. Several people skitter out of the way as one tire runs up onto the sidewalk and then thunks back down. He shifts in his seat, glaring at me. "Don't say that out loud again. Don't insinuate it. Don't even think about it when you're in Rocket's presence. You understand?"

"Do I look dumb to you?"

His nostrils flare, and his brows pull together.

"You didn't answer my question. I want to know why."

"Saying I want to be your friend isn't enough? Because that's all I've got. Maybe I recognize myself in you. Yeah? Maybe I see more than you want me to."

My heart hammers, knocking against my chest. I don't want anyone seeing me.

Magnum's lips thin as he takes me in. "Remember that we both have shit on each other, Kyla. I know you fucked Brawler."

"And I know you tried to get me out."

"Tit for tat. When two people share secrets, that makes them friends."

"That's...fucked up."

"That's how it is here."

He doesn't have to tell me twice. I already know.

I sit back in the seat while Magnum pulls the car back onto the road. Good thing all the windows are dimmed, and no one can see in. I'm heeding Magnum's warning on that. Spies are all over the Heights, and they would love to endear themselves to the Crew by turning in a backstabber.

Magnum pulls into a parking spot in the garage. It's a different one than he usually uses. The shadows in this area stretch through the whole corner. He sighs as he leans back in the seat. "I really am trying to be a friend to you. I know it's fucking hard because of where we are. I understand that things are usually never cut and dry. Johnny tasked me with keeping you safe, and that's what I'm going to do. Even if it is in a way he wouldn't approve of."

"You seemed shocked before...when you asked if I actually liked him."

He scratches the short, stubby hairs on his face. "I didn't see the connection at first, but I get it now."

My phone rings. I glance toward it and then back at Magnum's face. He's closed off again, looking alert and ready to make a decision at a moment's notice. I reach inside my bag and pull it out. It's Johnny. I bite my lip. Ever since I had the revelation about how he was going to take the news about his father being killed, guilt has been tearing at me. "Hey."

"Hey," he says. "Just making sure you didn't forget I wanted to see you tonight."

"I'm actually right downstairs about to come up."

"Excellent," he says, voice suave as usual. "Get your sexy ass up here."

I end the call and push the door open when Magnum puts his hand on my thigh. "Be careful."

He squeezes and lets go, and I glance back as I get out of the car, but he's already face forward, the bodyguard mask down over his face.

I take the elevator alone this time. When it pings on

their floor, the doors open to reveal a stunning Johnny. A smirk quirks his lips, and his posture is savagely confident, as if he knows he looks good. He's wearing a pair of khakis and a button-down shirt, the top four or five buttons undone.

His presence about knocks me over, and I have the sudden need to shower. Brawler's scent is all over me. His touch. His words, and here I stand in front of someone who wants to own me. Hell, he thinks he already does. He may have been able to capture a part of my heart, but he doesn't have it all. Not completely.

"Hey," I say, trying to plaster on an innocuous smile.

"There she is," he says, stepping forward. He reaches for my hand to bring it to his lips, kissing me on the knuckles.

Security steps forward, and he gives me a sheepish look, but lets them run their metal detecting wands over me. "There's a knife in my bag," I inform them, dropping it to the ground.

One of the men runs a wand over it, and the thing lights up with several beeping noises. They look up at Johnny who's smiling. "I told her to take it in case that asshole detective came around again."

They chuckle, handing the bag to Johnny so he can make the final decision. When they're done running the wand over me, Johnny hands the bag back to me. I take it from him, trying to keep my distance. If I can feel Brawler on me, I don't want Johnny to. "Glad I'm back," I say as we head toward his suite. "I need a shower in the worst way."

His chest rumbles appreciatively.

He opens the door to the suite, and I walk in and stop. Candles flicker on the square dining room table tucked to the right of the room. He never uses it as far as I can tell, but today, fancy white plates are laid out with heaps of steaming food. An ornate vase lies in the center, beautiful white roses bursting out of it in bunches perfectly arranged.

He grabs my hand in his, pulling it up to his face so he can kiss my knuckles again. He loves to do that. Always has. It reminds me of some debonair character from the old South. A true gentleman. The kind us girls only read about in books. It's such a sweet gesture that's so unlike him—but also very much like him.

"What is this?" I ask.

"Just a little something," he preens.

I turn toward him, and although I don't regret Brawler's touch on my skin, I'm burning from the inside out. Brawler doesn't know I care for Johnny and Johnny doesn't know I care for anyone but him. Telling them isn't an option.

"Speechless? That doesn't seem like you."

"I'm just...wow." I shake my head. "I'm underdressed. I smell like sweat." The need to take a shower remains in the forefront of my brain, even though whatever is on the plates smells absolutely delicious after all that training and sexing. My stomach growls in hunger.

Johnny chuckles. "Let's just eat. I happen to like the way you look after a workout."

He doesn't know the half of my "workout", which is a good thing.

I rise up on my tiptoes and kiss him on the cheek. "Just give me a minute," I say. Not giving him a chance to respond, I walk quickly to the bathroom and shut the door behind me. He won't give me enough time to take a shower, so instead, I take a washcloth, wet it down with warm water and wash my arms, neck, and chest. It's ludicrous to be thinking about Johnny detecting Brawler on me, but I have to keep Brawler safe. I can't bring him into this mess that way.

I pull my hair out of its tie and it streams down my back and over my shoulders. I reach for my hairbrush that's usually on the sink and stop. It's not there. I pull the drawers out, but still can't find it, so I settle with running my fingers through my hair until it looks presentable. When I come out through the bedroom again, I look for the bag of clothes I have, but can't find that anywhere either. What the fuck? When I actually want to change into something nicer than training outfits, Johnny—or his cleaners—have gone and done something to my shit.

Shaking my head, I walk back out into the main room only to find Johnny at the door. A hand pushes his chest, and he moves backward with the pressure. My hackles rise, ready to step in, but then a voluptuous redhead walks in, lips stained bright crimson. She giggles. "They told me I was needed."

Anger and jealousy whiplash through me. "Um, what?"

"Oops," the woman says, glancing over at me with a coy smile. She's older than I am, but she's acting like a giddy fucking schoolgirl, which infuriates me even more.

Johnny nudges her hand away from his chest. "There's been a mistake."

She shakes her head. "Don't think so," she singsongs, running her hands up him again like I'm not even fucking here. "Your dad sent me."

Well, this is fucking rich. "Your dad sent you a… whore?" I implore, crossing my arms and staring Johnny down.

The girl turns glittering eyes on me. "I'm not a whore." She flicks her hair over her shoulder. "I'm an escort. A pricey one too. Rocket and I are well acquainted, aren't we, baby?"

I stand there, hands fisting. I keep glaring at Johnny to see what his move is before I push this bitch out of the place. Or worse.

"It's a mistake, Clarissa."

Acid sours my stomach. "Oh, goodie. You're on a first-name basis," I deadpan.

Dagger-like eyes pierce me when he looks at me over his shoulder. "Clarissa, you need to leave."

Her mouth drops.

"Now," he says, pushing her out the door and closing it behind her.

"What the fuck, Johnny?" I explode as soon as the door is shut.

He turns a heated gaze on me. Rationally, I know I have nothing to be upset about considering Brawler's cock was just inside me but what-the-ever-loving-fuck! He dives a hand through his dark hair. "You heard her yourself. I didn't order her."

"*Order* her?" I laugh hysterically. I guess we're in a world where we can just order up whatever we want. Sex. Food. Murders. At least, that's how Johnny sees it. "Right," I say. "Your dad...hired you an escort. Well, isn't that...fucking insane?" I end. I'm too pissed to try to tiptoe around their father-son dynamics. What kind of father fucking does that?

"He thought he was helping."

I laugh again. I'm totally jumping straight into the deep end on this one. "Helping? That doesn't even make any fucking sense. He knows you're with me."

"Enough!" Johnny roars, shoulders tightening, muscles popping out of his jaw and arms. His ice-blue eyes cold and unfeeling.

I take a step back. The old Johnny just peeked his head out of the sand. Again.

If I was having an argument with a normal boyfriend, I'd get the fuck away. I'd take a walk. I'd calm down. I'd get the hell out of his face before I smashed it, but Johnny Rocket isn't a normal boyfriend. I glance around the suite and realize there's nowhere to escape. I can't get away from him. I'm just here to do whatever he feels like with me.

He moves toward me, and I back away. "Kyla," he growls out, a warning if I ever heard one. He takes another step toward me, and I do the same, getting just out of reach of his fingertips. He stops, glaring at me. "Don't."

I press my lips together, arching a brow in challenge.

He steps forward again, and I retreat. He makes a noise of pure exasperation, taking several quick steps forward. Each step he takes toward me, I take one back until my legs hit the side of the couch, and I end up planting my ass on the cushions, Johnny following after me. I try to push him away now, but he takes my hands and pins them over my head while he straddles my lap.

My chest raises and lowers with every rapid breath I take.

"Let me fucking explain."

"You can explain without touching me."

"No, I can't. Because I need to remind you of the connection we have." He lowers himself over me, his chest grazing my nipples. They peak to attention despite the fury brewing inside me. "Now, if you're settled," he says, placing both of my hands in one of his and using his other to cup my cheek. "...I'll fucking tell you what just happened."

Unwillingly, my heart skips a beat. Despite the fact that I've just worked out all my sexual frustration not an hour ago, desire returns between my legs. I try to stop it in its tracks. "If this is about you fucking other women, I already told you how I felt about that."

His touch circles around to cup my chin. His fingers bite into me a little before letting go just as quickly. He rubs his thumb over the sting and then cups my cheek again. "I wanted to have a nice dinner with you because we need to discuss things."

I swallow. His close proximity cages me in. I'm wrapped up in him again. He was right that we have this crazy connection. I just can't understand it.

"After what happened between us the other day," he starts, voice calming by the second. It's taking him great restraint, but the more he talks, the more relaxed he and his body become. "I had a talk with my dad. I asked him to explain the stipulations of his rules regarding us, specifically our romantic relationship. I told him that we both want to take it to the next level, but that we *both* didn't want to do anything to jeopardize his faith in me."

I couldn't give a rat's fucking ass about his pathetic excuse for a father and his archaic rules. I look away.

Johnny patiently moves my face back to look at him. "I reiterated that I want you more than ever. Not sexually, but in life. He suggested we move into separate rooms."

I blink, everything coming to focus. My hairbrush and clothes. I don't even need to look around to know that my shit isn't in this suite anymore. "That's why my things are gone?"

He nods.

My temple throbs. I'm constantly trying to stay ahead of the curve by making plans, but sometimes, I'm just too fucking tired. I never thought it would be this hard, but since real feelings have entered the picture, I'm constantly having to war against them. What's best for me and what's best for my ultimate goal are sometimes so completely at odds it's enough to drive me fucking insane.

However, anger has gotten me here now, so I lead with that. "So, because your daddy says we have to live separately, you're going to follow along? You moved me out of your place without even telling me, or hell, asking me?"

His icy blues flare at me again. I'm prodding the beast, but with Johnny, maybe I sometimes like it. Subconsciously, maybe I'm trying to make him into the terrible person I want him to be so I can completely write him off.

Or maybe I do just get off on this shit.

"You're the one who threw yourself at me."

"I've never had guys complain before."

He gets in my face, noses touching. My heart stops for a second. "Don't ever fucking talk about you with other guys again," he seethes. "You're *mine*."

Theoretically, getting out of Johnny's suite is a good move. More freedom, maybe. But I'm used to having someone around again. When I was at my aunt and uncle's, it was just me. Now I have people who care, and just because this one is psycho, doesn't mean he doesn't care.

"It's not right," I tell him. "You've told me before that your dad wouldn't be in our sex life, but he is. You told me we'd have freedom, where is it?"

"Give it time."

"Johnny..."

He strokes my chin then trails his fingers down my neck. "I'll try to move up the process," he says, fingertips grazing my chest. He pinches my nipples, and my thighs clench.

"What's the process?"

"It's best you don't know."

I lock eyes with him. "If I'm going to be yours, I can't be left in the dark."

He gives me a taunting grin, pinching my other nipple. Johnny must like to torture himself too because he's rapidly growing thicker between us. "Give it time," he promises. He lowers his head, pulling my shirt down to nuzzle in my chest, licking the curve of my breast that Brawler had his mouth on earlier. For some reason, that skyrockets my need, and I push my hips up to meet his. He groans. "I hope you understand how much I want you." He pulls my sports bra down, tongue rolling over my nipple.

"Don't you just want to fuck the rules?" I ask, voice breathy with want.

"I want to fuck a lot of things. This pussy." He lowers his hand, finding my clit to rub through my training pants. "This mouth," he adds, suddenly moving his head up to kiss me, making my head spin. He dives his tongue into my mouth, and I let him, kissing him back with as much ferocity as he's kissing me. His chest rumbles, and he pulls away. "You're like the sweetest drug," he murmurs. He moves backward, keeping my hands in his before pulling me to my feet after him. "Everything happens for a reason, Kyla. You'll see. I may not like the rule, but I understand it."

He's the only one, because I have a hell of a lot of frustration and damp panties that say otherwise.

17

*J*hate to admit it, but it was difficult sleeping by myself. I'd gotten used to Johnny wrapping his arms and legs around me as we drifted off. He's only a floor above me now. Over dinner, he promised he wouldn't take his father's offerings of escorts or any other devious way his father would try to get him to stay away from me. I'm not naïve enough to be positive that Johnny will stay true. His past is evidence otherwise even though I think he's changed, at least somewhat, in our time together.

I don't see him for breakfast, and when I text him, he doesn't respond. It's possible that after I left, he had to go to another meeting with his father. I guess Big Daddy K wants a sharper eye on the strip club and Joe Dunnegan. He doesn't have any proof he's doing anything wrong, only a gut feeling. Listening to Johnny talk about it over dinner only reinforced the fact that he is completely and utterly blind to anything bad his father could be doing. I guess that's not necessarily a shock considering it's been him and his father for a long time. The gang raised him, and his father has been at the top of that gang for a lot of those years. Of course, he would end up having some weird sort of relationship with him.

A knock comes on my door, and I assume it's Magnum because it's about the time he comes for me every morning to take me to school. Opening the door, I find him leaning against the frame, arms crossed. "I take it you probably knew this was happening," I say.

He looks behind me. The suite is set up a lot like Johnny's, but it's a little smaller. The decorating is the same. Everything is pristine with clean lines. The cupboards, medicine cabinets, and refrigerator were already filled with my stuff. All I had to do was plop my ass in bed.

He nods. "I didn't think you'd mind."

I shrug because I do...and I don't. Growing up with my aunt and uncle, I hadn't realized how much I craved the kind of relationships I have now. Relationship by fire. It's like throwing people into a shitshow and daring them not to get involved with each other. It's impossible. Relationships are formed, melded, and set to stone.

"Just so you know, I'm right across the hall, so don't hesitate to reach out if you need anything."

I look around his imposing figure. His door is shut, but

I'm desperately curious to see what kind of place Magnum has. Is it black? If that's the case, it would be different from the bright whites and grays of the other rooms I've been in in the tower. Black seems to be Mag's style though.

"You ready for school?"

I roll my eyes. "That makes me sound like I'm a little kid."

Magnum grins. "Well, you are young."

"I disagree. Age is just a number. We should be judged by our past, maturity, and wisdom. In that case, I'm probably older than you."

He wets his lips, and my body reacts.

I drop my stare to his mouth. "You don't agree?"

"I agree you're beyond your years, but you're not older than me."

"I guess we'll just have to agree to disagree. How old are you, anyway?"

"Twenty-five."

"All things combined, I'm like thirty, so I got you beat."

He chuckles. "You should grab your *book bag*, so I can take you to *high school*." He reaches out to pat my head, and I pull away from the chastising touch. It only makes him smile wider. "I'll give you a couple of years for your badassery in the ring, how about that?"

"We can keep discussing," I tell him, pulling my bag up on my shoulder.

We share easy conversation all the way to school, where

I try to convince him I'm actually older than what my real age would lead people to believe. I can't share many of the reasons why I think that way, so I tell him losing my parents aged me because I didn't have them to fall back on. He counters, telling me I play with the ripped holes in my jeans every day while he takes me to school. We go back and forth, him telling me why I'm still young and me coming back with reasons why, even though I'm eighteen, I should be older.

"You can't drink," he adds when we pull into school.

I laugh at him. He's already seen me drink. He's just trying to pull out anything he can think of. "Who says? Laws are for pussies."

He grins, pulling the car to a stop. Oscar starts toward the vehicle, and Magnum puts his hand over mine on the seat. "Be careful, and don't try to grow up too fast." All the banter dies between us while things get serious again.

I nod, not realizing what he's trying to say until I get out of the car and come face-to-face with Oscar. He gives me a smile, but I can tell by the shadows under his eyes, he's tired. He hasn't gotten much sleep.

Everyone grows up fast in the Heights.

I forget myself for a moment, reaching up to touch his cheek. "What's wrong?"

He dodges me, taking my fist in his grip and moving his head out of the way. He does it so fast it looks like I was trying to punch him. "There, there, Princess," he says loudly. "I'm just doing what I've been told to." He glares at me, and I instantly want to kick myself. The drive over with Magnum was just too normal, I almost forgot what world I was living in.

For what it's worth, Magnum is completely wrong. I'm definitely older than eighteen when we're talking about maturity. I've already gone through things in this life that some people never will. Don't get me wrong, I'm glad they won't. I don't want anyone to live through the hell I've lived through. No one should have to do that.

"Sorry," I whisper, but I pull my fist out of his grip like I'm actually pissed.

We turn to walk away together, still feeling Magnum's gaze on us all the way as we bypass security. No one's alerted to the fact that I have a knife in my bag. I need to ask either Magnum, Oscar, or Brawler to get me a gun. My first instinct is Magnum since hello, his name is Magnum, but at the same time, things are up in the air with him. I'm sure Oscar or Brawler could get me a gun, no questions asked.

"What's wrong?" I ask discreetly as soon as we enter the halls of Rawley Heights High. It's as normal as it ever is. At least there isn't a detective in the hallway ready to ambush me this morning. Not that I think that's the last I'll see of Detective Reynolds. He just has to be cleverer about how he approaches me. What he doesn't realize is that I'll never be his friend or helper when it comes to taking down the Crew. The Crew is none of my concern. Big Daddy K is. And since I'm planning on murdering him, me and cops won't mesh well.

Go figure.

Oscar pulls me into the boys' locker room. There's no one in here at this hour, but I barely notice that fact before he turns his dark gaze on me. "What the fuck were you thinking?"

I let my bag slip off my shoulder and drop to the floor. "I'm sorry. Fuck."

"As much as I want to be all over you, Princess, we can't be that friendly in school. Or anywhere for that matter. Johnny's a psycho when it comes to his things," he says dismissively. "No one ever touched Cherry, and she was nothing compared to what you are to him." He eyes me, questions glaring back at me.

"What?"

"I hear you moved out of his suite. Things getting too hot and heavy between you two?"

He must already know the reason behind it. The higher you are in the Crew, the more you know. "How did you hear that?"

"I heard them discussing it before the meeting last night." Well, that explains why Johnny didn't respond to my text this morning and why Oscar looks like shit warmed over.

"Well, it's none of your business."

"None of my business? Oh, I'm sorry. I thought there

was something going on between us. It was you pressed all up on me when I first came back, right?"

"Don't be an asshole."

"Then don't be dumb. Johnny is not your friend. He never will be. He uses things to get where he wants, and I don't care if you think he's in love with you, the fucker isn't capable of it, so stop being naïve."

I place my hands on Oscar's chest and shove him back. All these alphas are driving me fucking insane. "What I do is not up to a panel of judges. If you don't like it, walk away, Drego. I think you understand what it's like to live in a shit-hole of your own. Physically and mentally. Family-wise or otherwise."

"Alright, alright!" he growls, ceding the point. "I think about his hands on you, and I want to rip them off because here I am, and I can't even touch you."

The frantic beating of my heart calms a little. "Well, I have my own suite now."

"In the tower," he says. "It's not like you're living back at the other place. You're still under his thumb. Their thumb."

He's right, and it's one of the reasons why I didn't push Johnny too far last night. Yes, I hate the fact that his father is pulling the strings, but ultimately, my own place works in my favor even if it is still in the tower. I have a little more freedom, yet I'm still in close proximity. Johnny won't be breathing down my neck anymore, which allows me to think. To make plans. And hell, maybe even possibly open my life up some to explore things with Oscar and Brawler. There is no security on the floor I'm on. No metal detectors or bodyguards waiting just outside the elevator. The security is on the perimeter before you even make it into the building and then they have the extra security to protect Big Daddy K and Rocket.

"But I am safe there though," I tell him. If there is anyone left in Fonz's crew, which is information I'm not privy to, they won't be getting to me. Magnum's across the hall, and he escorts me around all day. Then when I'm here, I have Oscar and Brawler.

"Fonz's crew have gone into hiding," Oscar tells me, eyes finally softening. "They don't have enough numbers to fight against us right now. It's business as usual."

"Then what was the meeting about last night?"

Oscar eyes me warily. I still haven't told him why I'm here, but he knows something is up. I'm sure the fact that I'm asking about the Crew is a red flag. "K ordered all his guys over last night, talking about business in the future. There's talk of adding some, expanding others. It's the usual stuff now that the underground fighting isn't a threat anymore. There's even talk about expanding the fighting ring with heavy emphasis on you. You better win the fight this weekend, Kyla. K doesn't like it when people fuck with his plans, and right now, you're number one on his assets to exploit. If you let him down, consider yourself done. Consider whatever arrangement you have with Johnny over.

Consider whatever you're trying to accomplish here in the Heights over."

My stomach twists. I don't have any worries over the upcoming fight, but this just adds another layer of tension over everything. This is what I wanted though. I wanted Big Daddy K to count on me. To let me in, so I'd have better access to him. For as long as I've been staying in Johnny's suite, I've only seen him a couple of times. He's a difficult man to get an audience with, that's for sure. When I have seen him, he's never alone. I will not risk my freedom to take him out. I just have to bide my time.

It's not as if being here is a difficult task. Not as hard as I thought it was going to be, anyway, befriending the depraved members of society.

"I don't want to fight," Oscar says, coming closer. "You're right. We should all be able to find peace and enjoyment wherever we can in this fucked up place. I know I've desperately tried to figure out a way."

The bell rings overhead, and my phone buzzes in my pocket. I take it out to find a message from Brawler. **Where are you?**

I'm okay. With Oscar.

We all have to be careful about what we say in case Johnny checks my phone. Those messages shouldn't alert anyone. Johnny wants me with Oscar at school because he's the one tasked with protecting me here.

"Big Man upset because I'm with you?"

I laugh at his attempt to start a rift between Brawler and me. That's not happening. "Jealous much?"

He cups my ass. "More than you would fucking believe." He nuzzles my neck. "You know those movies where the quarterback always gets the girls? The ones where they're always on the sidelines cheering for them in tight ass little skirts and tops where their cleavage pops out?"

"Are you saying you want me to be a cheerleader? Because that's dead last on my list of things to do."

"I'm saying I want something normal," he growls.

My heart breaks a little. These guys—me—we've never had anything akin to normal. "TV isn't normal, and besides, you picked the wrong girl if you wanted a cheerleader."

"Aww," he sighs dejectedly.

"How about this? I'll dedicate me beating the shit out of this girl this weekend to you. You'll just have to pretend I'm wearing a cheerleading uniform."

He nips at my neck. "Maybe normal isn't better. The sound of that just made me perk up."

"You're depraved."

"You started it."

I think I'm already getting a feel for how Oscar will be in bed. Flirty. Fun. Not half as serious as Brawler is, and that's okay. Apparently, I like variety.

18

Friday rolls around. It's the night of my fight. I attend school like normal, though half the student body is studying me like they can see through me. Those who haven't seen me fight before are probably wondering if I'm worth all this hype. Those who have, are looking me up and down wondering if I can keep this up.

Crude posters adorn the walls at school announcing UPPERCUT PRINCESS vs. THE ROSE. Apparently, every fighter has a nickname. I'm pretty sure my name would even kick her ass, but we'll see tonight.

Like usual, the butterflies that started this morning stay with me throughout the day. At the gym after school, we don't do anything too heavy, just some light sparring and some core moves that I might need, mainly jabs. Jax found some amateur footage of The Rose on YouTube or something, so we watch that a little. She's okay, but as I've said before, I'm not worried about her. They can put anyone in front of me, and unless I'm standing opposite a fucking titled UFC fighter, I'm not going to shit my pants over it.

At least, that's what I tell myself to hype myself up. I don't care who you are, the moment you get close to a fight, even if you know by all intents and purposes the fight should be one-sided, you're scared as fuck. My stomach rolls. I'm super confident in my skills, but I need fighting to keep my spot in the Crew. With what Oscar told me the other day, I wouldn't be surprised if Big Daddy K is holding back on Johnny and me just because he wants to make sure I'm going to continue to be an asset for him. If I end up losing, he has no use for me, and that also means, he can't have his son with me either. They need to be strong on all fronts.

Fuck it. It doesn't matter. I'm kicking this girl's ass.

I'm in the back of the warehouse in the same room Brawler brought me back to that first night after Johnny claimed me in front of everyone. I still remember how he walked over Cherry's body to get to me, which should tell me everything I need to know about Big Daddy K and his family. There's always something shinier that might catch their attention. I have to make sure I keep being shiny to them.

The only people in the back with me are other fighters. Brawler comes by every once in a while to grab the next fighter. Each time he comes in, he watches me. If I'm feeling up for it, I glance over at the same time to reassure him I'm okay, but if I'm not, I shadowbox the air, pretending it's Big Daddy K's face. He's been all my opponents since the day I started fighting. It helps to keep it consistent. It helps fuel my fire.

I'm the last fighter in the room because my fight is the most important. As the night wore on, the buzz in the main room has entered earplug worthy territory. It's ten times what my fight with Cherry was. The warehouse is huge, but the area around the ring isn't big at all. I can only imagine how far back the people are standing. Some of them probably can't even see the fighting area.

The fight in front of mine is a long one, which makes my stomach twist even more in anticipation. *The Rose is my bitch*, I keep repeating. I'm not surprised they gave me a better opponent this time. I agree with Johnny on one thing. His dad knows what he's doing. He's got an angle on everything, and maybe he's truly trying to test me. Just like moving me out of Johnny's suite was a test, too.

After a few more minutes, the door to the room swings open. Instead of spying Brawler creeping in, it's Johnny. A huge grin pulls his lips apart. He's dressed in a dapper suit, like usual. A dark gray coat offsets his dark hair. "God, you're sexy as fuck," he breathes. "Maybe if you said you needed a good fuck to win, Dad would let up on the rule."

"Actually," I say, "there are more than a few fighters who

forego any sexual activities before big fights. The Gracies are known for it."

He makes a face. "That's terrible."

"I haven't bought into it yet," I tell him, winking.

His face darkens in lust. He pulls his hand out from behind his back and a royal purple robe unfurls between us. "Purple for royalty." He turns it over. On the back is my fighting nickname with a wrapped hand making the uppercut movement. "May I?" he asks, gesturing with the robe.

I nod, turning around so he can slip it over my shoulders. He puts one arm through and then the next, then moves his hands up to my shoulders to massage me there. Leaning down, he captures my earlobe and sucks it into his hot mouth. "Take her down, babe." He pulls me against his hard body, hand slipping noticeably low over my abs and toward the front of my skin-tight shorts.

My body melds into him. It doesn't take much to get me excited when I've started and stopped with him so many times. He lets out a breath and backs away from me. I'm relieved because whenever he's near, I'm caught up in him, just as I am when I'm with Brawler or Oscar. Hell, even Magnum can sweep me away into another time and place. I lose a little of myself to them as soon as I'm in their presence. It's unnerving, scary, but satisfying at the same time. It's nice that I don't have to bear the brunt of all the pressure myself. Finally. It's just too bad I only trust two out of those four people fully. Magnum and Johnny bringing up the rear.

"Is it time?" I ask, to make myself focus.

Johnny holds his arm out to me. "I think you'll find a few things have changed."

"Like?"

He grins before opening the door. We step out into the room. There's a clear path from the door to the fighting area this time. I don't have to push past people. People hold out their hands to touch me as I walk toward the ring. There's a girl already standing in the center, and I completely zone everything else out. A golden yellow bra and pant set completes her fighting outfit. It's completely different from my black on black. I'm not trying to be subtle about anything. I'm trying to tell everyone that I will fuck them up if I have the chance.

The roar of the audience is deafening, but it doesn't stop me from sizing my opponent up. She grins at me like she knows something I don't. Her mouth too wide and lips too thin to be anything but intimidation. I wonder how long she's been near the top of this ring. At least the female card. Brawler's at the very top of the male card, and he'd blow this girl away. Not that I think he'd actually fight her. Brawler's not the type.

This time, it's not Brawler in the center of the fighting area announcing the fights. It's a guy in his thirties, looking like he's trying to take a page out of Bruce Buffer's playbook.

When he speaks, his voice comes out of speakers. I glance up, noticing the new large speakers circling the room. Not only that, but there's also huge TV's in different corners of the room. I look down and straight into the lens of a camera. From my peripheral, I see myself on the screen, and the crowd explodes again.

The guy in the center of the ring announces The Rose first. She has a decent following. The yells and claps for her are genuine. Hell, I am the newbie. No one knows what could go down here. Most of these guys have just heard of me and not seen me yet.

When the guy gives me my introduction, Johnny slips the new robe off my shoulders. I bounce on my feet and shake off the tremendous uproar of the crowd that pierces through my focus. Johnny says something to me, but I can't even fucking hear him. He backs away, and that's the last time I feel his presence before the fight starts.

However, he's replaced with another presence I recognize. Brawler walks into the center of the room. He eyes us both coldly, like he doesn't have any sort of connection with either of the fighters. I lick my lips, and he holds his hand in the air, bringing it down in a swinging motion to call the fight to a start.

The Rose comes right for me. She doesn't circle or try to get a feel for how I fight. She's on the offensive from the get-go. I sidestep her, a little perplexed by her tactic. She's got some lady balls for sure. She probably wants to take me out as soon as she can to prove a point, but little does she know, I'm not going to let her get away with that. No fucking way.

When I duck under her attack, I throw a backfist into the back of her head. She whirls in an instant, coming for me again. I lift my guard to save me from her two crosses, and then retaliate, giving her a solid three count that ends in an uppercut instead of a cross.

The crowd fucking loved that one. Especially because I staggered her a bit.

With how many people are in this space, which must be double what it normally is or even more, the Crew—or should I say Big Daddy K—is making bank tonight. That's just on attendance. That doesn't even count bets where they skim a little off the top for allowing people to even place money on a fighter.

The Rose slows down now. She steps back, circling me after finally learning her lesson. If she comes straight at me, I will make her pay. So, I return the favor. I step inside, cracking my foot off her calf. She winces, and I move in, sending three good body shots to her midsection. When her guard lowers, I take it to her. I batter her face with punch after punch until she pushes me off.

That won't work though. She's scared now. She's circling but instead of looking for ways to get in on me, she's only focused on staying away. I have this fight. Now, I only have to finish it. The thing is, will the crowd want a beat-down of epic proportions? Or will they want me to carry this out a little?

Fuck it. I just want to kick her ass and get it over with. I want to prove my dominance. I can play with the next person if I think that's what they want.

I throw a stomp kick to her gut. As soon as her hands lower, I throw a right uppercut, rocking her. Her eyes roll back in her head, and I throw some quick jabs until she staggers, falling to her ass. I jump on her, backfisting her in the face. Blood spurts from her nose, staining my wraps. Then, two strong arms engulf me, pulling me away. Brawler's sweet scent surrounds me as he hauls me to my feet, but he lets go just as soon.

I move my stare up, watching the crowd go bananas. I catch sight of Jax and Finn in the crowd, and I smile. I had no idea they'd be coming tonight. I figured since they "unofficially" were fans of underground fighting and they have a very real business promoting real fighting, I didn't think they'd risk it. Instead, they're both clapping and shouting for me. Jax nods, but Finn looks like he's going to jump over the line between the ring and the crowd to celebrate with me until his brother holds him back.

Soon after, a silky robe covers my shoulders again, and Johnny squeezes me from behind. He raises my hand and walks me into the center of the fighting area. The announcer walks up, but Johnny gestures for the mic. "If you want to celebrate my girl's win, we'll be at Candy's."

I sneak a glance at Brawler who's helping The Rose to her feet. I shrug out of Johnny's grasp and move toward my opponent. She lifts her steady gaze to mine, and I'm relieved to find that she's not that injured. I hold out my hand, and she takes it. "Good fight," she says.

"Same," I tell her.

I glance up to meet Brawler's eyes. Adoration, respect, and pride seep through his turquoise shades. I nod at him, but people start to crowd me now. I guess not everyone has a brother to hold them back. Johnny holds out his hand, keeping everyone at a safe distance. "We'll be at Candy's. She's very thankful for your support. Thank you." The crowd opens a gap for him until we're safely back in the small holding room for the fighters.

Johnny doesn't waste any time getting his hands on me. "I'm impressed as hell with you, my sexy Kyla," he purrs, and then we lose ourselves in a kiss that has rivaled all our other kisses. It's the proof of two people who desperately want to share their feelings with one another but can't. It's a wild coming together due to our connection until an invisible barrier holds us back from the breech.

Basically, all I get is a lady hard-on with no way to release.

19

Johnny treats me like his princess as I ready myself for the celebration at Candy's. Kudos to him for thinking of it. He just marketed their strip joint to a bunch of rowdy customers ready for a good time. The plan is genius.

As of tonight, there's a whole cabinet of the shampoo I like in the shower area. There's also brand-new makeup: foundation, eyeliner, mascara. All that's missing is an actual closet with all my clothes, but Johnny's thought of that too. He holds up a skintight purple dress when I step out of the shower, a towel wrapped around myself. I dry my hair as best I can then run the towel over my body before dropping it to the floor. Johnny stares, gaze dropping until my nipples peak. Listen, if he's going to rev me up, he has to deal with the consequences, too.

209

He hands the dress to me, taking up a spot in the corner where he watches me shimmy into it pulling it over my hips and then pushing my arms through before making sure everything is in place. The fight didn't last long enough to get battered. My face is fine. My knuckles hurt a little, just as they do after every fight. Other than that, my forearms are a little sore from blocking her punches, but all-in-all, probably one of the better fights I've walked away from.

Johnny walks up behind me, wrapping his arm around my midsection, his other hand drifting up my thigh. "I don't think I'll be able to walk away from you tonight." His hand breeches the hem of my dress. A muscle jumps in my upper thigh as he gets closer.

I push my ass back into his hips, and he moves his other hand up to grip my breast. The dress is so tight, I can't use undergarments. I wet my lips and bite down to keep from uttering something embarrassing. I turn toward the mirror that's just over the sink and lock gazes with him. "Should I be pushing you away?"

He moans, dropping his head to my shoulder and playfully biting me there. It turns me on more than it should. "Yes," he croaks out. "You should definitely be shoving me away."

He steps back, giving me space. Perfect timing, too, because the door to the room opens. Johnny whirls to tell the person off, but it's Oscar who strides in. "Your father needs to see you."

I try to calm my beating heart. "Your father was here?"

Johnny straightens his shirt and rearranges himself. "He wanted to watch you fight again."

Yeah, sure. I bet that's all it is. I share a look with Oscar that I'm sure says exactly what I'm thinking. If Johnny hasn't seen it yet, he will soon. Then again, he probably already knows that his father is checking on his assets, and it doesn't make a bit of difference to him.

"Watch her?" Johnny asks Oscar. "I'll be back in fifteen."

Johnny cups my ass before leaving the room. As soon as he exits, Oscar locks the door behind him.

I glance at the lock. "What are you doing?"

"Protecting you."

He moves forward, and I turn to face him. He studies my burning cheeks. "You're flushed."

I could tell him it was from the fight, but I'd be lying.

"I watched you from the box, hiding a stiff one the whole time. Then again, I don't think I was the only man doing that."

He hooks his hands under my legs and lifts me until I'm sitting on the sink. He rolls the fabric of my dress back and pushes my knees apart. He trails a hand up my thigh, and my heart starts to pound.

"Let's see how much Johnny got you riled up." His fingers pass over my slit, and I tremble. "Damn," he says, jaw hardening as his hands find me slick with my own desire.

"Just for that, I'm going to make you cream for me." He plays with my slit and then pushes a finger inside.

I grip his shoulders. "Is this smart?"

"Is any of this smart?" he asks, pumping his fingers in and out of me at a steady pace. I pull him forward to kiss me, and he groans. His thumb passes over my clit, and then he pulls me closer to the edge of the sink to get a better angle. I gasp into his mouth and then bite his lip playfully. "Do you know how many times I've thought about this?" he asks, lips still against mine as he forms the words. "Too fucking many. I drive myself crazy."

"Mmm," I murmur into his lips. He's pulled taut with need, but his movements are still at expert status. He knows exactly where to touch me to get me off quickly, and it's working. "Fuck. Oscar."

"You won for me, didn't you?"

I nod. "Did you notice my outfit? I tried to get it as close to a cheerleader's uniform as I could." The bra cut was triangular in shape, thick bands for my straps and around my back. The closest I could find to make Oscar's dream come true. The little booty shorts are what I imagine cheerleaders wear underneath their skirts, too, though I don't have any personal experience of that myself.

"Aw, fuck, Princess." He keeps his movements steady, still concentrating on my clit, pressing circles there with the pad of his thumb until I'm gripping him so tight, I'm sure it must hurt. I straighten my fingers to keep from hurting him and then reach down, cupping his cock. It jerks in my hold. "Fuck." He pulls just far enough away to look at me. There's something there that yanks me over the edge, sending me into a spiral of the richest pleasure. Oscar holds me until I come down, but the look on his face when I touched him still lingers between us. Why did he look shocked?

Slowly, he removes his finger, and then pulls me off the edge of the sink. I slide down his body until my tiptoes hit the cement floor. "You should get ready. We don't want Johnny wondering what we've been doing in here if you're not farther along than you were when he left." He kisses my forehead and then reaches around me to wash his hands. He pulls out a few paper towels from the dispenser and frowns back at me. "This isn't going to be soft." He wets them, the towels turning a dark brown before he carefully runs them over the area he just played with until I came apart.

I watch him while he does this, awestruck by his compassion for me after the fact. When he finishes passing a dry paper towel between my legs, he looks up. "You should be getting ready."

"Why did you look at me like that?" I ask. "Why did you seem so shocked when I touched you?"

His lips form a thin line. "A story for another day."

"Oscar," I plead. Time's running out, and Johnny could be coming back any moment, but this is too important not to talk about right now. "Tell me."

I reach up to cup his cheek, and he holds my palm there.

His skin is hot, burning up. He turns his face to kiss the inside of my palm. "Let's just say I've been with a lot of selfish women." He squeezes my hand and then drops it, striding toward the other side of the room where he unlocks the door, ending the conversation.

I turn back toward the mirror and replace the skirt of my dress back down my legs. It isn't long, but it certainly won't bode well for Oscar and I if it remains around my hips. "I'll take that answer for now," I tell him, holding his gaze. I make quick work of my makeup as Oscar watches. The hairs on the back of my neck stand the whole time. I do a halfway decent job of blow drying my hair—yes, whoever set this up for me has thought of everything—but I leave it somewhat wet, touch up the powder on my face, and then coat my lips with a fun shade of red.

When I turn, Oscar's pants are still bulged in front of him. Johnny hasn't returned even though I'm sure the fifteen minutes is up. Neither Johnny nor his father is ever very good at telling people how long things will take.

"You're by far the most beautiful woman I've ever seen."

My skin sprouts with goosebumps. The urge to thank him for saying that overwhelms me. I want to thank him for pleasuring me by getting down on my knees and taking him into my mouth, but I don't even need to list all the ways that's a bad idea.

A knock sounds on the door, and Oscar closes his eyes briefly.

"It's Johnny."

Oscar mouths something to me. I can't be sure what he's said, but I read the word everything. *It's* everything? *You're* everything? I can't ask him because he's already opened the door, revealing a waiting Johnny.

Johnny's lip quirks up. Oscar studies us as he moves forward. His hand curls to the small of my back as he looks me over appreciatively. "Ready?"

I nod, fighting the urge to look at Oscar.

We walk from the room. "You too, Bat," Johnny says, calling for Oscar to follow us. "We're all celebrating."

I search the main area for Brawler and find him talking with a few people with cleaning supplies in their hands. When he sees me, his gaze zeroes in. "Nice fight, Kyla."

Johnny hugs me tighter, beaming. Brawler nods at Oscar, and Oscar returns it. At least in that they're on the same side. They can put aside their differences when they're worried about me. Though, they shouldn't be. Johnny's not going to let anything happen to me, even if it is more about his own ego than his love for me.

When we're seated in the car for the short drive to Candy's, Johnny makes sure I'm plastered to his side. There are a few other bodyguards in the back with us, including Magnum. "Nice fight," he says, echoing what Brawler just said.

"Did you catch it?" I ask.

He nods. "I was up in the box."

I grin at him, letting everyone's praise flow through me. This is the first time I've had people around me whose praise and encouragement I wanted. My aunt and uncle never used to come to my fights. Hell, they didn't even know about them. I've been in the underground circuit a long time. Just not here. They'd see me come home with black eyes, and I'd make up excuse after excuse. Bullying at school. Accidents. You name it, I used it just to get out of the inevitable conversation.

Sanctioned fights were never really my thing, but that could be because it's difficult as fuck to get fights in the normal competition circuits. There aren't a lot of female fighters, and I couldn't make a splash out in the real world where someone could easily trace me when I made my move to the Heights. I had to keep under the radar as much as I could. I cut my teeth on fighting back home though it was nowhere near what it's like here. Even when I fought Cherry, that was the biggest fight I'd had to date.

For Johnny's part, he's playing the doting, proud boyfriend well. Except, it's not an act for him. I know how proud he is of me. But it also sucks that he's got something to gain from my fighting, too. It makes his reactions not as genuine as the others, even though they very well might be.

The night at Candy's consists of rounds and rounds of alcohol being delivered to our table. The waitress keeps announcing who's bought me the next drink, but they are all names I don't recognize. Except for Joe Dunnegan. I recognize his. He lifts a glass to me, and I do the same, taking a sip of the dark amber liquid before turning toward Mag and whispering, "Told you I could drink."

"I know. Fuck the rules," he whispers back.

Tonight at Candy's isn't a normal night though. Sure, there are women dancing on the stage, but there are more bodies in here than ever, all of them writhing against one another, dancing with each other instead of focusing on the stage. Johnny was the only reason we could score a booth to sit in. The regular customers don't seem to mind all the newcomers because scantily clad women accompanied all the bloodthirsty men from the warehouses, and those ladies aren't as untouchable as the ones on stage. Tonight is more like a nightclub with naked entertainment than a chill place to sit back and get your rocks off while watching women dance.

"Look what you did," I tell Johnny, gesturing toward the bodies in the room. "You know what you're doing, don't you?"

Even Dunnegan himself couldn't look more pleased. He's already returned to our table a few times, telling Johnny that Candy's should always host my after parties. Johnny looks to me as if I have a say in the matter, but I agree anyway. It just makes good business sense.

Why I'm worrying about making the Heights Crew money is beyond me. I tell myself it's not for them at all. It's for Johnny. Just like he watched me kick that girl's ass, pride beaming from him, I feel the same as I watch everyone in this room have a great time because of him. I bet this place has their best week yet. Not that it's not always a money-maker. Sex sells. I'm not naïve about that. But tonight, Johnny dropped the cover charge, and the liquor is flowing like nature's waterfalls.

An hour into our celebration, the crowd is pushed back as more of the Crew's guys filter into our space. I almost stop breathing when a familiar face follows a horde of black-clad bodyguards. Johnny nudges me so we can slip out the side of the half moon table. Johnny lifts his hand to greet his father with a handshake while K inspects the room. "Good job, my boy," he says, his other hand landing solidly on his son's shoulder.

"Kyla," he says, addressing me with a short nod and smile. "You fought very well tonight." He slides his gaze down my body. It's only cursory, but it slips a wedge of unease through me. No one wants to be ogled by their boyfriend's father unless their boyfriend's father is Jensen Ackles. Let's get real.

Whether Johnny notices or not, I'm unsure, but their conversation turns to business as Big Daddy K takes a seat with us at the half circle table. It might just be my percep-tion, but Magnum moves closer to me on the edge of that half circle seat. I'm more secure with him here as K informs Johnny that they had their best night ever at the warehouse. He even tells him they had to turn people away, and they definitely don't want that. All signs point to the fact that they'll be getting a new venue for the fight ring.

While they talk, I search the room for Jax and Finn, wondering if they made it to my after party. Jax doesn't seem like the type who would want to come to a place like this, but Finn definitely does. Naked girls? Dancing? Hello. He'd be on board, as would most males.

Johnny's hand moves up my thigh. He squeezes me a little to get my attention. "Want to dance?"

He nods toward the gyrating bodies of which I was staring after. In actuality, I'd moved on to looking for Oscar who'd only stayed for a little while after we got here. He probably couldn't stand not being able to be close to me, so he decided to leave. I can't blame him.

Johnny excuses himself from the table, and we move to the outskirts of the bodies pressed so tightly together. People give us a berth as we start to dance. Johnny's got moves. Within a few minutes, my cheeks are flush, and my body is telling me it likes Johnny's touch far too much. His hand roams over my ass. "Have I told you how much I like this ass?"

"I thought you were more of a breast man myself."

"Ugh, don't remind me," he says, nipping my earlobe. He spins me around, so my back is against his front. He maneuvers my hair over one shoulder and drops his hand to my stomach. I grind against him, looking at him over my shoulder. The crowd has pulled back a little, and more than a few people watch us. "I forgot you weren't wearing any panties. Bad move on my part."

I grind against him, only to look back to see the lust in his light blue eyes. He spins me until I'm facing him again. I look up. "Everything okay?"

Conflict sears in his gaze. He drops a kiss to my lips. "Perfect."

The song ends, and Johnny helps me off the makeshift dance floor. Magnum avoids my gaze as we walk back. However, Big Daddy K motions for me to scoot into the booth first. It was bad enough when there was a body between us, but now that I'm next to him again, I can't stop replaying what he did to my parents over and over again in my head. No matter how many times I try to push it back so I can concentrate, it comes to the forefront.

"You put on a good show out there, you two."

Johnny hugs me to him, and I'm grateful for the few extra inches of separation between his father and me. I'd be happier if it was a few feet, but I'll take what I can get.

Big Daddy K taps his lips. "People couldn't keep from staring at you."

"It's all her," Johnny says.

"That's what I'm saying." Big Daddy K leans forward, and Johnny follows him. "What do you think of Kyla working here a few nights? A fighting stripper." He raises his eyebrows in quick succession. "They'd go nuts."

The air in the room shifts. Everything goes quiet around

us. I want to reach out and slap the fucker, but I know what that would mean for me. My heart holds still until it waits for something else to happen. For Johnny to reply. For him to kick his father's ass. Just something.

Johnny laughs, and my heart kicks back into gear. "You better be joking," he says, practically hauling me into his lap.

"Remember it's all about business, son." The leer he gives me sends shivers down my spine.

Just what the fuck is Big Daddy K getting at? And whatever it is, I hope this is one of those times that Johnny will tell him to fuck off.

20

*J*ohnny's chest rumbles. "It's not business with her. I already told you."

My stomach clenches. I've only ever heard Johnny argue with his father once, and that was when Big Daddy K wanted me to fight Evan. Big Daddy K glances at me as if I'm going to stick up for myself like I did that time, but I press my lips together. I am not fucking stripping.

Big Daddy K shrugs, but there's a noticeable tick in his jaw. He can't stand the fact that Johnny just didn't go along with his plan.

"Not that I would ever buy into that," Johnny says, "but doing that to Kyla would sexualize her even more than she already is. People won't come for the fights. They'll come hoping to see a show any girl could perform here on any other night."

"But not by her." Big Daddy K circles the whiskey glass in front of him.

"And it won't ever be by her. Would you have let Mom strip?"

Big Daddy K's face reddens. Johnny's body goes stiff beside me. Even I know he crossed over a line there. It seems Mrs. Big Daddy K is a sore subject for the both of them.

Johnny ignores his father's reaction, jutting his chin out, and I want to clap for him for finally taking control. "Exactly," he says. "No one gets Kyla but me."

Big Daddy K looks from his son to me. He maneuvers out from around the seat and throws a wad of bills on the table. I don't know why. Maybe out of habit. He owns the place, so it's not as if he has to pay for his drinks. "We'll talk more about this privately."

Big Daddy K's bodyguards follow him out. Johnny pretends nothing is bothering him, but I'm not dumb. I turn to him. "You okay?"

His jaw tenses, and he stares at me like he's looking for a lifeline.

"You can talk to me about things, you know?" I sound like a broken record, but he needs to trust me. I grab his hand under the table. "Anything at all." Even though I should be saying this to look for some sort of aspect to get to Big Daddy K, it's coming from a place of wanting to help Johnny. I hate that he's under his father's thumb. I lean over and whisper into his ear. "No matter what it is, I'm siding with you."

That's probably the truest statement I've ever said to Johnny. He just doesn't know that I'd take anyone's side over his father's.

"Another round," Johnny says, catching the attention of a passing waitress. Then, he licks a trail up the curve of my neck to the hollow under my ear. "You're in my bed tonight."

I bite my lip. Someone wants to defy their father.

We drink the final round of drinks and then Johnny indicates he wants to leave. It's only a half hour away from closing time anyway, but instead of making a big deal about it, we try to slip out the back again. Once we succeed, we're back in one of the fancy black cars heading toward the tower. With Magnum as an audience, the only thing Johnny does is hold me close to him. Once we're ushered through the exterior security, we pull into the underground parking lot and Johnny helps me out of the car. I've had a few drinks tonight, so I'm a little buzzed. I made sure not to drink all the drinks that were purchased for me because if I had, I would've been out a while ago. I attempted to stop the drinks from even coming, but Johnny told me to let them. They wanted to show their appreciation for the fight, and plus, it's more profit for Candy's.

The elevator opens on Johnny's floor, and he pulls me

past Security. "She's been with me," he tells them before they can even move forward.

"Plus, I don't have any place to hide anything in this dress," I call out to them as we sneak by.

Johnny's grip tightens on my wrist. He pulls me inside his suite and presses me against the door. "God, I fucking want you." The need in his eyes is almost unbearable. He rubs his cock against me. The dress is so thin that if he wasn't wearing his suit pants, I'd be able to feel every last hard ridge and curve.

"You're not thinking straight." That's saying something because I'm also pretty inebriated right now.

"I'm thinking straight," he counters. "He can't take you from me."

I press onto his shoulders. "Does he want to take me from you?" That would be news to me, and I don't like the sudden twist to my gut that thought provokes.

"He thinks women are playthings. He doesn't understand my feelings for you. He hasn't felt for another woman since my mom left." His stare dips down my body. He palms my tit, then squeezes my nipple. "I don't want to fucking talk about that."

He rolls the dress up over my hips, palming my bare ass with his hands.

I moan into him, then work on unclasping his pants and shoving them to the ground. He rests against me, his cock hard. "Christ," he growls. "I've denied myself you for too long."

His hand skates between my legs, fingers brushing over my apex. I drop my head back, resting it against the door. He gets close, toying with my pussy until he pulls his fingers to his face and licks them. He closes his eyes as he savors my taste.

I work on the buttons of his shirt, throwing the fabric back as he wrestles out of it. He slips his shoes and socks off, standing in front of me like a concoction of my own making. A specimen I would dream up for myself while I brought myself to orgasm.

"You always look at me like you could pounce," he breathes.

"Not sorry," I say.

He grins, pulling my dress over my head. Once the dress is free of my hands, I'm completely naked. He cups the underside of my breast. "I think I'm a tits and ass man because of you."

I reach out, sliding his boxers down his muscular thighs. "I'm a cock girl."

He strokes his dick in front of me. Cum beads at the top.

I take his hand and lead him to the couch. After pushing him down, I straddle him. My core heats as it brushes against his cock. I should be sensible and ask about condoms and birth control, but the brains are out the window. I take him in my hand, replacing his, stroking him to my core. "Fuck, fuck," he breathes. "You want to ride me, don't you?"

His tip touches my entrance. "So fucking bad," I moan.

He grips my hips and pushes me to the couch cushions until he's hovering over my body. He rests his forehead against mine as he stares down, moving closer and closer. Every time he touches me, he retreats, driving me crazy. At first, I think he's doing it on purpose to drive us both crazy. I know I'm about ready to grab his ass and make him stay, but then I look into his face and read the conflict etched there.

I still.

"Fuck," he roars, moving off me. He forces his fingers through his hair. "I want you. Don't think I don't."

I peek at his cock. That much is evident.

I close my eyes, trying to keep my cool. This is the second time he's driven me to the edge and pulled back. "I want you too," I say.

"You sound frustrated."

I smile. "Wouldn't you be? I'm horny, Johnny. I want you."

Torture lances his face. He strides quickly toward the door, opening it before I can barely even blink. He drags a figure inside, and I try to cover up with nothing but my hands to aid me.

When Magnum looks up, the confused look on his face washes away, and he stops. "Fuck her," Johnny orders, pointing at me.

"What?" I screech.

"You're fucking horny, and I can't." He turns toward Magnum again. "Fuck my girl. Make her come."

Magnum holds his hands up. "No. I won't do that."

"You took an oath to do what I say, and right now, I need you to mount my girl until she screams."

"You don't want me to do that, J. You really don't."

Johnny moves toward one of the tables by the side of the couch. He whips the drawer open and pulls out a gun. "I said…" He spins toward Magnum, raising the gun to point directly at Mag's chest. "…fuck my girlfriend. If she isn't screaming by the time you're done, I'm putting a bullet in your head."

"Johnny," I cry, moving up the couch. He's completely lost it.

I slip off the side, but Magnum says, "Stay back, Kyla."

"No, Kyla. Move forward," Johnny orders. "Remember how you just wanted to ride me. Ride him." He peeks at me for a moment. "I'm so sorry I keep doing this to you. I deserve it, don't I? I fucked that whore in the dress shop. You know you want to do this to me. To get back at me."

"You'll never forgive yourself, man," Magnum says. "You don't want this." He seems to assess the room. Every time I move, he jerks his gaze back to me, giving me a warning look.

"I said—!"

Magnum moves forward, making quick work of getting

the gun away from Johnny. He takes it from his grip and slips it into the back of his pants before planting his hands on his forearms. "You don't want this, man. That's your girl right there. You're scaring her."

Johnny's whole body trembles. Magnum shakes him and then shoves off.

I move forward, wrapping my arms around Johnny as Magnum backs away. Now that pretty much everyone has seen my goods, I blow out a breath, eyeing the two of them and just hoping that it's over now.

"I'm sorry," Johnny says into my ear.

"Shh," I say, motioning to Magnum that I'm fine.

"No one hears of this," Johnny demands the second Magnum's hand grabs the knob to exit the room.

"I wouldn't do that to you."

When Magnum leaves, I take Johnny to the couch and cuddle next to him. My mind still races from the quick turn of events that I can barely wrap my head around. Was it a test? Or did Johnny just completely go insane for a minute?

A lost stare meets my gaze. "I'm completely fucked in the head. I can't fuck you because I hear my father's voice telling me I can't even though I so badly want to tell him to fuck himself. I love my father, but fuck." His muscles tighten. "It's like he takes pleasure in taking things from me. My mom. You."

Now we're getting somewhere.

"Just because people are related to you, doesn't mean

they're what you need in your life," I say, speaking from experience. My aunt and uncle were always there, and they were good to me, but whether it was in my own head or not, I was never theirs. Maybe Johnny's feeling the same right now. His dad is good to him. In his eyes, he's probably given Johnny the best life, but sometimes, that's not enough.

"You can't repeat any of this."

My jaw hardens. "My allegiance is to you," I say.

His stare almost knocks me off my feet. He grips my hips. "I can't believe I just told Mag to fuck you. I would've killed him."

"I think he knew that."

All the pressure Johnny is under is threatening to explode in different ways. I don't know that I've noticed it before. The truth is, Johnny's still young, but he runs areas of his father's business with skilled, experienced hands. The one thing he has apart from that is me. Yet, I'm also a part of that too.

"I'm yours, okay? We're a team," I state, reinforcing it for him. Not because I'm playing an edge, but because I truly mean it. "I can certainly restrain myself if you need me to," I say. "Let's just not take it so far next time," I hedge. The last thing we need is Johnny forcing Magnum in here to fuck me again.

Warmth simmers in Johnny's light blue eyes. "I was so, so wrong, Kyla. I hope you can find it in you to forgive me."

"I think you're just lost," I tell him truthfully. "You need someone to talk to who's apart from everything going on. Open up to me. You know I don't want to just be the girl who's holding onto your arm every night like I'm some model. I want in. Let me in," I plead.

For the next few hours, Johnny spills some secrets to me. He pulls a blanket off the edge of the couch and holds me to him. It's like an exorcism off his cold, dark heart. Someone who's truly good, but who's been forced into something bad. He tells me about the people he's killed at his father's behest. About the conflict he always feels when it comes to his father. He pours every last part of his soul out to me, and I soak it in through my pores, sharing the burden with him.

By the end of the night, we've melded into one person, and I've suddenly gained a whole new insight into how Big Daddy K ticks. His son isn't spared the gory details of his treatment of others. He's manipulated everyone. He uses dirt he has to get what he wants. He's a sick, sick person, and how Johnny was able to escape *some* of his monstrous ways is beyond me.

That isn't to say Johnny's an angel. He's not. He loves the Crew. He loves his life. There's no getting around that. He'll be forever tethered to them in more ways than one.

But there's a chance he could survive without them, and that's what I'm banking on.

21

Johnny and I fall asleep on the sofa. In the middle of the night, he moves us to the bed where we lie with one another until the first rays of sun poke through the curtains in his room. I get out of bed, stretching, making sure not to disturb Johnny and his angelic, sleeping face. I don't know how he'll react this morning to telling me things he probably didn't mean to. Though, I'm glad he did. Now, I'm one hundred percent certain it will take a lot for Johnny to ever defy his father. The manipulation, the puppet strings, it's far too deep. It's for the best if we don't take our relationship further.

I slip out of his suite. Different guards line the hall in front of the elevator, and my stomach tightens. I need to find Magnum and talk to him. Prolonging the inevitable will just make me queasy. Wordlessly, I take the elevator down to my new floor. Instead of stopping at my door on the right, I turn to the left. Looks like I'll get the chance to see his apartment after all. I bite down on my lip and knock on the door.

I stand there in Johnny's oversized t-shirt and a pair of sweats. I run my hands through my hair as I wait for him to answer—if he's even home. I'm about to turn and hide in my place for the foreseeable future, but at the last second, I decide to knock louder.

I step back when he pulls it open. He stands in front of me in low-slung joggers. Black, of course. Rivulets of sweat drip down his naked chest. His damp copper hair stuck to his head. My stomach tumbles over itself. Magnum always looks so put together, so to see him like this is...captivating to say the least. Jaw-dropping even. Then again, he saw every last inch of me last night, so he still owes me.

He takes a step back, allowing me access to his space. As I thought, the neutral bones of the apartment are there. Light walls. Same silver finishes. However, Magnum's motif is darker. Everything he's added is either black or dark blue. The perfect contrast.

The door clicks shut behind me, so I turn. "I just wanted to say..." I pop up on my toes. Never in a million damn years did I ever think I'd have to have a conversation like this. "...I don't know, I guess. Um..."

"It's okay," Magnum says.

"No, no, it's not. Johnny pulled a gun on you last night, and that was just—" My mind works to try to find a word other than insane, but it keeps getting hung up there.

"Are *you* okay?" Mag asks. His hazel-green eyes penetrate through my hardened exterior like usual.

"Great," I say, smiling. "Everything's fine. I just thought we should have a conversation since Johnny ordered you to have sex with me last night. And you know, that you, in general, saw me buckass naked."

Magnum's eyes turn molten. He doesn't allow his stare to move lower, but it feels like he's undressing me with his gaze, anyway.

"Thanks for, you know, for *not* doing that," I say. I eye his perfectly chiseled chest. "Not that sex with you would be bad. It's probably good. It's just—"

His lip quirks. "Having your boyfriend demand you fuck someone in front of him isn't your cup of tea?"

"Right." I say, smiling, and glad that we're on the same page. "Not my cup of tea. Nor would I imagine it's yours, but stranger things have happened."

I start to tremble. I can put all the false bravado I can muster on, but it doesn't change the fact that what happened in Johnny's suite last night was scary as fuck. Also, these feelings for Johnny aren't just going to go away even though I know they're a terrible idea. I can't share it with Brawler. Not even with Oscar. Magnum is the only one who knows about *all* of them.

"Come here," he says, beckoning me forward.

I blink up at him and cock my head to the side.

He gestures his fingers for me to come closer.

I eye his sweaty chest. There's a barbell and bench in the corner, the likely culprit of Magnum looking this damn sexy this morning.

"Come on, you're not a stranger to sweat," he says, moving forward himself. We meet in the middle, and he puts his arms around my shoulders, holding me to him. "My Grams used to say that hugs could cure almost anything. It's less about the hug and more about the human connection."

I close my eyes, allowing myself to be held in his arms. It's tense at first, but then I relax more and more, and my own grip on him strengthens, holding him to me. His grandmother was on to something. "You should start a Share-A-Hug business," I tell him. "You're really good at it."

"And miss out on looking all badass?"

I huff out a laugh. "And the black clothing? I can see why you'd stick your nose up at it."

His chest rumbles with laughter, and it's a welcome distraction from everything. Magnum's like a chameleon. He can change his persona to suit what others need, it's just that they usually need him to be an ass-kicking security guard. Who knew this nice, funny guy was lurking inside him somewhere? "Let me make you some tea. Or hot chocolate."

"Ohh," I say, stepping back. His mood must be rubbing

off on me. "You had to throw in the hot chocolate. Why? Because I'm so young?"

He shrugs. "Figured that's what kids your age liked to drink. I don't have any chocolate milk."

I glower at him, but all it does is make him laugh harder. "I'm not the one who has hot chocolate in my place."

Lies. I actually requested hot chocolate when Johnny had me put together a grocery list when I was staying in his suite. Considering how observant Johnny is, I'm sure if I went through the cupboards in my new place, there'd be some hot chocolate there, too.

Magnum lifts a single shoulder like he's a tough guy and can take everything I throw at him. I definitely agree with that. He's already saved my life once. I would like to know how he keeps all these muscles hidden under his shirts though. Brawler's got a bit of size on him, but Magnum's build is more the quick and deadly type. Lethal. Agile. I should know. The way he diffused the situation with Johnny last night was awe-inspiring from a tactical point of view.

I sit on Mag's couch as he busies himself in the kitchen. I expected his place to be squeaky clean since he always looks so put together, but his apartment looks so lived in. Johnny looks like he's barely there. Mine already has clothes strewn around it, and last I knew there were dishes in the sink, though I'm sure those have already been taken care of by housekeeping, but Mag's place looks homey despite all the stark lines.

In a few minutes, he joins me on the couch with his own mug of cocoa. We sit back, and I take a sip. I don't know where he got this hot chocolate, but it's ten times more chocolatey than the stuff I have. I take another sip. The steam rises in front of my nose and billows toward the ceiling.

"You're sure you're okay?" Mag asks. He lifts an eyebrow as he studies me. "He didn't hurt you, did he?"

I shake my head.

Relief is palpable on his face. "I didn't think he would, but I was worried all night. I almost didn't want to leave, but I know staying wouldn't have calmed him down."

My cheeks heat, and it has nothing to do with the temperature of the drink I'm swallowing. "Has he done that before?"

Mag quirks a brow. "Asked me to sleep with his girlfriend?"

I burst out laughing, almost spluttering the hot chocolate out of my mouth. "Well, no. I would hope not!"

"He hasn't even had a regular girl before."

"Regular?"

Magnum looks away. "You know, someone he keeps around. Someone he asks us to watch. Someone that if something happens to, he'd lose it. He threatens us daily that if you get hurt, we're done, and he doesn't mean he's firing us, Kyla."

I nod, feelings welling up inside. I can't dwell too much

on that sentiment because I don't know what to do with it. My gut tells me it'll likely be impossible to get Johnny to go against his father. Even if it is for me. Plus, I can't shake the feeling that I'm going to be doing the same thing to him that his father did to me. At the end of all this, I am killing his loved one.

What kind of person does that make me?

"Well, I was hoping he hadn't done that before," I tell Magnum honestly. "I meant has he ever freaked out on you?"

"On me?" Mag shakes his head, taking a sip of his hot chocolate and setting it down on a coaster on the coffee table in front of us. I glance around the room, noticing one weird thing. There's no TV in here. That's just...odd. "That's not to say I haven't seen him do other questionable things."

"Will he hurt me?" I have a gut feeling I know the answer to this, but I want to make sure my feelings are correct.

Magnum shakes his head slowly. "Everything in my gut tells me no. You'd have to do a lot to get him to hurt you. I mean, physically. There are a lot of ways people can hurt you that aren't physical pain."

"Like banging a girl in a fitting room?"

His expression turns serious as he nods. "And like ordering someone to have sex with you."

It's hard for me to wrap my head around that. If I had to

analyze what was going through Johnny's head last night, I'd say he was trying to help in some fucked up way. He felt bad that he kept bringing me to the brink only to pull away at the last minute. He so badly wants to follow his father's rules that he was trying to solve a problem. Girlfriend needs relief, and he can't do it? Grab the closest person he could find.

I shift in the seat, and Magnum puts his hand on my knee. "I hope you don't feel uncomfortable with me now."

I take a deep breath and meet his eyes. "It wasn't your fault, but it was awkward as fuck. Not to mention scary. Don't you agree?"

Again, Mag focuses on my eyes even though it feels as if he's peeling the layers of my clothing off. My body flushes, and I finally put the hot chocolate down, so I can disseminate if it's Mag who's giving me hot flashes or the drink itself. "I would rather he hadn't freaked out while you were in the room."

Seeing that desperate side of Johnny helped me see who he really is though. I lick my lips, eyeing Magnum. "You said we're friends, right?"

He nods.

"How far does that friendship extend?"

He lifts his brows, already trying to figure out where I'm going with this.

"I'm not asking you to fuck me."

His cheeks turn a soft shade of red, easily recognizable even with his copper scruff. His skin is so light that it shows everything. "I'm wondering if it extends to me saying something about Big Daddy K?"

Magnum stiffens.

Well, that's my answer. "Forget it," I say, reaching for my mug.

"No. No," Magnum says, and I don't know if he's convincing me or himself. He squeezes my knee again. "You're misinterpreting my reaction." He gives me a solid nod as if to tell me to continue.

I take a deep breath. "After you left last night, Johnny opened up to me. You know I'm new here, so..." The lie churns my stomach after just confirming with Magnum that we were friends, but I'm pretty sure I just can't go off spouting to one of the Crew's bodyguards that I want to murder the Crew leader. "...well, it made me think twice about the kind of person he is. Johnny seems to look up to him so much, but to be honest, with what he told me last night, he sounds like a master manipulator. Someone maybe Johnny shouldn't be around." I don't dare mention the fact that K thought it would be a good idea that I take up stripping. That can't get around. Johnny will lose his shit.

Magnum brushes his scruff with his hand. "Big Daddy K is ruthless. You have to be to get to the top of the Heights Crew. I'm sure you figured that out already." He eyes me, doing one of his bone-deep gazes again. "If you're asking if Johnny should get away from him, the answer is, he can't." Mag shakes his head. "Nor would he probably want to."

Sourness churns my stomach.

"You haven't lived your whole life here, so you don't get it. The Crew is family. It's all they know. For Johnny, it's double that because the Crew leader is actually his flesh and blood. Johnny's been indoctrinated into this way of life since he was a baby. Most of us, we don't come around until we're teenagers. We make our own decisions. Even those of us who had siblings or parents in the Crew, it's not the same as having someone like Big Daddy K in your family."

"You had a family member in the Crew?"

An intoxicating mix of pain and guilt crosses Mag's face. "My father."

"Is he still in it?" I ask, wracking my brain to see if I've encountered anyone who looks like Magnum. It seems like the red hair would be a give away.

"No," Magnum says simply. "He's dead." He runs his hand through his copper mane. "That's why I feel so protective of you, Kyla."

I cock my head. I don't know what his father's death and protecting me have in common.

"Over and above what I'm ordered to do, anyway." He runs a hand over his chest absentmindedly. "You remind me of my mom." He takes another sip of cocoa again before putting it back down on the coffee table. "She didn't want my dad—our family—associated with the Crew, but my dad was a smart businessman. He wasn't a thug or one of these low lives you see out on the street. He was cunning and smart. That's not to say he didn't do questionable things. If you're in the Crew, your morality will be called into question. Even mine," he says, piercing me with a glare. "But my mom was an innocent. My dad hid who he was working for from her until it was too late. You can't just get out of the grips of the Crew."

My mouth is suddenly dry. "You sound as if you don't like the Crew. Yet, your job is to literally keep them safe."

"Protecting people is my responsibility, Kyla," he says, gaze burning. "I understand that just because you might do something wrong or bad or illegal, doesn't make you a bad person. Just as if you go to church every Sunday and preach religion doesn't technically make you a good person. There are gray areas. Hell, a lot of life is a gray area."

I lean back into Magnum's couch. He's right about that. My whole life is a gray area. "Maybe it's your individual decisions that make you good or bad?"

"In the end," Mag says, "My dad made the right decision. It cost him his life, but..." He shrugs.

"Your mom?"

His jaw hardens. "I don't see her anymore."

His tone ends the conversation. He looks away, and if what he told me about his mom in the beginning of this talk holds true, I bet she doesn't want to see him because of who he works for.

If she was able to get out, more power to her. I hope she's safe. Just as I hope to be her one day, as long as living in this world doesn't corrupt me. I like the idea of being gray. Gray, I can handle. The darkness, I can't.

2 2

─────────

For weeks, my life is a replay over and over again. School. Training. Fighting. Getting in as much time as I can with Oscar and Brawler while solidifying my relationship with Johnny. He and his father must have come to a conclusion about what pissed Johnny off at Candy's because me stripping is never brought up again and every time we have an after party at Candy's, his father doesn't show up even though I'm positive he comes to all my fights.

I don't trust his intentions.

My door drifts open. I'm half asleep on Monday morning, but I shoot straight up in bed.

"It's me, it's me."

I blink at the doorway to find Johnny there. It's early,

but he's already dressed in a suit with his dark hair perfectly coiffed. "Hey," I croak out.

Since the night he pulled a gun on Magnum, all we've done is kiss, even though I try to avoid doing that. He strides over while I try to get my hair to calm down. "You," he says, taking my hand as I run it through my hair. "Are beautiful no matter what."

My face heats. Johnny is intense, and I crave it. I crave him. Every word he says feels like it's perfectly chosen just for me. The conversation we had that night has only strengthened our bond, though I know it's stupid. "You know just what to say to a girl," I tease.

He beams back, and the bed depresses while he sits. "I have to leave for a couple of days."

"Couple of days?"

He brings my hand to his lips and kisses my knuckles. "Something came up. We'll be back on Wednesday. My dad has a dinner that night. Some other higher-ups in the Crew will be there. He wants us both there."

Johnny can't keep the smile off his face. "What is it?" I ask.

"He's going to move forward with me moving up. He's liked my business choices lately. It won't be long until we can take our relationship to the next level. Officially. And unofficially," he says, running his fingers up the inside of my arm. My skin tingles in his wake. I can't help the way my body heats. I've been able to spend more intimate moments with Brawler and Oscar, but that doesn't diminish the way I want Johnny. No matter how recklessly stupid it is.

"That's great news."

Johnny can barely hold his excitement back. He presses me down into the bed and hovers over me, feathering soft kisses over my face. Before long, he finds my mouth, delving his tongue inside for a short, hot kiss. We both know not to push each other. It's just enough. Johnny groans and pulls away from me. "Magnum's going to watch you. You're safe with him."

"I know."

"And I'll call you, so have your phone on you."

"Of course," I promise.

He nuzzles my neck. "Bye, babe. Think of me." His lips linger on my neck before he leaves the room. When he's gone, I begrudgingly throw the covers off and pad toward the shower. Johnny leaving could mean two things. One: I'll be bored as fuck. Or, two: I'll have more leeway and can spend time with Oscar and Brawler. Even Magnum. He and I have become quite friendly. When Johnny is at long meetings and I happen to be at the apartment without an excuse to leave, we often find ourselves in one another's company. Sometimes, we just talk. Other times, he lets me use his weights. He never comes into my apartment though, and every time I try to invite him in, he tells me to come over instead.

I wash my hair and lather up my body. I'm under the

spray when a noise grabs my attention. Johnny is the only one who comes into my apartment unannounced. Alarm bells sounding off inside my head, I shut the shower off, pausing where I stand only to hear another clicking sound.

I step out, careful to be as quiet as possible as I wrap my body in a towel before moving into my bedroom, going to my bag, and taking out the knife Magnum gave me. I keep it steady in my hand as I exit my room. I stalk through my apartment and stop. The knob of my apartment door moves. I shoot forward, ripping the door open and thrusting the knife in front of me only to find a surprised Oscar standing there. I look both ways down the hall. "What are you doing?" I hiss.

He grabs a hairpin from the lock on my door and pushes me inside my apartment, avoiding the knife shoved toward him. "Surprising you." He takes the blade from me, closes it, and sets it on the kitchen counter. "I heard the big bosses were off. They left a little while ago."

"I know," I confirm. "Johnny came in to tell me he wouldn't be back until Wednesday."

Oscar devours me with his gaze. When he gets to the top of my head, he smirks. "You didn't finish washing your hair."

"I thought someone was breaking into my apartment," I whisper yell. "Of course, I didn't finish."

Oscar completely ignores the part that I would have a reason to be cautious and goes right for teasing me. "Why are you still whispering?"

I grin and shake my head. "You love doing that, don't you?"

"What?"

"Working me up."

He reaches behind him and locks my apartment door. He stalks forward, gaze penetrating mine. He eyes the knot in my towel like he wishes it would just fall apart. Oscar and I haven't had a lot of time together. Only at school. The football season is coming to a close. Not that you'd know it when you walked into school. No one cares. Oscar, however, puts all of his attention into it like his team is going all the way.

Oscar shakes his head. "Not sorry. I swear I didn't come over for a booty call. I just knew we'd have a chance to see each other without fear of anyone dropping by."

I take him in. He has on a backwards hat lower over his forehead. His tan skin highlights his dark features. Oscar has confident badass down to a T. "It's a good thing you didn't come over for a booty call because you wouldn't be getting one by calling it a fucking booty call."

I arch a brow at him, and he smirks.

"Hmm, is that a challenge?"

At school, girls flock around Oscar. Nevaeh is out of the picture, of course, but he's still a hot commodity. High up in the Crew. Gorgeous. Football quarterback. Plus, he's genuinely a nice guy once you get through his sarcasm.

I turn. "I don't have time for this. I have to finish my shower. Creeper."

He's following me, and I love it. I turn the shower back on and drop my towel. Oscar moans behind me as I step inside the stall, the distorted glass hiding my true figure. I continue washing the soap off my body like he didn't even interrupt me. Through the glass, though, I find Oscar leaning up against the wall, staring. Once I'm done with my normal shower routine, I run my hands over my chest, squeezing my breasts while I eye him from the corner of my eye.

Oscar groans. "Seriously?"

"You're the one who barged in on me this morning."

"You always touch yourself while you're taking a shower?"

"Mmm, maybe," I say, flicking my nipple. He can't see exactly what I'm doing, but he gets the gist.

"Fuck it," he says. He moves forward, opening the door. He pulls me out of the spray, carrying me to his chest. My drenched body soaks right through his clothes as he takes me to the bed, laying me out there, my feet hanging over the side. He gets to his knees, shoving my knees apart while he buries his face between my legs.

"Oh God," I pant as his delicious tongue laps at me.

He licks the length of me, swirling around my clit. "Now tell me I can't have you. Tell me you don't want this."

Fuck me for thinking this, but it's nice to have Johnny gone. I can act on all my fantasies. As long as we're behind closed doors, anyway. I pin Oscar's face to my core. "If you move, I'll shank you."

He chuckles, but the humor dies as he devours me with his mouth. Oscar has an expert touch in this arena. It's not long until I'm warning him I'm going to come. I'm too far gone to want him to pull away, but if he wants to be inside me while I orgasm, then that's fine, too. He just needs to hurry.

He doesn't pull away. He renews his attentions, the tip of his tongue flicking over my clit until I come so hard I see stars.

Oscar stands. He starts to step away, but I pull myself up and reach for his shirt, grabbing it so he doesn't get too far. Desire floods his ravenous eyes.

"You're not getting away," I tell him. I carefully unclasp his jeans, forcing them down his muscular thighs. His boxers tent in front of me. I run my hands up his strong legs before grabbing the top of his boxers and moving them over his hips until his cock springs free. I lean forward, licking his slit.

"Princess," he warns.

With a tight grip on his hips, I move him back as I sink to my knees in front of him. With one hand clasping his ass, I reach the other one up, nails scraping against his washboard abs. I've sucked dick before. I don't know that I've ever wanted to do it this badly though.

I lick the underside from balls to tip, and he jerks in

front of me. Precum oozes out, and I lick that too. Oscar runs his hands through my hair. "You don't have to."

"I'm well aware, thank you. Is the notion that I want to suck you off until you come inside my mouth new to you?"

He groans as I close my lips around just the bulbous tip, my tongue teasing his silky skin.

"Fuck me," Oscar says. "Are you even real?"

My nails curl into his chest as I take him all inside, hollowing out my cheeks. He guides the rhythm that he likes, thighs quaking the entire time. I lap him up, taking pleasure in this. The more sounds that slip through his always contained exterior, the hotter I get. Oscar is vocal, and I love every fucking second of it. I start playing with my clit, rubbing it when he increases the pressure and pace.

"That's right, baby. God, you're a fucking sight. Are you turned on?"

I nod. I'm almost ready to come apart again. I swirl my fingers faster until the pressure builds and builds. Oscar keeps rocking into me, taking more control of the pressure until I come undone. I start to scream, but Oscar holds me there, his hips jerking into my hot mouth until liquid spurts from his slit.

I swallow and keep swallowing until he's given me every last drop. I pull my lips away, and he drops to his knees in front of me too. "Fuck," he says, gaze sliding all over me. "Are you okay?"

"Am I okay? I loved every fucking second of it," I say, the

after-sex hazy feeling encompassing my body. "You don't have to worry about me."

He helps me stand, hands roaming all over my sensitive skin. He palms my breasts, a flirtatious glint in his eye. "These are fucking amazing, by the way. You should be proud."

I peek down at his dick. "Likewise."

He cocks a grin. "Fucking hell, Princess. What am I going to do with you?"

This feels nice. Special. Like in the midst of all the crazy, we can find times like this to let the stress roll off our backs and explore our feelings for one another.

"I really didn't think that was going to happen when I came in this morning. I mean, I've jacked off to it. About every night, but—"

I put my hand over his mouth. "Don't ruin it," I tease, even though there's nothing he could do to ruin this moment. It's because of who he is that I'm even standing right here naked in front of him. He appeals to my dark, sarcastic side. The gray area, if you will. Brawler's mostly light. Johnny? It'd be so easy to classify him as dark, but I'm not sure that's the truth yet.

Magnum's face filters through my brain, but I push it back. He's made enough insinuations about my age that I don't think that's where our relationship is headed. Don't get me wrong, I like him. The more I talk to him, the more his barrier walls come down, revealing the real him underneath.

I'd be lying if I said he wasn't easy on the eyes. Damn, I'm a greedy bitch.

Maybe I shouldn't be thinking about being attracted to another, especially since one doesn't know about the others, and when he finds out, it could mean the end of all of us.

Oscar and I are still staring at one another when a knock comes on the front door. A flash of fear rises inside me, but it dampens when I remember what time it is and what I should be doing on a Monday morning. "Shit. It's probably Magnum."

Oscar stands, pulling his pants up. He looks down at me as another knock comes. "You better get dressed."

I grab panties and a bra and start to put them on as Oscar leaves the room, fastening his pants. I yank my panties on and just hook my bra when there's a sound at the door. I freeze, but I don't have time to do anything because Oscar comes stumbling back into the bedroom, almost falling on his ass.

"Where is she?"

My heart beats rapidly in my chest. Magnum peeks his

head inside the room just as I pull the straps up on my bra, concealing my breasts. Not that he hasn't seen me buck-naked before, but still. As soon as Magnum sees me, he sighs in relief. His gaze skirts lower, lower than it ever has, but then pops back up.

"Get the fuck out of her room," Oscar growls. "She's not dressed."

A fierce look crosses Magnum's face. He pushes Oscar up against the wall. "What the fuck were you thinking opening the door? And with her inside like this?" He holds his arm over Oscar's trachea, the veins popping out on his forearm.

Oscar fumes. His nostrils flare while Magnum continues to pin him. I move forward, still in my panties and bra and grasp Magnum's arm to pull him away. I don't agree with his reaction, but he's right. "We're sorry."

Magnum lets go just enough so that Oscar pushes him the rest of the way off. "We're not fucking sorry. How dare you come into her room?" Oscar's trying to posture. He puffs his chest out, and his gaze narrows. I'm sure he's forming an excuse in his head that he can give Magnum so the bodyguard doesn't run to Johnny. Little does he know he doesn't have to. At least, I've pretty much bet our lives that we don't have to worry about Magnum turning us in. If I'm wrong, we're all dead, eventually. But for now, Magnum has kept my relationships with Oscar and Brawler a secret.

"Don't be a fucking idiot," Magnum growls. "I could

have been anyone. You don't think they'd be suspicious of you in Kyla's apartment? You need to play this smart."

Oscar looks at me, brows pulling together. I stand in the middle, looking between them both. I understand why Magnum is so upset. It was stupid of Oscar to get the door. What was he going to say he was doing? Especially since I was in here practically naked. It wouldn't look good for us at all. But Oscar deserves an explanation. "So, Magnum knows about you, Brawler, and me."

Oscar's dark eyes round in surprise, but then he shuts off, his face becoming dark. "First, it's you and me, and you and Brawler. It's not all three of us. Second, what the fuck?" He eyes Magnum warily.

"He won't say anything."

"And why's that?" Oscar asks, not even attempting to look at me anymore. He's glaring straight at Magnum as if he's trying to intimidate him. "Why would you keep this a secret?"

"You don't need to know why. All you need to know is that I've done so, and I'll continue to do so."

Oscar shakes his head. His badass Oscar "Bat" Drego attitude is about to come out in full force. He doesn't trust Magnum. "I don't think so. That answer isn't good enough. What is it?" He gets up in Magnum's face. Magnum has an inch or so on him, but they're about the same build. "You're going to use this against her at some point, huh? You won't live to do it. I can promise you that."

"Whoa. Whoa," I sputter out. When the threats start coming out, I need to act.

The look they're sharing makes me think the sentiment goes both ways.

"I could say the same for you, Drego," Magnum lilts, confirming my suspicions. He crosses his arms in front of his chest, taking on his bodyguard stance that's ripe with testosterone. "You could be playing Kyla too."

I glance between the two. I don't think either of them are playing me. At least, I fucking hope not. Actually, no, I know they're not. The way Oscar and I just came together doesn't just happen with two people who don't care about one another. Also, who would risk it? Johnny would likely cut his dick off just for touching me even if he was doing it to play me. Oscar's a lot of things, but he's smart and has a healthy dose of self-preservation. That's just something you acquire when you grow up in the Heights.

"Alright, alright," I say, trying to calm the two of them. "I trust both of you. Oscar, you probably shouldn't be opening my door."

Oscar's jaw hardens. "And he shouldn't just waltz into your room." His pallor softens. "Unless..." He swallows. "Great. You fucking want her, too." He pales. "Or you've already had her."

"Oscar, come on," I say, my face heating.

"I'm making sure she's safe," Magnum states. "That's all."

"Because Johnny told you to, or because you have a vested interest?" Oscar challenges.

"Both."

I take a step back, getting sick of this. "Listen if you're going to fight, fight. Let me know. I'll grab some popcorn. If you're not, I should really get dressed in case anyone else wants to come into my apartment unexpectedly."

Oscar and Magnum glance over at me. Their heated stares collide with my flush body. The bra and panty set I grabbed isn't sporty. In fact, it's the sexiest set I own. It's damn near lingerie. It was in one of the bags Glo brought over right before she tried to kill me.

Magnum's throat works. I can tell he's trying not to peek. He's trying to be the gentleman in the room and not take an eye full, but he's losing the war with himself. "Yes, you should get dressed," he finally says.

I pad back into the bathroom, picking an outfit as I move past the closet, then disappear behind the bathroom door and lock it behind me. I turn off the shower since I left it pretty rapidly when Oscar barged in to carry me out. Then, I start to get ready. I pull on the pair of jeans and shirt I grabbed, then work on my hair and makeup.

A half an hour has passed by the time I exit the room. Oscar and Magnum are no longer in my bedroom, which is fine. Better, probably. Though, being in a quarterback-body-guard sandwich sounds like good times. Yum.

I walk into the main living area to find Magnum in the

kitchen and Oscar sitting on the couch. Magnum brings a mug over to me, and I can tell by looking at it that he must have gone back over to his own apartment to get me the good hot chocolate. I confessed the other day that his was better than the stuff I had at my place. Oscar has his legs propped up on the coffee table, feet crossed at the ankles. Magnum eyes him, distaste evident on his face. It looks like everything about Oscar pisses Magnum off, which is kind of funny.

Magnum slices Oscar a look, but then turns toward me. "I was coming over to see what you wanted to do today. I heard Johnny and his dad left this morning."

"Where did they go exactly?"

"Chicago. They have some business dealings there."

"I knew that," Oscar pipes up like a petulant child.

"Yeah, and you wasted no time trying to put Kyla in jeopardy once you heard they were gone."

A look of absolute rage transforms Oscar's face. His hands ball to fists. "I would never put Kyla in jeopardy."

I'm struck he didn't call me Princess, but more than that, his emotions are one hundred percent real and true.

I place my hand on Magnum's arm and squeeze, telling him silently to lay off him. Oscar turns his attention to where I'm touching Magnum though, so I pull my hand from his shortly after. "Wait until Brawler hears this," Oscar says, laughing to himself.

I swallow. "Hears what?"

"How Mag wants you too. If you thought he was pissed when—"

"Okay," I say, silencing Oscar. I shoot him a look, trying to tell him Mag doesn't want me and the only thing he's doing is making it awkward as fuck for all of us to be around each other. I run my hands through my hair. "I was hoping to get some freedom out of Johnny being gone," I hedge, staring at Mag.

He nods. "I thought you'd want that."

"By the way," Oscar says, pulling out my cell phone. "Brawler texted you. He says he's wondering if you're going to school today, which is probably code for, 'I can't stop thinking about you. Come suck my dick.'"

He lifts a brow at me in challenge, and I stalk forward, yanking my phone from his grip. I don't get very far because he grabs my hand and pulls me into his lap. He settles me there until we're staring into one another's eyes again just like we had after I sucked his dick. I'd planned on telling him not to fucking read my texts, but instead, it comes out, "Don't read my texts." For good measure, I throw in, "Asshole."

He grins.

Magnum clears his throat behind us. I scramble out of Oscar's lap and try to figure out what I want to do.

"I know you probably want some freedom, but I just ask that I drive you places and that I'm around wherever you want to go, so I can make sure you stay safe. Things tend to get a little less formal when Big Daddy K and Johnny leave, but I need to make sure you're secure."

"No," Oscar answers, his tone haughty. "I can keep her safe."

"Oscar," I say, rolling my eyes at him.

Oscar lowers his voice. "I was thinking *we* could hang out today."

"I won't intrude on any private moments," Mag says tersely. "But I'm going with Kyla wherever she goes. She's *my* responsibility."

I fix him with a look. "As long as I get some freedom, I'm fine with that." Magnum is more like a friend than security personnel right now, anyway. "You know what I'm dying for?"

Oscar waggles his brows at me, staring down at his crotch suggestively.

I shake my head. "Bacon. Real bacon."

"We could go out to eat," Oscar offers.

"We'll have to go someplace beyond the Crew's reach," Mag says, voice taking on his bodyguard persona. "I can think of a few places."

"Great," I beam. "I'll text Brawler and tell him to skip school. Actually, Oscar, you text him." That way it doesn't look suspicious that I'm telling Brawler to skip school.

Within the hour, we pull to a stop a couple of blocks away from the school and Brawler gets in the back with Oscar and me. I'm wedged in the middle, but I don't mind one bit. "Hey," I say, greeting him. He has on a Golden Gloves boxing shirt that clings to his muscled torso.

"So, what's going on?" he asks, gaze shifting to Magnum who's left the divider down.

"We're going out to breakfast," I tell him, squeezing his knee. "Johnny and his dad are away on a business trip. They'll be back Wednesday."

Brawler's face softens, but then he freezes when I squeeze his knee. He darts a look at Magnum.

"Oh, don't worry," Oscar says, speaking up. "Apparently Magnum knows that we're both into Princess. He's being a pal and not sharing this info with the Crew." Brawler's face pales. His gaze moves to mine, but before I can say anything, Oscar interrupts again. "I'm pretty sure he wants to fuck her, but—"

"Jesus, Oscar. Shut the hell up."

"Notice how he hasn't denied it though."

Mag meets my gaze in the mirror. "Brawler, I can understand. That one," he says, gaze drifting toward Oscar. He shakes his head in response, which tells me exactly what he thinks about Oscar and me.

"That's what I said," Brawler grumbles.

Oscar peers around me to stare Brawler down. "Just when I thought we were becoming close."

"I told you," Brawler states. "I'll do whatever Kyla wants because I'm here for her. Nothing more. Nothing less."

I blink, gazing between the two of them. "You had a

discussion about this? Without me?" Damn. We haven't even gotten to the breakfast place yet, and I'm feeling completely outnumbered.

"More like we fought over you until both of us decided we weren't giving you up." Oscar's voice loses all its edge as he looks at me, his words seeping into my skin.

He might feel differently if he knew what I was planning on doing. Oscar's in the thick of everything. It'll be hard for him to leave the Crew, even if he's not associated with what I plan on doing. I know why he joined, but still the overwhelming sense of being stuck swallows me. It's an awful way to live.

Brawler pulls me closer to whisper in my ear, "You sure Magnum's cool?"

I nod, locking gazes with Magnum in the rearview mirror. "He's good," I whisper back as Oscar threads his fingers through mine. I place my head on Brawler's shoulder, loving being next to all of them at the same time. If Johnny were here, it would be even better. Honestly, I want him here. The good Johnny would fit in so well with these guys. I want to show him that life can be better than the Crew. You don't need hundreds of people under you—fearing you—to make your life worthwhile. You just need a few on the same level, supporting you, because I haven't felt buoyed like this since my parents were alive. I haven't felt this safe, this loved, since my parents left this Earth, and it's all because of Brawler and Oscar and the friend I've found in Magnum. Sure, it's not easy. We've had to make sacrifices, but I know they're with me.

Oscar squeezes my fingers as if he knows what thoughts roam through my head. Brawler told me I should tell him my plans sooner rather than later, and I need to. I just don't know how to bring it up. It's not that I don't trust him with the information, it's that I hate to put any more pressure on him. It's easy for Brawler to know. He's barely involved with the Crew, but Oscar is. However, it hasn't escaped my notice that getting to Big Daddy K might be easier with his help, seeing as he's already in the Crew, anyway.

I close my eyes, promising myself I'll tell Oscar while Johnny and Big Daddy K are away. That will give him time to get his shit together before he sees them again.

I can't think about the consequences if he defies my trust. It would break me.

2 4

The next day, there's no pretense of going to school either. Since Brawler can't come into the tower without raising suspicion and we can't go to Brawler's apartment because his mom is unwell, Oscar grudgingly invites us all to his place. When he lets Magnum and I in, he's shier than I've ever seen him. "Hey," I say.

It's a little awkward to be invited into these guys' homes. It's like unraveling another layer of who they are. I had a pretend life when I was living in the apartment down the hall from Brawler. Nothing in there was anything I ever would have chosen for myself. It was fake. But here—and at Brawler's—I get another sense of who they are and how they were brought up.

Oscar and his mom live above a corner grocery store. The apartment isn't as nice as Brawler's, but it's clean.

He smiles at me as I enter but gives Magnum a begrudging look that he doesn't even notice. "Your mom's not here?"

He shakes his head, but a line of concentration appears in his forehead like he's trying not to show emotion. I want to ask him about it, but he won't open up with Magnum right here. I always thought they got along, and they did, up until yesterday morning. I just hope Oscar can shelter his thoughts when the others come home.

"I've got some snacks, but if we want anything else, we'll have to run downstairs. Actually, I'll run downstairs," he says, gazing at me. Magnum was extra careful about who was around on the street before we slipped up the entrance to Oscar's apartment.

A few minutes later, Brawler shows up. We congregate in the living room where Oscar finds a few fight replays on TV that we can all agree on watching without arguing. Mag stays off to the side. He watches us a lot but doesn't insert himself into the conversation, which makes me sad. Yesterday, I started wondering about the kind of guy Mag was when he was younger. I'm sure he wasn't always the silent, perfectly-fine-to-be-sitting-in-the-corner-to-watch type.

Oscar, though, takes complete control over the dynamics in the room since it's his space. He pulls me onto his lap, arms wrapping around me. Brawler's jaw ticks, but out of the two of them, he'd be less likely to start shit. I don't know how I feel so at ease, knowing they're both here, both watching me, both wanting to touch me. I have feelings for them, but it's not like these relationships are the societal norm. However, even though it isn't, this just feels natural to me. They just need to get on board with what's happening and stop trying to make the other guy jealous.

Oscar winds his hand around my stomach and kisses the side of my head.

Brawler's shoulders stiffen.

Oscar grazes a kiss down the side of my neck.

The vein in Brawler's temple pops out.

I'm about to tell Oscar to stop when Magnum gets to his feet. "Looks like you need to have a conversation. I'm stepping outside."

As soon as the door shuts behind him, Brawler gets to his feet. Oscar starts to chuckle like he hasn't a care in the world. He was trying to get Brawler going, but the warning glare Brawler sends him makes Oscar's laughter die off. "I didn't agree to you feeling her up in front of me, dude." Before Oscar can counter, because that's what Oscar does, Brawler says, "You wouldn't go for it either."

Oscar puts his hands on my hips. "Your boyfriend's mad," he teases.

I give him a look over my shoulder and then stand. "Listen. *Both* of you," I say, glaring at each of them so they know I mean business. "I like you both. There's no reason for jealousy because just as much as I want Oscar's hands on me, I want yours, too, Brawler. We've all lived shitty lives, right?

Can't we just do something that feels good without adding extra pressure to us? Can't we grab onto something that's good for us and go with it? Fuck what normal people think. Let's not be those people. You don't need to be jealous when I want you, too. And you," I say, turning to Oscar. "Don't need to push buttons."

"It's what I do," he says nonchalantly, like he's bored with this conversation already. He presses his tongue against his teeth. "Does this mean you're really not going to pick one of us someday?"

My head whiplashes back. "Um, no. I never planned on it. Actually, I didn't plan on any of this, but now that you ask, no, I'm not choosing. It's up to you guys whether you want in or not. If you don't, that's fine. Just tell me now."

Oscar looks me up and down, lips losing color as he presses them together.

"I'm in," Brawler says. "I'll tone down my possessive side. Okay, I'll try to tone down my possessive side."

"Oscar?" I ask, quirking an eyebrow at him.

He swallows and shifts on the cushions under my scrutiny. For a second, my heart freefalls to my stomach because I think he's going to tell me he can't do this. "I need you to cough up your secret. About why you're here. Brawler got what you wanted out of your apartment for you. Right? I've been left to sit here wondering what's happening. I've been waiting for you to tell me, but you haven't."

I exchange a look with Brawler.

"See!" Oscar explodes. He gets off the couch.

The door to the apartment opens and Magnum sticks his head in, eyeing the situation.

"Jesus Christ," Oscar curses. "I'm not going to fucking hurt her. That's the last thing I would do."

Mag looks at me for confirmation. "It's okay," I tell him. Oscar won't hurt me, but he's hurt right now. "Brawler?"

He nods. "I'll go get us some stuff to eat at the store."

Brawler and Magnum leave the room, and I turn toward Oscar. "I'm so sorry," I say. "I only told Brawler because he found what was in my apartment. I absolutely did not tell him because I like him more than you."

The raw truth of how much I hurt him is splayed all over his face though. That's why he's been a dick to Magnum. That's why he was goading Brawler just now. He wants to see where he stands in the pecking order of things, and from what I was giving him, he thought he was last.

"I've been fucked around my whole life," he says, teeth gritting. "I care for you, Kyla, but if you're going to do that to me, we can end this right now."

"No," I say, reaching for him. "I didn't tell you for any other reason than I wasn't sure how you would react. Okay?"

"You don't trust me?" He steps back like I've slapped him in the face.

I shake my head. "I do. It's just...fuck, Oscar, it's difficult, okay?" I retreat and breathe. It's not Oscar's fault he's feeling like this. I brought it on.

"Women use me," he says. His jaw ticks, and he's trying to wrangle in his emotions. "At first it was because I was a quarterback, and then it was because I was in the Crew."

"Nevaeh?" I guess.

"Nevaeh, yeah, but she wasn't the worst one." His face darkens. "There was another girl who treated me like shit. I'm not saying I'm a saint. I've done shitty fucking things, including when I was with her, but she played me big time. The nice have never liked me." He rubs the back of his neck. "When you actually wrapped those pretty little lips around my cock, I was shocked. I thought maybe you were fucking with me, too, because who would want me when there's someone else?" He hikes his thumb toward the door as if he's insinuating I would prefer Brawler.

"Don't say that," I tell him. I wrap him in a hug. "I'm not playing you. I promise."

"Then you need to tell me what's going on. I can't stand that I don't know shit."

"Okay," I say, closing my eyes. It looks like I'm about to have that conversation with him right now. I don't even have the chance to think about what comes from my mouth, I just have to come out with it. "The two things Brawler found in my apartment were a picture of my parents and a burner cell."

"Okay..."

I push him back to the threadbare couch ar
his lap. I place his hands on my hips and put my
chest. His heart thumps underneath his ribcage.
didn't find was a gun that I also had stashed there.

Oscar's lips thin. I can tell he's trying to put
these things together in his head. How they're lin
had them. Why I really wanted them. How
honest, it's not all that odd for people to be pack
the Heights.

"The phone links me to my aunt and uncl
over my care after my parents died. They don't
I've come here or even where I am specifically
better that way. I don't need this life knowing a
They're the only family I have left in the wor
Oscar's eyes, hesitant to go on.

"You can tell me," he says, sensing my appreh

"It was difficult for me to tell Brawler too," I
to placate his worries. I blow out a breath. "It's in
one knows about them because once I get anoth
shoot a glance toward the door and lower my voi
get a gun, I'm going to kill Big Daddy K."

Oscar stills. Flashes of different emotions s
his face.

"He murdered my parents when I was twe
continuing to whisper. "He took everything from
going to take everything from him."

I fill Oscar in on the finer details about my pa

ersects with Kingston Marx on that fateful night. He
ocably changed my life, but he didn't realize it. He
't understand the monster he made in that moment.
wound festering inside me until I decided to do some-
g about it.

Joanne?" Oscar laughs, his abs tightening under
ouch.

glare at him. "They used to call me Jo, but yes, that's
eal name. This is all beside the point," I say, temper flar-
"I'm not her anymore. I'm someone completely
rent."

He screws his face back to normal. "Right. Sorry. It's
that name doesn't suit you whatsoever."

drop my head back. "Tell me when you're ready to
ιss the important shit I just told you."

Oscar grips my hips. "I love it when you get angry. It
es me hot."

bring my head back up and glare at him. "Do you see
I was worried about telling you?"

He slides a gaze to the door this time. Voice low, he asks,
ause you want to take out the biggest crime lord in this
? No, I can't imagine why you didn't want to say
hing to me."

glare at him, and he grins.

"Princess," he says, pushing the hair off my shoulder. "I
ght you were crazy before, but now I know you're
fiable."

I swallow. "I know you're in the Crew, so I'm begging for your silence on this one. You can decide you don't want to be mixed up in this certifiable crazy—"

He pulls me down, pressing his lips to mine briefly to shut me up. "I like my chicks crazy." He kisses me senseless for a few seconds and then lets me go. "You know I didn't join the Crew out of any loyalty. I joined it out of sheer desperation. I had to. I had to protect myself and my mom." His gaze hardens again. "A lot of fucking good that did because she can't be here without getting mixed up in drugs. She was fine when she was in Spring Hill. Here? The moment we fucking got back, syringe in her arm like a damn crack whore."

I cup his face. "Is that where she is?"

"I haven't seen her in a month, Princess. The Crew pays my rent. When she gets like this, she stays away because she can't stand for me to see her all doped up, but she isn't strong enough to get out of it."

My heart fissures. "Can we send her to get help?"

"I've tried in the past. It doesn't take."

"Maybe the Crew will help her?"

Oscar's face darkens. "How do you think she gets the drugs, Princess? Nothing happens in the Heights that the Crew doesn't control."

My mouth drops. I hadn't thought of that.

"They don't advertise it," he continues. "They have different levels of businesses. They have legal ones like some of the small businesses in the area like grocery stores and dress shops," he says, pinning me with a look. "Then they have the illegal but not terrible ones like the underground fighting ring. Then they have the businesses that ruin people's lives."

"How can you even stand to be around them when they've done that to your mother?"

He traces his fingers over my skin absentmindedly. "I understand that it's just business for them. Besides, it's my mother who keeps putting the needle in her skin. They're not standing over her with a gun to her head, telling her to shoot up or else. It would be easy to blame it on them, but ultimately, it's her decision."

I run my hands through my hair and then clutch his shirt in my fingers. "I'm so sorry, Oscar." I swallow. "And I'm so fucking sorry if I made you think you were anything less than what I feel for you."

A lot of people have let Oscar down. That's the running theme in the Heights. Come here only if you want to be kicked in the nuts repeatedly.

This place isn't for me, and it's not for the guys I care about. As soon as I end this, I'm taking them and their families away from here. We just have to make sure the job gets done before then, so there's no one around to follow us. Like Johnny said, take out the big guys so the smaller ones are too afraid to regroup.

The only problem is: I have feelings for one of the big guys, and I won't sacrifice him either.

A little voice in my head tells me I might be forced to. I try to kick its ass out of my brain, but I can't.

Depending on what happens, I might be the monster in this story.

After Brawler returns with snacks, we—including Magnum—sit and watch TV again. I don't let him stay in the background. I make him sit next to us like he's actually a part of our group. I'm sandwiched between Oscar and Brawler again though. Oscar's fingers trail over my thigh, and Brawler's feet rub mine absentmindedly. I can't deny that my heart is full sitting here like this. It's easy to forget how I met these two, and why I'm here. It's more difficult to forget Johnny though. In a way, I do. I forget how pissed he would be if he found us like this, and instead just miss him.

During a female fight, Oscar's phone starts blowing up. Message after message pings through. He sighs, pulling it out of his pocket. I scoot closer to Brawler, putting my head on his arm. I don't mean to peek over at Oscar's phone.

Okay, I kind of do. Not because I'm a jealous bitch, but because I'm wondering if the texts have something to do with the Crew. They don't.

"Who's that?" I ask, referencing the girl named Jaz who keeps texting him. The picture next to her name is all cleavage.

"A chick at school. Apparently, there's a costume party at Candy's tonight."

I share a look with Magnum. That's interesting. They're hosting events at the strip club that aren't focused on naked dancers.

"Could be fun," Oscar says.

I glare at him.

He returns it, undisturbed by my murderous eyes. "I meant if we all go."

"You're forgetting I can't go anywhere," I tell him. "With you guys," I add even though a lot of the time it feels like I literally can't go anywhere.

He smirks. "You could to a costume party."

I sit up, and Brawler's hand clenches in mine. Call me crazy, but I haven't had the typical teenager life growing up. I haven't been to many parties, and a costume party sounds like a hell of a good time. I can be whoever I want to be. I can dance with Oscar and Brawler. I can—

"No," Magnum says.

I turn to look at him. "No?"

"It's a terrible idea."

Well, now that someone's told me no, I think it's a fucking great idea. I stand. "I'm going. You can come if you want."

He stands right along with me. The fight on TV already forgotten even though it was an evenly matched killer fight between two badass chicks. "Kyla, come on."

"We should live a little," Oscar says, not helping the situation.

"Don't listen to him," Mag grumbles.

"Oh, come on." Oscar gets to his feet now. "There are three of us. She'll always be around one of us and no one will know who she is. Nothing will happen."

Mag implores me with his hazel-green eyes, but I'm all for this. I'm one hundred percent on board. Not just because I want to do this, but it will be good for Oscar and Brawler to get out too. To have fun.

"That chick better not think you're hers," I say, sashaying away from Oscar.

Brawler holds back on my arm. "I'm not sure it's a great idea either."

I back up until I'm facing him and then rise to my tiptoes, kissing him solidly on the mouth. "Trust me," I tell him.

Oscar beams as Brawler's shoulders relax.

"Sucker," he throws at him.

Brawler flips him off, but Oscar's right. "Don't worry," I

say, pecking Brawler on the cheek. "Now I just need something to wear. No one will know it's me."

I tap my chin, but Oscar runs to a room in the back of the apartment. Before long, he comes out with a Mardi gras like mask. It's purple and silver. Almost bird-like. The nose comes out in front, a slight rounding on the end until it ends in a sharp point. Feathers plume off the top, and it sparkles in the light.

I suck in a breath. "It's beautiful."

"My mother went to a Halloween party when we were in Spring Hill. She wore this."

"I have just the dress to wear with that back at my place," I say, anticipation starting in my feet and winding its way through my body. As long as I can keep the mask on, no one will know it's me. It'll be so dark in there, as well as the stage lights flashing, that it will be impossible. I look at Mag. "You'll have to wear something too. You're recognizable."

"This is a terrible idea," he argues again.

"I think it sounds amazing," I say, not able to hold back. Butterflies flutter in my stomach? What? Just because I'm here on a revenge mission doesn't mean I can't have fun.

"I've got something at my place for Mag," Brawler says.

I pop up and down on my toes. "This is going to be so much fun."

Brawler smiles softly while Magnum still looks less than pleased. He makes sure I know all about it as we head down the apartment steps to get in the car, me clutching onto the mask. "I'm just worried about your safety. I'm worried what will happen if someone spots you."

"No one will know it's me. I promise." I get in the car and wait for him to get in on the driver's side. I'm acting overly confident on the outside, but I understand that it's a risk. But, it's a risk I'm willing to take. I haven't been able to do anything since I got here, and being with the guys, makes me want to live. Maybe it's a false sense of security, but I want to throw caution to the wind at least for one night.

His jaw ticks. "I'd love to tell you no, but you'll find a way to go anyway so let's hope both of us are well-concealed."

I squeal and reach over the seat to kiss him on the cheek.

His cheeks darken to a shade of crimson, and he looks away.

We're silent when we head back to the tower. We stop in my apartment, and Magnum waits in the living room while I grab the dress and head into the bathroom connected to my bedroom to get dressed and put on a face full of makeup, so no one knows who I am.

I pull the purple dress with the sequin-studded bodice and tulle skirt on. It was one of the dresses Johnny bought for me that day I found him with the girl at the clothing store. I imagine he went back in afterward and told them to get whatever they had in my size and this happened to be one of them because I have no idea where he thought I was going to wear something like this unless it was to a costume party.

The mask and the dress are only a shade off, so it's damn near a perfect match. I pull my hair up, placing it into a bun with the hairs underneath flaring out in a circle-like pattern. I darken my eye makeup so that they really stand out in the mask and then put a layer of lipstick on I would never normally wear. Then, I round out the outfit with a pair of black boots. Stepping back, I mostly look like a conglomeration of things, but I'm also hoping I look like a badass bird.

Ha. I don't know.

I stand by the door. I haven't heard Magnum on the other side even though I know he's there. "Hey," I call out.

"You need something?" he asks. The answer is immediate, and I smile.

"Close your eyes," I tell him. "When I tell you to open them, tell me if you can still tell it's me."

"Okay," Mag says without hesitation.

This should be a good test considering Mag's seen me in a variety of different clothes, including sweats. Hell, I forgot, including stripped naked. "Remember it'll be dark at Candy's."

"Got it. I'm ready."

I pull the door open to find Magnum standing there, all dressed in black like usual. He has his eyes closed just like I asked. I take a moment to really look at him while his discerning gaze is closed off from me. His jaw is angular.

Fierce. But the area around his eyes is kind when he's not studying everything in sight like it could potentially be a threat. His beard is longer than I remember it being. A little disheveled. He needs a trim to shape it up.

"Are you out here?" he asks.

I shake myself out of my reverie. "Yeah, you can open up now."

Magnum's eyes flit open. He's struck for a moment. His lips part incrementally. There's a host of feelings in that blip of a second, but ultimately, his features school together again. He walks around me, taking me in from every side. Magnum definitely takes his job seriously. "In looks, you would pass as any other beautiful girl."

My stomach seesaws, but when I chance a look at Magnum when he turns to face me, he has his bodyguard face on. "So, you approve?"

He nods once. "That doesn't mean we shouldn't still be diligent. We'll keep to ourselves in the shadows. Don't do anything to bring attention to yourself."

"I wouldn't put us in jeopardy."

He pulls his phone out, bringing up the video feed to the tower there. He checks it until it looks like we can leave and get down to the parking lot without being spotted. When he thinks it's clear, he ushers me out the door. He relaxes as soon as we get in the elevator and then relaxes even more when we're in the car. We're picking Brawler up from his apartment since he has something Mag can wear, and Oscar is meeting us there.

We park a couple of blocks away from the apartment building and Brawler ambles toward us. He gets in the back with me and then hands a long black, thin piece of fabric to Magnum who holds it up. "What's this?"

"I played Westley from *The Princess Bride* a few years ago for Halloween. Oh," Brawler says, also handing over a toy sword. "This, too."

Magnum takes the fake, plastic toy and laughs. "I think I'll just use the mask. Thanks." He pulls it over his face, lining up the eyeholes. The black piece of fabric covers his forehead all the way down to the tip of his nose. His beard is still showing, but it also acts as part of the disguise too. Magnum can't possibly be the only red-haired guy with facial hair.

"It's a good thing you have a penchant for wearing black," I tease, noticing the black tactical pants and black shirt he has on match the mask perfectly.

He glances at me through the rearview mirror. It's still his eyes, but with the mask on, he oddly looks like he's letting more of himself come through. His lips quirk up. "I knew the black attire would come to my rescue one day."

Brawler puts his arm around my shoulder, squeezing me to him. "You look beautiful."

"As do you," I say. I've only ever seen Brawler in t-shirts, so it's something else to see him in a button-down shirt. He's not wearing a mask or any sort of costume, but it also won't be odd for him to be out at a costume party in the Heights. The same with Oscar. It's only Mag and I who have to worry about being spotted.

It doesn't take us long to get to Candy's. Instead of parking in the back where Mag usually parks for Johnny and me, we ditch the car a couple of blocks away and walk in. The closer we get, the more it's apparent we're headed in the wrong direction. There aren't a lot of costumes, per se, but there are a lot of women in scantily clad dresses. There are a few who are wearing masks like mine, but none of theirs are as intricate as the one I'm borrowing from Oscar's mom.

"Follow my lead," Mag says. Because we're not associated with the Crew tonight, we wait in a line like everyone else. The up and down look I get from one of Dunnegan's security guys makes my stomach churn, but I'm also pretty sure it's the reason why we're let in. The guard takes my hand and pulls me beyond the rope. I grip onto Magnum's hand because he's the closest to me and I want to make sure he and Brawler get in as well.

"Save me a dance, sexy."

Both Brawler and Magnum eye the guard, but as soon as we're inside, he hits on the next girl. Magnum moves in front of me, still gripping my hand in his so I can easily follow him through the thick crowd. There might even be more people here than there were for my first after party.

What a great thing for Johnny. His after parties have really been helping to bring Candy's to the forefront, and I'm also excited that it's turning into less of a strip club and more of a nightclub.

Brawler takes my other hand, and we move into a booth in the back. It's one of the only ones left, and it's definitely secluded, which is probably why no one else has taken it before us. People don't come to these things to hang out in the back, unless they want to be concealed.

As soon as we sit, Brawler takes his phone out and messages Oscar where we are. I handed my phone off to Magnum earlier, so he could keep it safe, but also in case Johnny calls. The last thing I need is for Johnny to call and me be too busy to answer. He'd be suspicious right away.

Oscar strides to our booth five minutes later. He's slicked his hair completely back. The shorn sides high-lighting his mop of dark hair on top. He's also wearing a skin-tight Superman shirt, a big S dominating his chest. He stands in front of us, fists on his hips. He looks off in the distance like he's just finished saving the world. "Not to brag but I'm kind of important."

I bark out a laugh, falling into Brawler's lap with the force of my mirth. Tears dance at the corners of my eyes. It feels good to have the pressure off for just this one night. I trust them to keep me safe, just as I hope they trust me to keep them safe.

Oscar beckons me with his fingers. "Come, sexy bird.

You and Superman are about to get freaky on the dance floor."

Brawler lets me scoot around him while Oscar takes my hand, holding mine firmly in his. Oscar takes us to the edge of the floor where we're still in view of the table we scored, and we dance to the house music pumping in around us. My pulse jumps as he brings my hips solidly to his, swaying us to the music. He dances differently than Johnny, but not any less sexy. His fingers clutch my ass right through the tulle, and I press into him, tongue gliding up his neck. "You're bad," I tease.

"I'm just thrilled I get to touch you in public. I have one night to lay my claim."

"No one lays their claim on me."

"So, we noticed," Oscar says, nudging his nose over my fake one. "One guy claims you and you start dating two on the side just to prove a point."

Another laugh rips from me. "I guess I did, didn't I? Let that be a lesson. Who knows who else I'll attract if you start getting possessive, Quarterback?"

Oscar nuzzles my neck. He kisses me there, leading a trail to my earlobe before sucking it into his mouth and biting it softly. "Remember when I licked your pussy until you came?"

I bite my lip. Of course, I fucking remember. "Are you trying to turn me on in the middle of a dance floor?"

"Maybe voyeurism is my thing," he teases, biting my

earlobe again. He kisses his way along my jawline and then crushes his hips against me, his cock hard between us.

I almost turn to putty in his hands. "When we get out of here," I whisper straight into his ear. "We'll be able to do whatever we want."

"Get out?"

I step back and look Oscar straight in the eye. "When we escape after I get my revenge."

Emotions swirl in Oscar's dark gaze. He blinks a few times before tilting his head. He almost has to tilt it horizontal to get past the beak on my mask, but then he slides his lips over mine, kissing me like he's pinky swearing my face. It's a promise. A signed, binding contract.

No one has ever tried to help Oscar selflessly before. But I will. I'm not leaving him behind in a life he never wanted in the first place. I try to hold back thoughts of what we could be, but I see him in the middle of a huge stadium, a college football uniform on with his helmet in his hands. If I can give him that, I will.

scar, Brawler, and I make use of the freedom we're given. It takes Brawler a little while to relax, but he does eventually. He doesn't dance with me like Oscar, but he pulls me against him while we're sitting. He runs his fingers up and down my inner thigh like he and Oscar have a pact that they're going to drive me absolutely insane while we're here. Johnny's not the only one I have explosive chemistry with. I just felt his first because we're allowed to touch each other. We're allowed to take it to the brink whenever we want. I haven't been given that chance with Oscar and Brawler until now.

Like the nice person I am, I give it back to them whenever I can. "Accidentally" rubbing against their hard-ons. Using my body against them wherever I can.

During one song, Brawler joins Oscar and I on the

dance floor. He doesn't do much but stand behind me, gently swaying, his cock nestled on my ass, but it's enough to overheat me. Especially since Oscar is grinding against my front. My fingers sink into his ass, and Oscar and Brawler lock gazes above my head. Before I know it, I'm being led up the stairs. "What is this?" I ask, trying to forget the fact that my panties are damp.

"Private areas," Oscar whispers. "It's for lap dances and for parties when you don't want an audience. I'm hoping the rooms will be free tonight."

My heart jumps in my chest, but my excitement is short-lived. The rooms aren't free. We weren't the only ones to have this idea. In fact, the majority of them are spoken for. I catch glimpses as Oscar peels back the curtains just an inch to see if the room is free and then we move down the line after finding each one occupied. Finally, he finds a free room and pulls me into it. I have a hold of Brawler's hand, so he comes in afterward, making sure the curtain is closed behind us.

"What now?" I ask, breathless. I'm not naïve. I understand why we came up here. In fact, I'm fucking salivating for it.

"Just don't think, Big Man," Oscar says to Brawler over my head. "Do."

He moves forward, angling his head again to kiss me. Brawler's hot breath hits my neck, and my own breath hitches in my throat. I'm sandwiched between them, their hard bodies pressing against mine. Brawler pulls my dress zipper down, letting his fingers trail behind it over my spine while I kiss Oscar harder for the pleasure. Once the dress is fully unzipped, Brawler moves the straps down my shoulders. I stand straight until the material skims past my hips and pools by my feet.

Brawler's hands perch on my hips, pressing me forward while Oscar grinds on me. "Christ," I say, coming up for breath.

Calmly, Brawler unclasps my bra, pushing those straps down too. I reach up, grabbing my bra between the cups and yank down, throwing it to the side until my bare breasts are pressed against Oscar's Superman shirt. Brawler pulls me back though. He skims his hands over my hips and palms my breasts, his fingers teasing my nipples. "Oohhh," I moan as my panties soak through even more.

"Fuck," Oscar growls, biting his lip. "You're so fucking hot." He steps back to watch Brawler play with my breasts, fixating on his movements. He raises a lust-filled gaze to me. "How does that feel?"

"Fucking amazing," I purr, pulling him back to me. His hands move to my hips, then down, edging past the elastic in my panties until his hands skim over my slit.

"She's so wet, man. So fucking wet."

He pulls my panties down and spins me, arms banding over my abs while one reaches up to cup my breast. He pulls me back until he sits on a couch, placing me on top of him.

He makes sure I don't touch any part of the couch itself as he spreads his knees and puts my boot-clad feet on top of his thighs, forcing my legs open. "You should check," he murmurs to Brawler.

Brawler only has eyes for me. His stare takes me in, my peaked nipples, my throbbing pussy. A dim, red light in this room casts everything in a fiery-like glaze.

"Do you want Brawler to check?" Oscar asks, his voice husky in my ear.

I nod, opening my own legs farther, giving Brawler ample room.

Brawler hits his knees, hands running down my thighs. The pad of his thumb passes over my folds, and he curses. "So fucking wet."

I whimper. This is the hottest thing I've ever done, that I've ever even imagined. I want Brawler's mouth on me and Oscar's fingers teasing my nipples. I lock gazes with the fighter in front of me. "Fuck me with your mouth, Brawler."

"Oh God," Oscar moans, pumping his hips into me, his hard cock nudging me from behind.

I move Oscar's hands to my breasts. "Play with me. Don't stop."

"Fuck yes," Oscar growls. His fingers play, squeeze, and pinch as I watch Brawler. His gaze heats the more he takes in the scene in front of him. At first, I'm unsure if he'll play along, but I'm pleasantly surprised when he leans forward to dart his tongue across my clit.

"Fuck, fuck, fuck," I moan, my hands diving into Brawler's hair. "Oh God."

"That's right," Oscar says. "Tell Brawler how good that feels."

I hold him to me, panting as he slides his tongue up my slit swirling around my clit. Trembles overtake my body. "Keep going," I murmur.

Oscar kisses my neck, nipping here and there while he tortures my breasts.

"Tell our girl what she tastes like."

"Like fucking heaven," Brawler groans, before diving forward, humming over my clit.

"Yes, God. More."

Brawler's hands join the fold, tracing over my folds while his tongue plays with my clit. He pushes a finger inside me, and I gasp. The feelings are almost too much. I'm caught between wanting to hit that height of climax and wanting it to last as long as it can. It feels that good.

"Yes, Brawler," I tell him, urging him on.

He rumbles, sending erotic sensations straight to my core.

"This is so fucking hot," Oscar breathes. "Princess loves it. She's dying to explode, I can tell. Aren't you, baby?"

I let out another moan. My core tightens, and my body starts to lock up. "Yes. Yes."

"She's so close."

"Fuck," I breathe.

Brawler looks up, and the moment, our gazes connect, my orgasm hits. It tumbles over me so fast and hard, I open my mouth in an almost silent scream until I breathe out again, my pleasure coming out in a long moan spliced with expletives.

Oscar holds me to him as Brawler gives me one last chaste kiss to my pussy. I tighten up at that briefest of connection. He sits back on his heels like a man starved. "If we weren't surrounded by people, I would take you right now."

I feel the truth of that statement in every square inch of my skin his eyes graze. Oscar's hands cup my breasts, smoothing over my sensitive nipples. "I didn't realize I'd get such enjoyment out of that."

I smile. Nothing could make me come down right now. I'm on cloud nine. I swear I'd probably run away with these two right this moment if they asked. I'm too high on endorphins. "Let's get Princess dressed," Oscar says. "Next time, I'm tongue man. You can be breast man."

Brawler doesn't answer. He feels around on the floor until he finds my panties and skims them over my ankles and knees until I lift my ass. Oscar helps them on the rest of the way as they work in tandem.

He kisses my neck. "I'm pretty sure you soaked right through my pants, too."

I'm too high to even be embarrassed.

Brawler brings me my bra next. He holds it out, and I

slip my fingers through the straps until Oscar clasps it behind my back. I straighten the mask on my head and then Brawler helps me stand. I hug him while Oscar grips my ass in the palms of his hands. "Thank you," I whisper, so just he can hear me.

He holds out my dress, and I step into it, pulling the straps up while Oscar zips me from behind. "I'll be jerking off to that tonight," Oscar muses.

"Glad I'll take a starring role in your fantasies," Brawler quips.

Oscar doesn't even get mad. "If you saw things from my point of view, you would too."

"Act cool around Mag, okay?" Brawler asks. "My gut tells me we can trust him, but—"

"Act cool?" I ask, skin still buzzing. "No way, I'm telling him you ate me out while Oscar egged you on."

Brawler turns a fiery glare toward me, but my answering smile tells him I'm just joking. I would never say anything. Obviously. Though, Magnum isn't an idiot. He'll know why we disappeared.

"You go out first," Oscar says. "We'll follow you. Don't go too far."

I peck each one on the cheek and step beyond the curtain. I look left and find no one, then look right, realizing that's the way we came up. I move a couple of steps until a woman stumbles out of one of the sectioned off areas. She falls on her ass and laughs. She's older, but she's got everything you need, which is painfully obvious with her breasts hanging out and the G-string she's sporting. "Come back," a male singsongs from behind the black curtain. "I got the good stuff."

I peer down at her then, noting the glazed look in her dark eyes. She has dark hair and wrinkles around her temples. I imagine she would've been very pretty at one point in her life, but it's obvious she's on something and has been for a while. She has that rode hard, put away wet look. She blinks up at me. "Do I know you?"

I reach my hand out to help her up. "I don't think so."

She leans on me as she struggles to get to her feet. It's the crazy high heels she's wearing. She's not very steady on them at all, which I guess is realistic if you were doped up out of your mind and trying to walk on what are essentially short stilts.

"You okay?" I ask her. I peer toward the curtain, hoping whoever's in there isn't taking advantage of her. I don't know if this woman would even be able to help herself if he was. She's too far gone.

"I know," she says, her eyes shimmering. "I don't know you, but I had a mask just like that."

Warm hands surround me from behind. They still for a moment and then grip my hip. Brawler curses under his breath, but I don't understand anything is wrong until Oscar's choked voice hits me. "What the fuck?"

The woman peers from me to Brawler to Oscar and then back to me.

"Come on, babe. I'm ready, and I got just what you ordered. A little blow for a little blow. Come back here and let me feel those pretty little lips."

The woman's face tilts. "That's my mask." She lunges for my face, scratching her nails down my forehead until she clumsily steals the mask right off my head, the elastic snapping in the back. "Bitch."

"Don't fucking touch her," Oscar hisses as Brawler pulls me back. He's trying to push past us, but Brawler shoves his hand out.

"She stole my mask. She stole from us, baby."

Us?

Oh shit. I gasp as the revelation hits. Oscar finally gets around Brawler, and his mom clings to him, nakedness and all. The vein in his neck looks like it's about to thrum right out of his skin.

He pushes her away. "You're fucking high."

"Bitch," a male voice growls. The curtain to the side of us opens. Brawler steps in front of me, but I get a good enough look to peer over his shoulder. She's not the only girl the guy has in there. There's two already passed out on the floor. White powder lines grace the top of a table under a soft lamp. The guy, who must be in his late thirties to early forties, grips Oscar's mom's arm and yanks her back into the room. "Mine first," he says, slicing a deadly look to Oscar and Brawler.

My stomach heaves. He thinks Oscar wants a shot with his mom.

"Give me half an hour."

Oscar roars. I want to go to him, but Magnum appears at the top of the steps, pulling Oscar back. He says something into his ear, and Oscar yanks out of his hold, then turns and flies down the stairs behind them. It takes Magnum all of a few seconds to glimpse the scene and know what's going on. Oscar's mom is exchanging sex for drugs.

The guy closes the curtain behind him and the women as if nothing happened. He probably can't think straight either. I come out from behind Brawler and Magnum curses.

"We can't leave her there," I hiss, pointing toward the closed curtain. My heart aches for Oscar to have seen that. Plus, that guy didn't seem nice. What if he hurts her?

"We don't have a choice." He frowns at my now mask-less face.

"Fuck that. That fucker—"

"Shh," Magnum demands. "Put your hair in front of your face." He guides my head to Brawler's chest. "Pretend you're sick. Don't let go of her," he orders Brawler.

We walk past more rooms. Some of them don't even have the decency to pull the curtains completely closed. Oscar's mom's room isn't the only one that is laced with drugs. Two women at the end of the hall come stumbling out of a room. Their eyes tell me everything I need to know. They're high, too. They probably don't even know where they are.

Brawler hides me until we're all the way out to the car, and I'm safely inside. I wait until Magnum gets in. "We need to find Oscar."

"We need to get you home," Magnum says.

"Fuck that. You saw what Oscar just saw. He's going to be fucked in the head. Please," I beg, desperate now. I can't imagine what he's feeling.

Brawler sighs. He kisses me on the temple. "I'll go find Oscar. Promise." He pushes the door open and gets one foot outside.

"No, wait," I say, trying to get out with him.

"Kyla," Brawler says, piercing me with a look. "I've got this. I won't let anything happen to him, okay? We'll both call you later."

He slams the door, and my stomach drops. Mag turns around in the seat. "Did they see you?"

I shrug. His mom definitely saw me, but I doubt she knows who I am. "They were so high; I doubt it matters." I hold my head in my hands, worry paralyzing me.

Magnum pushes his door open. He gets out, and I glance up when the door to my left opens. He beckons me out, and I follow. He takes me around the back of the car and makes me get in the front seat. Then, he closes the door behind me and gets in on the other side again. After taking a deep breath, he places his hand over mine on the seat. "It's going to be okay."

I meet his gaze. His eyes track over my forehead. He reaches out, fingers trailing over the stinging skin there. "She ripped the mask off my face," I tell him.

Magnum frowns. "Let's get you home. Johnny called while you were with them, so you need to call him back."

I slump back in the seat. Magnum rubs circles into my hand with the pad of his thumb as he drives me back to the tower. I can't believe I thought I'd have a nice night out with my boyfriends. Nothing good ever happens in the Heights.

My phone rings while I'm in the shower. I hurry to shut the water off and then dive for it. Magnum told me Johnny called once already. I can't not answer a second time.

"Johnny?" I ask as soon as I pick it up. My heart is in my throat. It's all the events of today. I'm stressed. Worried. Furious.

He chuckles. "Hey, babe. I called earlier." His voice doesn't betray whether he's trying to check up on me or not. It's just conversational.

"I saw." I swallow, hoping I can say this convincingly. "I was training. I must not have heard it."

"Training this late?"

I close my eyes and pinch the bridge of my nose. "Just making sure I give everyone the best fight." Here's to hoping he doesn't check with Finn and Jax. Or if he does, they've seen enough to just go ahead and agree that I was there. We haven't come out and had any sort of discussion with them, but they know who I'm dating. Hopefully, their alliance is to me and not the Crew.

"That's my girl." His words poke me in the chest. Not an hour ago, Oscar had referred to me as 'our girl', and even though I was in the heights of pleasure, those words made me warm and fuzzy. In fact, they only added to my excitement. "You okay? You seem out of breath."

"I was taking a shower, but I didn't want to miss you. You know how I like to take showers after training," I say, only trying to drive the point home that he shouldn't be suspicious. At the same time, I feel like shit for doing it because he has every reason to be suspicious. It's becoming clearer I'm going to hurt Johnny in more ways than one.

He moans. "Mmm, I miss you."

"Me too. Tomorrow," I say. I have two minds about him coming back. I've enjoyed the freedom while he's been gone, but I miss him too. If Johnny were in any other city. If he were born to any other parent, God, he'd be fucking perfect. It's not fair.

"Actually," Johnny says, disappointment lacing his voice. "That's what I called to tell you. I won't be coming home tomorrow after all."

I grit my teeth as my heart sinks. "No?"

"I'm sorry, Kyla. We thought we'd be done, but something else came up."

"But the dinner?"

"We'll reschedule."

I sigh, aware Johnny can hear my true disappointment. None of this is an act. I rub the side of my face. My wet hair drips down my back. I usually squeeze it out when I get out of the shower, but I didn't get the chance. I grab a towel and wrap it around myself before I pad toward my bedroom and lie down on the soft bed.

"You okay?"

"Just bummed," I tell him.

"Me too. It helps to think about you though." He takes a deep breath and lets it out. "I want to put your mind at ease about something. I know I fucked up once. I let my privilege work its way into our relationship in the beginning, but I want to let you know the only woman I'm interested in is you. Dad thinks I'm crazy, but he's respected my wishes." His voice goes quiet. "I got thinking that you might be worried about that. You know, while I'm gone that I might do something."

The thought had crossed my mind, and I'm relieved to hear his words. At the same time, I'm holding back from him too. When I finally tell him about Brawler and Oscar, I hope he doesn't... Well, I hope he doesn't kill us. If he's into me as much as he says he is, I'd hope he'd understand. I'd hope he'd give it a chance. Us. Them. Everything.

But I'm asking a lot because this is probably going to be after I murder his father, so he won't give a rat's ass about what I'm doing with Brawler and Oscar. He'll hate me for taking something from him.

I wish I'd been able to keep feelings out of this relationship. I really do.

Instead of answering him, I change the subject. We talk for a few more minutes about what we've been doing. I make up a few more lies about training and school and then he tells me he's heading to bed because he has an early morning meeting.

I stay on my bed, my phone clutched in my hands after I end the call. Guilt hits me full force in the chest, but I close my eyes, reminding myself that these are small prices to pay to execute my plan.

My phone rings again, and I'm surprised until I bring it up and realize it's Brawler on the other end. My fingers shake as I answer. "What's going on?" I ask right away.

"Hey," he says. "I got Oscar. We're at his place."

"Is he okay?"

"He's..." A cracking sound reverberates through the phone. "He's mad."

"Can you put him on the phone?"

"I'll try," he says. "He's in the middle of destroying the place though." They talk in the background. Brawler has to tell him a few times that I want to talk to him before he actually hears what he's saying.

The line goes dead for a moment, but then Oscar comes on. His breathing fills the connection, so I know he's there. He's just not saying anything. "Hey," I say.

"My mom," he says, like he's explaining who the woman was.

"I know."

"Did she hurt you?"

"A few scratches." If Johnny comes home before they're healed, I'll shrug them off as training injuries.

"She didn't mean it."

"I know. She was high."

"That fucker, Gregory," Oscar growls.

My stomach pitches. "You know him?"

"Easy on the phone," Brawler warns in the background.

Oscar ignores him. "Yeah, I know him. K won't be fucking happy when I tell him what's going on in that fucking place."

Dread forms a knot in my stomach. "What do you mean?"

Oscar fills me in on his suspicions, including Dunnegan's right-hand man—the one his mom was with—plying women with drugs for sex. In their place of business.

My throat goes dry. "She wasn't the only woman I saw like that there, Oscar. Not even tonight. When Johnny and I went before, he had to speak to Dunnegan about a few girls who were high. He didn't want them working when they were like that."

Oscar laughs like he's going insane. "This fucker thought he could do this while they were gone. I'm going to nail his ass."

"Wait, wait, wait," I say. "You don't think any of this is sanctioned by the Crew?"

"No," he huffs. "Gregory should have been scared shitless that I found him, but one, he was toasted. Two, he probably thinks I'm going to be his little bitch. I'm not. Fuck him. He probably didn't even realize that was my mom he was with, but I'm going to make him pay."

My mind starts to whirl. Johnny keeps a good eye on these businesses. If what Oscar is saying is true, he'll want to know about this, but we can't just bring him something so small. What if it's a one-off? I bite my lip. I know what I want to say to Oscar, but I don't want him to think I don't care either. "I need to talk to you about this. Meet tomorrow? Don't do anything about it until I've spoken to you. Okay?"

"What's going on, Princess?" he asks, more alert now.

"Just trust me, okay? Can you do that?"

"You know I do. I'm so fucking sorry you had to see that today."

"I know, but hey, remember, the objective is to get the fuck out of here, right?" I ask, giving him something happy to focus on. My goals have changed, I realize. I'm taking Big Daddy K out. That plan hasn't gone anywhere. In addition to that, though, we're all leaving the Heights, so we can get out of this hellhole.

"Right," he breathes out.

Tomorrow, I'll tell him we can use this information we have on Candy's to our advantage. Tomorrow, I'll tell him that if we find out Candy's is really doing something against K's wishes, we'll get that much closer to the inside of the Crew. The closer we get to Big Daddy K, the sooner I can end this, and then the sooner we can get out of this shithole. They've all told me I should leave, and I plan on it. I'm not going without them though.

Right now, we don't need suspicions of what's going on. We need evidence.

We have to go back.

As planned, Brawler sets me up with an impromptu fight the next day. He got Johnny to agree by saying some girl was running her mouth about how she was going to kick my ass. Whatever he told Johnny, Johnny agreed.

Which was all we needed.

I can't go undercover to Candy's again without the pretense of the costume party, and I can't go as me without word getting back to Johnny.

I make quick work of my opponent. One of these days, I'll draw a fight out. Despite the fact that it's a last-minute fight, they have to turn people away at the door again. The atmosphere holds the same thirst for blood it always does, which is why the crowd doesn't care if I annihilate my opponent or not. They just want to see someone suffer, and I give that to them.

Though everything else is the same, I'm different. I'm edgy for a whole slew of reasons that have nothing to do with it being a fight night and have everything to do with figuring out what's going on at Candy's. Oscar's quiet, and I want to help him. In the same token though, I'm pissed someone would do this to Johnny. He and Dunnegan acted like good buddies. Imagine if Dunnegan is playing him.

No one fucking plays the people I care about. If Dunnegan is doing something behind the Crew's back, I'll be the first to step up and spill my guts, so he gets what's coming to them. Not to mention that they're using distraught, desperate women to carry this out. Oscar's mom is broken. It doesn't make her a bad person. It makes her a person in need of help. And here we are, treating her like the scum of the earth, exploiting her weaknesses to use her.

The thought makes me sick.

The crowd surrounds me the minute Brawler calls the fight. I may have dislocated a knuckle or two on my right hand, but it's the least of my worries. I play the part, acting like the cocky winner, accepting my Uppercut Princess robe with a cocksure smile. Usually, fighting makes me feel alive, and maybe it's because of that that everything feels so urgent right now. I don't want to sleep on this another day. I just keep picturing the glazed, lost look on Oscar's mom's face. I don't know her. Not really. But I know Oscar. I know the type of person he is underneath all the layers of hurt and bravado. He's a good person, and it killed him to see someone he loved like that.

Magnum takes Johnny's place, ushering me into the back where I can shower and change to start what tonight was really all about. Right before I hit the locker room door, Brawler announces that we're headed to Candy's tonight. We figure the more bodies there, the better. We'd stick out less and have more opportunity to snoop around to see what's going on.

Magnum shuts the door behind us and flips the lock. "Nice fight," he says.

I wish I could remember. I only have bits and pieces, mainly the scared look on the girl's face when I pounced on her. We definitely threw her to the wolves, but Oscar didn't just make up the part about her bashing me. Apparently, he'd heard a rumor, so we went with it, whether it was true or not.

I shrug the purple robe off. To my right, there's a bag with the outfit I'm wearing tonight. I'm shaking. Usually, the fights help calm me, but since that wasn't the main point of tonight, I still have all this expectation built up inside me.

Magnum's hands settle on my shoulders, and he starts to massage them. "Relax a little."

My posture droops as his fingers delve deep between my muscles.

"You take too much on your shoulders."

He doesn't even know the half of it. I shared what we thought was going down with him this morning. He wanted to call Johnny right away, but I convinced him I didn't want to bring it to Johnny if it was bullshit. He doesn't know I have another reason for wanting to do this, to ingratiate myself even farther into the belly of the Crew. To stick myself so far up the Crew's ass I'm practically Big Daddy K's daughter.

My stomach roils. I hate the fucking thought of that, but if he lets his guard down around me, he's toast. I'll have him wasted before he can even blink. The worst thing that could have happened over the last several weeks was Johnny telling him we couldn't control ourselves around one another. I'm sure that made me look like a pathetic female, which is nowhere near how I want him to view me. Maybe this sick part of me wants him to like me too. It'll feel that much sweeter when I kill his ass. Knowing I got one over on him. That he isn't the high and mighty leader of the Heights Crew. That I took him out. A no one. I can almost picture the look of betrayal in his eyes.

"You're tensing up again," Magnum murmurs.

"Lots on my mind."

"You're worried about Oscar." It's not a question, but a statement. Magnum sees everything. It's like he has a direct line to my brain. I've never met a man who was that observant before. My uncle, as good as he was to me, was clueless when it came to my aunt.

"No kid should have to see their parent like that," I whisper, my voice cracking.

"It's a sad reality here."

"But if Dunnegan is doing that to them..."

Magnum moves to my neck. He massages his strong hands up the base and down the curve to my shoulders. I close my eyes because it feels that damn good. He sighs, and his breath hits my neck. Goosebumps sprout over my body. He's standing so close.

"Have you thought that maybe Big Daddy K and Johnny already know about this? That maybe this is sanctioned by them?"

My mouth parts, and a solid brick falls to the floor of my stomach. Magnum stops massaging me for a brief second and then keeps going. "I—I hadn't thought of that," I admit. "Maybe briefly, but I don't think they would do this."

"You know they're not good people."

"But Oscar's mom."

"They're not good people," Magnum reiterates again.

I want to ask him again why the hell he's working for them then? But that's not fair. Oscar's the same way. He's in the Crew even though he really doesn't want to be. Maybe Magnum's the same way. Maybe he's stuck. The Crew took his father and mother away from him too.

It's not easy to get out of the Crew. It's virtually fucking impossible.

Magnum moves his hands downward, the pads of his thumbs digging into my shoulder blades.

"Do you think that's what's going on?"

Magnum's silent for a moment. His movements don't stop, but they let up while he thinks. "I think the only reason they'll care is if they're losing money on this. If Dunnegan has a side business going that he's cutting the Crew out of, that's what makes it a big deal."

"I hope Johnny doesn't know," I confess. It's one thing to have underground fights. It's one thing to own a racetrack. To own a strip club. But it's completely different to be involved in using prostitutes to satisfy someone's sick sexual craving by holding drugs over their heads. The flip my stomach does only solidifies the fact that I don't know if I would be able to get past this if Johnny's aware.

"Me too," Magnum says. "Johnny's on a seesaw right now. Let's say the left is his father and all the terrible shit he does and let's say the right is you and what you represent."

I swallow, his words forming a lump in my throat. He's acting like I could be Johnny's salvation.

"Right now, he's got two legs on either side of the pivot point. One toward his father and one toward you. I hope he chooses you, but he may as well be brainwashed. You have a headache in front of you if you want it." Magnum steps closer, his chest grazing my back. "No one would blame you if you don't want to take this on."

Magnum and I stand in silence. Neither of us moving.

The thumping of my heart reverberates in my ears. My back pricks each time Magnum takes a breath and his chest brushes my skin for even the briefest moment.

He moves closer. His hot breath caressing the dip of my neck. "I mean that, Kyla. No one would blame you." His lips are scant inches from my skin. It feels as if Mag and I are on a seesaw too. One move away, and it stops everything. One move closer, and it'll start something else. I remain frozen in place, terrified one way or the other.

I take a deep breath, my shoulders rising with the motion. His lower lip brushes my skin. Neither of us breathe.

A knock sounds on the door. Magnum's hands tighten on my back for a split second, but then peel away. "I'll get that."

When he steps back, a breeze of cold air surrounds me. I take the bag of clothes I brought with me and head toward the shower area. I could use a shower about now. I need to wash these thoughts away before they take hold of my brain. Focusing on what's going down at Candy's is what I need right now.

I take the quickest shower of my life. When I towel off, I dress in the clothes I brought with me. No dress and heels this time around. I pull on a pair of skintight leather pants, boots, and a halter-top instead. This way, it's easier to get around if I have to, and I won't have to worry about showing my goods to anyone if I get in a compromising position.

When I walk back out into the main area to do my makeup and hair at the sink, Magnum acts like nothing happened between us just now, so maybe it was all in my head. I imagined the whole thing. The tension between us. The underlying meaning of his words.

Oscar's in the room now, too. Magnum is trying to draw Oscar into a conversation, but it isn't working. He's been in his own head since yesterday. I can't imagine knowing that your mom was about to pleasure some fucktard for drugs. That's got to mess with your psyche.

I finish up, and Brawler walks in. "Ready?"

We all head out. While we're in the back of the car, I pull Oscar's hands around me and lean into him. "We'll figure this out," I whisper. He hugs me to him, kissing my temple.

"I kind of figured what she was into, so I don't know why it's hitting me this hard."

"Because that's your mom," I say. "And that shit ain't right. We protect the people we care about." Or we seek vengeance for the people we care about. I get exactly what Oscar is feeling. He's in that phase where he's trying to wrap his head around it, but when he comes out the other side, he'll want to make someone pay even more so than he did last night.

Magnum pulls the car up to the back of Candy's like we would on any normal celebration night. I send Johnny a quick text letting him know I won. It's too bad he couldn't have come home today, but it's also a blessing. He wouldn't let me out of his sight if he had, and I'm determined to help Oscar figure out what's going on with his mom and the connection to Candy's.

We don't really have a set plan, except that Magnum and I will be taking a look around to see how the workers act tonight. We'll also occupy Dunnegan and any of his workers, so that Oscar and Brawler can search the office. We even talked about heading upstairs again to see if it's happening right under our noses. What Magnum said to me in the locker room rears its ugly head, and I hope that Johnny has no idea what's happening with these poor women. I'm disgusted already. Sick to my core.

He better not be involved in this because that's crossing a line I refuse to cross with him. I give him leeway because of the life he's lived, but I won't go there.

Magnum paves the way for us inside Candy's. Like normal, Dunnegan is there waiting for us. He's always struck me as an intelligent, well-mannered man. Then again, on the outside, no one would guess the shit that Big Daddy K has done. His exterior is made up of fancy suits, cocky smiles, and brash—often logistical—business decisions that make them a lot of money. Maybe Dunnegan should have the same classification as him?

He gives me a slight bow. "Kyla, I hear another round of congratulations are in order."

"Thank you," I tell him. I make a show of looking

around his showroom. "Looks like Candy's is the place to be again."

He beams like this was all his doing. It wasn't. This was Johnny putting Candy's on the map as something other than a respectable strip club. There aren't even any strippers on the floor right now. There are dancers, and the dances they're performing are sexy, but the dancers themselves aren't naked. Johnny's completely changed the face of Candy's. For the better.

I return his smile, although it's pretty muted compared to his. "Johnny is still away on business. Do you mind having a drink with me?"

Dunnegan stands straighter. He's pleasantly surprised as he offers me his elbow, and we walk onto the floor together. He leads me to our usual table in the midst of all the cheers sent my way. I wave politely, but I don't lose focus of what I'm doing. I'm keeping Dunnegan preoccupied so Oscar and Brawler can get into his office to see what he's up to. If they are doing the drugs/prostitution as a business, he'll have records. Profit and loss statements. Bank accounts. Anything that we can use in our favor to prove to Johnny that Dunnegan is doing something behind their backs. Like Magnum said, if the only way Johnny and his father will care is if they're making a profit off it and not sharing, we have to bring them that proof.

Let's just hope nothing we find ties Johnny to this. It doesn't seem right to me. Why would he go to so many lengths to bring a different crowd of people here if he knew what was truly going on?

Unless he wants more people around to hide what they're actually doing.

Magnum brushes up against me. I glance his way, and he nods.

I take a deep breath. Right. Stay focused.

Dunnegan escorts me to my side of the booth. I slide in while he goes around the other side of the half-moon table, unbuttoning his suit coat so he can sit. A waitress approaches. She has a crop top on with long sleeves. The shirt itself is covered in sequins with the word Candy's splashed over her chest. It's much different from the outfits the waitresses were wearing the first time I came here. "Boss," she says, nodding to Dunnegan. "Princess," she says, nodding to me.

I gnash my teeth together. If people are going to call me Princess, they shouldn't forget about the Uppercut part. I swear I should start slamming my fist into everyone who dares call me just Princess. "Kyla's fine," I say tersely. "Can you get me an Amaretto Sour and whatever your boss usually likes to drink?"

The waitress's gaze cuts to Dunnegan. He waves her off. "Can't drink while I'm working, I'm afraid."

I lean back in the booth, pretending to look out over all the sweaty, dancing bodies. "This place has made such great strides. What a great accomplishment," I tell him, stroking his ego.

"We've tripled our quarterly income in just thirty days," he says. His gaze almost twinkles as he looks out over the floor.

I note some of the waitresses. The one we had was clearly fine. The others carrying drinks and empty glasses around us look clear too. There's no outward signs of drug use like there was before when Johnny and I were here. The crowd has shifted from casual on-lookers to more participatory. "You've probably had to increase security."

He nods. "Different clientele, different rules. But we're still far and away in the black."

I like that he's being so upfront with me. He's not just saying, "Sales are good, little girl. Don't you worry your pretty little head about it." That would definitely cost him an uppercut to the chin.

"You seem interested in the Crew's assets," he throws out.

I smile at him because this isn't hard to discuss at all. "I'm afraid Johnny's beginning to realize I'm more than just arm candy," I tell him.

"You have brains," he says, smiling knowingly. "I bet he likes that."

The smile that moves my lips farther apart is genuine. "I think he does. Or he's beginning to."

"The partner you choose is exceedingly important."

"You married?"

He lifts his finger to show off his wedding ring. If he's involved in this prostitution ring—if that's what it is—I feel terrible for his wife. To know that someone you love would do that to women is just disgusting.

"Good for you," I say. "A smart businessman like yourself chose wisely, I'm sure."

"The foundation starts in the home," he tells me, gaze drifting to the crowd. "If that's broken, good luck making anything of yourself."

Dunnegan says all the right things, but what kind of person is he, really?

The waitress who called me Princess comes back over and sits my drink in front of me. "We've named that the Uppercut Princess. We sell out of it every night."

"Yeah?" I ask, using the small straw to stir the drink. I guess I've made it. I have a perfectly fine alcoholic drink named after me.

Dunnegan sets his hand on my arm just as I'm about to bring the glass to my lips. "Sorry I can't sit with you any longer, but I have something to attend to. Please let me know if there's anything I can do."

My smile turns tight. Fuck. I was hoping I could occupy him for longer. "Of course. Thank you."

As soon as he disappears in the thick crowd, I pull my phone out and shoot Brawler a text to get out of his office if he's in there. Then, I send the same thing to Oscar. If Oscar got caught in there, it wouldn't be too big of a deal. He'd most likely be able to talk his way out of it, but not Brawler.

My stomach is in knots, so I tip the drink back, swallowing the sour liquid. "See anything out of the ordinary?"

"I don't think what we have to worry about is down here," Mag says. "I'm pretty observant, and I didn't notice anything off until we were upstairs yesterday." That leaves us with how we're going to get upstairs. Before I can even look over my shoulder at the staircases that leads to the floor above us, Magnum says, "Looks like security is standing guard today."

I see it now. Two men in black polos with Candy's written on the upper right chest guard the bottom of the steps.

Oscar and Brawler approach the table. It's so weird that they can't sit at the table with me right now when yesterday, we had so much fun here not being ourselves. Well, maybe it was just me not being myself, but now, they have to stand at the front of the table like we're merely acquaintances instead of two people I know intimately.

"Anything?"

"I grabbed a file," Oscar said, patting his jacket. "I didn't get a chance to get a good look, so I don't know if it has anything important."

Before I can get upset that we're literally failing at this, I say, "We need to get up to the next level to see if it's still happening."

"You can't go," Oscar says, piercing me with a look that begs me to defy him, but I know he's right. "Magnum can't either because he's watching you."

"I'll go," Brawler says, voice like stone. What we saw up there yesterday affected him, too. I bet he sees his sister in every victim's face.

Oscar looks like he wants to tell him he can't, but Brawler's the logical choice. If Oscar goes, it makes it Crew business even if it isn't. If Brawler goes, he's free from any ties. "Be careful," I tell him. "Take pictures."

"I got it," he says.

He turns, leaving the table. He doesn't go directly for the stairs because that would be obvious, but he lingers at the bar for a few minutes, warding off advances from older women that get my hackles up. I lose sight of him when two couples approach the table to talk about my fight. That's basically what these after parties are, so I sit and talk with them for a few minutes before Magnum makes it obvious the conversation is over. When they leave, Oscar's left too, and I can't find Brawler in the crowd anymore.

"We should probably wrap this up soon," Mag says, gaze darting around the room.

I nod, not knowing at all if we have what we need. Regardless of endearing myself to the Heights Crew, we need to get this prostitution drug operation shut down. I'll even sneak the information to the police so they can get it shut the fuck down.

I'm still looking at Mag when his body freezes. I track his gaze across the floor and try to find what's caught his attention only to find Brawler's arm around someone, a head on his chest. It reminds me of how he walked me out of here yesterday, and my heart takes off like a rocket.

I stand, eyeballing the two leaving not just the upstairs but Candy's altogether. The weird part is, I recognize her. At least, I think I do.

What in the fuck?

part of me knows Brawler wouldn't do something like that, but another part of me is saying that this is just what happens in the Heights. The place I brought myself to. The place I infiltrated and made myself one with.

"Come on," Mag says, his voice gruff. He helps me out of the booth while I'm still staring at the spot where Brawler and another girl just left.

I pinch my thigh, but no, I'm still in Candy's. Still trying to figure out what is going on around here.

He puts his hand on my lower back as he guides me through the crowd. We finally get to the hallway that leads out the back door. We start to pass Dunnegan's office, but he calls out my name, so we have to stop. "Thanks for coming," he says graciously. "Tell Rocket he better hold on tight to you."

It might be me, but his smile looks forced this time. Then again, my head isn't completely in the game since it's on Brawler's hand around another girl. "I'll tell him," I say back, trying to manage a smile, but I'm not sure it comes out at all.

We head outside. I search the area for Brawler and slow when I don't see him at first. Then, my phone vibrates in my pocket. I slip it out. **We're inside the car.**

We.

I march that way, trying to set aside my ridiculous jealousy, telling myself that he must've found someone who knows something. I pull the car door open and slip in. Thankfully, we brought one of the bigger Crew cars tonight that has seats facing each other. It came in useful earlier because Brawler, Oscar, and I could sit in the back together without being squished, but now it's coming in even more useful.

As soon as I slide across the seat across from him, Brawler says, "I had to get her out of there."

I glance over at her. Recognition tickles my throat. How I know her is on the tip of my tongue, but I'm just not sure. First of all, she's made up to the hilt. Fake eyelashes. Bright eyeshadow that looks caked on. She's also wearing a short ass skirt, her legs wide open. The red lacey panties she's wearing are practically a neon sign.

The door opens again, and Oscar gets in. Magnum and I move over to accommodate him. "Thanks for telling me we were taking this party elsewh—" He shuts up as soon as he sees the girl in Brawler's lap. She's out cold right now, eyelids fluttering like she's dreaming.

"So, I act the part," Brawler begins. "I tell the guy at the bottom of the stairs that I heard there was some fun shit happening upstairs. He gets this twinkle in his eye. I hand him over a twenty, and he lets me up. I'm directed to a room with her inside," he says, staring down at her. "She's awake, barely. Slurring her words."

"She's on something?" I ask.

"Something, but I don't know what." He shakes his head. "It wouldn't have struck me as odd except I fucking recognize her. She goes to the Heights."

Oscar's gaze narrows. Much like me, I'm sure he's probably trying to look past the caked-on makeup to figure out who it is. "Fuuuuuck," Oscar breathes. "That's the chick that actually cares about school."

I glance at her again. I don't know many people at school, but as I said, I feel like I know her. I turn my head, tilting it at the angle the girl is facing, and that's when it clicks into place. This is the girl who walked me out my first day at the Heights. The one who told me to stay away from Nevaeh and to not leave the school out the front doors when everyone else had left because the guards were handsy.

"Shit."

"Natalia," Brawler says. "She lived around the corner

from me growing up. No way would she be doing this. Her grandmother was so strict with her."

Oscar rubs his face. "I hate to say it, but you never know."

"I'm telling you," Brawler growls. "She seemed confused. She seemed not to know what was going on. I slipped the guy at the top of the stairs a hundred dollars and told him I wanted to take her home."

I glance at Brawler. How he even had that much money on him, I don't know. But I do know he needs that money for him and his mom. He must be certain about this.

"So, what's your plan?" I ask him.

"When she wakes up, we're going to ask her what she's doing there. If we have a witness to what's happening, even better."

Magnum and I exchange a look. He must still be thinking that the Crew knows about this.

"Oscar, the file?" I ask, holding my hand out.

Oscar pulls it out of his jacket and starts leafing through it. He shakes his head. "It's tough to know because I'm not privy to what Candy's numbers actually are. It's not like there's a sign here saying this is the money we're keeping away from the Crew, don't tell anyone."

I roll my eyes at his pure Oscar remark and then take the file to flip through it myself.

Magnum reaches through the divider and pulls a bottle of water back through. "Sit her up," he instructs.

Brawler does so, making her sit up in the car next to him. She stirs. Magnum leans forward, holding the opened bottle of water to her lips and tips it up. Some of it gets in her mouth and some of it dribbles down her face.

Her eyes blink rapidly and then they open. Immediately, she's on high alert. "Where am I?" her gaze darts around to us surrounding her. "What's going on?"

"Natalia, it's Mack," Brawler says. "You were at Candy's. I noticed you were kind of messed up, so I got you out of there. Are you okay?"

"Candy's?" she slurs. "Okay..."

She starts to go back to sleep, and I snap my fingers in front of her face. "Hey. Stay with us."

She looks me up and down. "You."

"Me," I say. "We were worried about you."

She shrugs. Her head lolls around on her neck like she has no control over it. When it points down, she frowns. "Whose clothes are these?" She picks her hand up, then brings her finger down on the short leather skirt she's wearing. She pulls it up, flashing us all her panties again like we couldn't see them before. "Whoa. Is it Halloween?"

I pull her skirt back down. She's totally out of it. I don't know Natalia like Brawler does, but I think his instincts are correct. The girl who walked me out of school that day would not do this.

"I look like a slut," she slurs.

I jab Oscar in the ribs.

"What?" he exclaims.

"Don't even think about making a joke."

His gaze narrows at me, but he doesn't say anything.

"This could be a victim like your mother."

"I've been around my mom enough to know that she does this shit to herself. The way I see it, it's all too easy. Don't do drugs, and you wouldn't be caught in the fucked-up situations you find yourself in."

"Natalia's not a druggie," Brawler says, voice firm. "She wouldn't be caught dead in a place like that."

I eye him again. He gazes softly down at her. He definitely knows this girl and is worried about what happens to her. He's got such a good heart.

But I will cut a bitch if I have to. Just sayin'.

Magnum drives to a corner store to pick up a few things and then to a park just outside of town. We stay there until Natalia starts to come around again. She's in and out of it, and no matter how much I want to slap her to get her to wake up quicker, I agree this is the humane way. It's just that the more we wait to see what's happened to her, the more the same thing is happening to someone else.

An hour and a half later, Natalia's eyes shoot open. Her cheeks blow out, and she covers her mouth. "Fuuuck," Oscar says, backing away.

I grab the shopping bag Magnum came out of the store with and shove it in her face. She expels the contents of her stomach into it over and over, gagging. The air in the car turns putrid. We throw the car doors open. Oscar and Magnum even leave while Brawler and I stay with her.

I hand her the water, and she takes it gratefully, sending me a short-lived smile. Her hands shake as she holds the bottle to her lips, gulping the water down. I tried to keep it cool, but she's been out for too long, so I doubt it's stayed refreshing. It doesn't seem to matter to her though.

She lies back on the seat, throwing the bag out of the car. She turns her gaze to Brawler and then to me. "What am I doing here?"

"You were at Candy's," Brawler says. "We were there for Kyla's after party and you looked messed up."

She clenches her stomach. "I work there," she says.

Brawler and I eye each other.

"I just started as a waitress," she continues. "I don't know. They're not doing the strip club thing anymore, so I thought what the hell. The last thing I remember is getting a drink before my shift started. We heard you had a fight that night, so we knew we were going to be busy."

Her drink. They must have put something in her fucking drink. "You don't remember anything after that."

She shakes her head, but the look on her face is telling me things are still fuzzy. "Fuck. Do you think someone put something in my drink? Fucking Gregory handed it to me."

I refuse to look at Brawler. That's the evidence we needed. I think. He's Dunnegan's right-hand man. He was in there with Oscar's mom last night. If he's orchestrating this sort of sex ring with women who are too out of it to notice, Dunnegan has to be in on it too.

I glance up at Natalia who's drinking the water again. How do I even tell this girl what's going down at Candy's? Or what I think is going down at Candy's? I don't want to alarm her for no reason, but she wasn't upstairs for the fun of it.

"We found you upstairs, Natalia. Upstairs at Candy's."

She shakes her head. "That doesn't make sense. We're not allowed upstairs. It's where they used to have the private stripteases and shit, but since they're not doing it anymore, it's off-limits."

I put my hand on her knee. She looks down at herself, frowning at her outfit. Recognition starts to spark in her gaze. "Natalia, I think you were drugged. Brawler found you upstairs in one of the rooms." As I'm talking, I'm a half second behind her thoughts because before the next thing even slips out of my mouth, it's as if she knows what I'm about to say and is already dreading it.

She sits up straight. "I want to go home now."

"Natalia," I say, squeezing her knee.

She pushes my hand away from her. "I want to fucking go home. Now."

We sit back. Brawler puts some space between the two of them. Magnum and Oscar must have heard what she said because Oscar gets in and shuts the door while Magnum gets in the driver's seat and starts the car up. I close the last door, the sound ricocheting around the interior as a pool of dead weight sinks to the bottom of my stomach.

I feel for this girl, I do. Who knows what unimaginable things were done to her before Brawler walked into her room? I watch her as we drive and see the moment each terrible thought strikes her. One thing's for sure. Natalia's fucking strong, but her strength can't hide the truth. Just as mine could never hide what happened to me.

30

Magnum follows Natalia's directions, pulling up to a house that's been turned into many apartments. The shudders are falling down, and the siding is peeling and chipping off. The glow from the porch light lights the rundown house in starkness.

As soon as Magnum parks the car, Natalia glances down at herself. She clutches her stomach. "I can't go in like this. My grandmother will kill me."

Brawler pulls the shirt off his back and hands it to her. She gives him a wobbly smile and yanks it down over her head. It pools around her until it's basically an oversized dress.

"Natalia," I start, pausing until she meets my gaze. Her eyes are like stone, and I can tell she doesn't want anything to do with us or what happened to her tonight. She wants to bury it so deep inside her that it never comes back up. "We should talk."

"Nope," she says, throwing the door to the car open. "I'm good." She pierces us all with a look before walking away. She didn't give us the order not to open our damn mouths, but it was implied. Like we would ever say anything.

She runs up the porch steps, straightens her spine, and pulls the rickety storm door open before disappearing into the apartment.

"Son of a bitch," Oscar curses.

"They're doping up girls who didn't even sign up for it," I say, testing the words out on my tongue because it doesn't even seem like something that should be said. How could someone be that heinous?

"And using others," Oscar deadpans.

Magnum pulls away from the curb. It's only a short drive to the apartment building where Brawler lives. I move to his side of the car and wrap my arms around his waist. He literally gave Natalia the shirt off his back. He has too big of a heart for the Heights. "We need to get these fuckers," he says.

I nod into his chest, agreeing wholeheartedly. There has to be something we can do. I have to hold faith that this would bother Johnny. If I take it to him, he'll deal with it. He'll make sure the guys under him will be punished, right?

Brawler kisses the crown of my head. I scoot away from

him, and he gets out, his broad chest naked as he walks up to the apartment doors.

Oscar moves over to my side of the car now, pulling my head down to his chest. He filters his fingers through my hair, playing with the ends until he starts all over again at the top.

"She's going to be fucked up from this."

He nods.

A little while later, my phone buzzes, and I pull it out of my pocket. Brawler sends me picture after picture he took of Natalia while he was in the room with her. He made sure to get the full room, so it was apparent it was taken at Candy's, but he also blurred her face out. Or in closeups, he cropped the picture so it cut her head off. Only Brawler has the originals, and if I know him, he'll have gotten rid of them so none of this traces back to Natalia. He probably saw his sister in her. An innocent bystander being hurt by the Crew again.

Then, a recording comes through of the conversation we had in the car. I can tell who the voices are because I was here for the actual moment, but he's hidden Natalia's identity for anyone who wasn't there, and I fucking love him for it.

"Jesus, he's smarter than I give him credit for."

I nudge Oscar in the ribs. "Not helping."

He blows out a breath and leans back against the seat.

"Alright," I say, "Tell me straight. What's the likelihood the Crew knows about this already?"

"Unlikely." His eyes apologize as he says, "I get that they're bad people, but they're well respected by people around here. If people knew they were doing this, they would get so much shit. At least when it's my mom, she's doing it for drugs. But being drugged and taking an innocent girl to be someone's plaything. No fucking way. In a sense, the Crew is like Robin Hood. Taking from the rich and giving to the poor. People around here have a healthy dose of respect and fear for the Crew, but look how much good they bring? They give people jobs. They give people safety." I balk at that, but Oscar shrugs. "In here they do. I know that hasn't been your experience with them, but I'm telling you, if you ask people if they like or hate the Crew, most will say they like them. Crew guys are like fairy tales in the making. Johnny, Mag, me, and a ton of other guys went to Rawley Heights and are doing better than most of the other guys who graduated from the Heights and didn't join up. We have people trying to get in every fucking day. That wouldn't happen if people didn't like them."

I hope he's right for Johnny's sake. I want to think he had nothing to do with this. In fact, I'm mentally praying he's oblivious. Yes, I've seen him do some fucked up things, but hurting young girls? I just can't wrap my head around it.

"What about the money aspect?"

"The Crew has limits."

"But they've murdered people in cold blood."

Oscar shuts his mouth, jaw tensing.

Magnum pulls into the underground parking lot, passing by security. "I'm coming up with you," Oscar says. His hand slides down my thigh.

It's just as well. I don't want to be alone tonight. I shudder to think about what happened to Natalia in her doped-up state. If she doesn't remember now, I hope she never does.

We take the elevator up to our floor. Magnum watches Oscar and me warily. He hasn't said much since this all went down, and I'd love to ask him what he thinks about it, but that will have to wait until tomorrow.

The elevator opens, and Magnum, Oscar, and I split. I wave my hand as he turns toward his door and I turn toward mine. "Goodnight."

"Night," he says.

He waits until I open my door, and Oscar and I walk in. The door shuts behind us, and I search for the light switch.

"I was thinking," Oscar says, grabbing my wrist.

"Yeah?" I finally get the light on and freeze. Johnny is standing just two feet from us. His gaze drops to where Oscar grabbed my wrist and fury erupts.

"You motherfucker!"

He rushes Oscar, the force of his attack breaking our connection. He pushes Oscar up against the door, pummeling his fist into his face. It all happens so quickly I don't have time to think, let alone move.

"I'll fucking kill you!"

His words rattle me. "Johnny, Johnny!"

Oscar's gaze meets mine. He doesn't fight back, but there's a steeliness in his gaze. Johnny cracks him in the nose and blood spurts from it, running down his lips. His eye is already swollen. Johnny pulls him off the door and pushes him to the ground.

"Johnny," I say, moving forward, grabbing his hand as he kicks Oscar in the ribs. "What are you doing? Stop!"

Johnny turns his bloodthirsty gaze toward me. "I came home early to be with you." He kicks Oscar again, and Oscar groans. My heart splinters down the center. Fissures crack all the way through. "And I find you with him!"

"We just came back from the after party," I say, trying to calm him down. "I didn't know you were coming home, or I would've skipped it."

He brushes a bloody hand over his lips. "What's he doing in your apartment? Where's Magnum?"

"Johnny," I say, trying to win back his full attention. He keeps looking back at Oscar who's writhing on the floor in pain. I pretend he's not there, so I don't give myself away, but inside, I'm breaking. "Hey," I say, once his ice chip eyes meet mine. I grab his cheeks. "Nothing's going on here."

"He touched you."

"I'm sorry," Oscar chokes out. A pool of blood from his nose and mouth forms around him on the floor. He's fucked up. Damnit! "It wasn't meant as anything," he sputters.

"She's mine," Johnny growls.

"I know, I know," Oscar says again. "I was just watching out for her like you asked me to."

"That's why she has Magnum here. Magnum in the tower. You at school. Do you need another fucking reminder, Drego? To think we fucking saved your sorry ass."

Oscar pulls himself up to a sitting position, clutching his side. He's pale, a hell of a lot paler than his darker skin ever is. Hell, he's practically my shade of white. "I meant no disrespect, Rocket."

"Apologize to her that your meaty fucking paws ever touched her."

"I'm sorry," Oscar says, eyes glued to the floor.

Johnny gets down to eye level with him. "To her fucking face, Drego!"

Oscar meets my eyes. I bite the inside of my cheek to keep from making a reaction. "I'm sorry I touched you, Kyla," Oscar says. The light recedes from his eyes, shadows replacing every last dark corner. "It won't happen again."

I swallow and nod, then look at Johnny to see if that's going to be enough for him. I hope to God it is because Oscar can't take another kick. He probably already has broken ribs, and his last fucking football game is this weekend. My eyes well with tears, but I hold them back. This all just got so fucked up.

Johnny stomps toward the door, whipping it open. I can't even meet Oscar's eyes. Not that I have that much time anyway because Johnny comes back within thirty seconds, Magnum in tow. "Now, I fucking said no one else in her room but me. How the fuck did Drego make it past you?"

Magnum stands tall. "They were discussing school. It didn't pose a threat to me."

"I said *no one* else, and I fucking meant it."

"It won't happen again," Magnum says simply.

He doesn't look at Oscar nor I, but tension wafts off him. The guard I got in trouble last time was severely punished. If something happens to Magnum on top of Oscar getting his ass kicked, I don't know what I'll do.

We pushed the boundaries, that much is true. Now we're suffering the consequences.

"Get Drego out of my sight before I fucking drop him."

I hiss in a breath, but Mag walking toward Oscar covers it up. If the Crew drops Oscar, he'll be fucked again. He'll be in so much trouble. He'll have to fucking leave. He'll have to run so far away they won't ever find him.

Magnum helps Oscar to his feet who hisses in a breath as he attempts to stand tall. He hobbles out of the room and as soon as they're clear, Johnny slams the door shut. He turns devil-filled eyes on me. A whole tidal wave of apprehension slams into me. He's got that look in his eye that reminds me of the Johnny before. I try to keep a level head, but I also set my jaw. He's not going to do the same thing to me that he did to Oscar. No fucking way. I already feel like shit that I couldn't intervene on Oscar's behalf, but if he thinks he's going to give me a beating while I take it like Oscar, he's got another thing coming.

I step back as he approaches me, and Johnny growls. "Don't run from me."

"You look mad," I say, throwing out the obvious.

His face morphs briefly, enough for me to see the guy underneath I hope will come out permanently. "I'm not going to fucking hurt you."

"Could've fooled me," I say dryly.

Johnny's chin sets. "That's not fair. Everyone knows the rules. Oscar broke them."

"We were just talking," I say. In a way, I hope I can get Johnny to come around to the idea that I can have friends. Or more, actually. That would be ideal. At this stage, I don't want to give any of them up. Brawler and Oscar have a truce already. Johnny is practically a caveman with his territory, but — Maybe it doesn't matter. "Actually, we had something we wanted to discuss with you until you went off the deep end."

"Went off the deep end?" Johnny quirks a brow at me. He grabs my wrist and pulls me to him. "I think I've made it abundantly clear that I'll do all that and more for you, Kyla. I know you don't want me to claim you, but you're too innocent around these vultures here in the Heights. I have to claim you, and I have to show them who's boss, so they can't get to you."

I wiggle out of his hold. He'd stuck up for me before with the guy at the racetrack. I hadn't minded that so much because I didn't know that guy, but this is Oscar. *My* fucking Oscar. "Oscar's a good guy," I say. "You know that. That's why you trust me with him. I'm already isolated so much."

"You like him?" Johnny's voice is a cross between a threat and disbelief.

"As a friend," I say. "Is that so bad?"

"You can have girl friends," he says, his tone broking no further argument.

But that's not me. "This jealous, possessive routine is getting old," I tell him, pushing my luck. I'm hoping to show him that this is all so stupid, but I guess to do that, I have to show him that he's the only one I want. It's a must if I want to save Oscar or Brawler, or hell, even Magnum. Anyone else and I could give two shits about. Johnny opens his mouth to say something, but I place my hand there. Then I take his hand and pull him to the couch. I push him until he's sitting, then I straddle his legs, placing my arms around his neck. "Wasn't it me that was begging you to fuck me the other day?" I pin his hands above his head. "It was me panting for it. Taut and ready. Do you think I give a fuck about Oscar?"

God forgive me for this lie, but it's necessary right now.

Johnny tries to free his hands, but I hold on tighter. "Nuh-uh. You're a naughty boy."

"How's that?" he asks, voice cracking.

"You come home after being gone for days, and instead of just wrapping me up, placing your sexy as fuck lips on me, you decide you want to get in a fistfight."

I drag my finger over his lips.

"A one-sided fistfight, I might add," I say, reminding him that Oscar didn't even fight back. He took it like the good little soldier boy he's supposed to be. I lean over to brush my chest against his. I'm trying to work on him, but that doesn't mean I'm also not working myself up too. They're called hormones, and they peak when Johnny's around. There's nothing I can do to stop it.

"Did that turn you on?" he breathes.

I shake my head, and he pouts. "What would've turned me on is if you'd picked me up, carried me into the room, and showed me how much you missed me."

"I did miss you," he says, finally freeing one hand despite my attempts to try to keep it locked up. He brings it to my hip, splaying it over the bare skin between my halter and leather pants. "I hurried home because I missed you. I've been waiting."

"And you got antsy and started making up reasons in your head for why I wasn't here," I say. "Whereas, if you had just called me, I would've made Magnum bring me straight here to see you."

"I was trying to surprise you."

"I would've liked that," I tell him, nudging his nose with

my own in a playful gesture. "But I was at Candy's helping your business like a good little girlfriend."

He traces his fingers over my stomach and then to the apex of my leather pants. He presses his thumb down there, and I moan. "I want to bury my head here," he says, tweaking my clit right through the thick fabric. "To thank you."

I nip at his lower lip. "Someday soon," I tell him. I crack a smile. "Now it's that time to back away before I get myself in trouble."

He groans as I move back but grabs my ankle as I move to the other side of the couch, stopping my retreat. "Take your clothes off, Kyla."

My heart hiccups.

"I'm so sick of jerking myself off in the shower thinking of you, I'm going to watch you play with yourself. Imagine it's me." He arches his hips up into his hand. The bulge in his pants is unmistakable. I completely downplayed the situation. I'd be giving myself more props except for the fact that I'm turned on too.

I lower the zipper at my hip and shimmy out of my stiff leather pants.

"Your panties are damp," he groans, getting restless on the couch. He puts his back against the arm, facing me, so he can get a full-on view.

"Is it that obvious?" I breathe.

He reaches his hand under his waistband and gives himself one long stroke.

I watch as he does it, and more juices flood my panties. Unclasping the back of my halter-top, I pull it off. Johnny's hips jerk up. "You're not wearing a bra. Fuck."

I sit there in my panties, watching Johnny run his hand down the length of his cock in the inside of his pants, biting my lower lip. "Can I see you?"

He fumbles with his zipper only because he's trying to take it down quickly. He shoves his pants and boxers down and his cock springs free. I hook my thumbs around my panties and move them over my knees, shucking them to the side.

"Spread those knees, baby," Johnny orders. "Pretend it's me."

I do as he says, giving him ample view as I reach my hand to my clit, swirling the pad of my finger there. I buck, biting down on my lip.

"No, no," he says. "Let out those beautiful sounds. I want to hear everything."

I do as he asks, releasing my lower lip, watching as he strokes his hard cock in movements that match mine.

"Pretend I'm licking that slick pussy."

"Ohh," I moan, thrusting my hips in the air and swirling over my clit faster. I've always needed clitoral stimulation to come. It's just my body, and from personal exploration, I know it won't take too long to throw myself overboard by concentrating here. "I want you," I tell him, locking eyes briefly before I return to watching him pleasure himself. His movements become more hurried too. "Fuck, Johnny."

"Do I feel good?" he asks, eyes laser focused on my wet folds.

My toes curl into the leather. I imagine him forgetting everything and just coming over, entering me bareback. "Yes," I breathe, throwing my head back. "Fuck, fuck, fuck. Yes, it feels good."

His breathing quickens. I peek at him. I've never watched a guy jerk off before and it's hot as fuck. Especially because it's Johnny losing all his inhibitions. Letting his guard down for once. Just living in the moment. I've no doubt he's an amazing lover.

I reach with my other hand to tweak my nipple and let out a low cry.

"You're so fucking beautiful like this."

I work myself faster. My orgasm is within reach, coming up fast. "Johnny, I'm going to," I warn him.

"Yes, come on me, baby."

It hits, and I'm suspended in air for a moment. Johnny's gaze trained on my fingers makes the heights of my pleasure that much more. I cry out. "Yes!" My fingers still swirl, urging every last wave I have in me to hit. Before mine's even finished, Johnny opens his mouth. The noises he releases are so fucking hot that my core still throbs. Rivulets of cum squirt onto his shirt.

We stare at one another. I don't know what the fuck I'm going to do with Johnny Rocket, but he's imprinted on me now. If I lose him, whether it's to him being a terrible guy or to me being a terrible person, I'll be heartbroken.

31

It's Johnny who remembers I wanted to discuss something with him. So later that night, I tell him everything we saw. Then, I back it up with the pictures and the audio of us in the car. I tell him all of us were trying to help the Crew until I think he officially feels like shit for punching Oscar. Okay, maybe only a little like shit. He's definitely not going to be knocking Oscar's door down to apologize but it's a start.

I keep Oscar's mom out of it because I can't tell him we were at the costume party, but I do tell him we were so concerned that they were fucking over the Crew that Oscar broke into Dunnegan's office to steal some files because of his loyalty to Johnny, not to Dunnegan.

"Who has the files now?"

"Oscar," I tell him. "I think. Unless he gave them to Magnum."

I watch him carefully, and it's apparent he knows nothing about what's going down at Candy's. He can barely stomach when I tell him that the girl—without using her name—was obviously drugged up.

Johnny pulls me closer as we lie together in bed. "I don't want you going anywhere near Candy's until I get this straightened out. If they did that to you, I'd burn the fucking world down."

"If your dad doesn't know about this, he's got to stop them."

Johnny pierces me with a look. "There's no way my dad knows about this."

I swallow. I saw the man fucking kill someone by shooting them pointblank in the face, but Johnny never saw that the way I did. Like his father, he believed it needed to happen. What if his dad thinks this needs to happen? What then? Will he try to talk Johnny to his side?

I just have to pray that Big Daddy K's sick ways don't go that fucking far. Not that murdering innocent people is any better.

Suffice it to say, I don't have as much confidence in his father as Johnny does.

"I can't believe you did all that for me," Johnny says.

I look away. It wasn't technically all for him. It was for the victims, and it was for myself, but yeah, as fucked up as it is, it was Johnny who I told first, not the police. But I guess that's normal behavior in the Heights even if it is far from how I grew up to think. Except, I don't have the best faith in the police myself. They couldn't take Big Daddy K down even though they knew he was the one who killed my parents, so why would they be able to take care of this? The Crew has the reach to make this right. Let's just hope they fucking do.

"I said it before. I want to be your partner, Johnny."

"You're definitely not Trophy Wife material."

"Unless that's me winning fighting trophies and bringing them home for our mantle, that's a no."

"I like having a partner," he admits. "A beautiful soldier." I know he likes that part. The shit he told me about how he grew up, whether he realizes it or not, is fucked up. Subconsciously, he needs me to be by his side, whether he'll actually admit it to himself or not.

"You know I want to be here for you," I tell him. "I really wish you wouldn't beat up my friends though."

Johnny glares at me. I probably shouldn't be bringing this up so soon, but it needs to be done. I need to open his heart to them. "What's done is done."

I turn his face back to mine after he looks away. "Just imagine not only having me, but others you can count on no matter what happens."

"That's what my dad's for," he says.

A trickle of unease climbs up my throat. I can still work

on him, but as I suspected, it's going to take a lot to get him to see the kind of person his dad truly is. If I lost Johnny to him, I'd be devastated. I want to save all of these guys, and it's possible Johnny is the one worth saving the most. I can't stand that he's basically been brainwashed his whole life into being a terrible person.

I smile at him, then lay my head on his chest. "I'm glad you're back."

He holds me to him, squeezing me to his side. "You have no idea."

My eyes dart open at the change in his voice. "Is everything alright?"

He kisses the top of my head. "Nothing for you to concern yourself with."

I want to protest, but I'm exhausted and worried and I've already pushed Johnny far enough today. His father has had twenty-plus years with him. I've only had a couple months. Turning him won't be an easy task, but I'm also not going to give up.

***

THE DINNER THAT WE WERE SUPPOSED TO HAVE ON Wednesday has been moved to today. Apparently, there are now fewer people attending since the date's been changed. When I wake in the morning, Johnny's already gone, but it's the text he sends me later that alerts me to the fact that there's still a dinner. I spend the rest of my day in my apartment, climbing up the walls and wondering what's happening over in Big Daddy K's suite. Is he telling K what the guys and I found out? Did he already know? Is he as furious as he should be? I'm almost giving myself an ulcer and wish I could be there to know what's fucking happening.

In the same token, I'm also not a fan of spending time in Big Daddy K's presence. Which, I know I'll have to get over. Keep your enemies close. I mean, that's like the moral of every gangster movie. Hundreds of people can't have gotten it wrong.

I talk to Oscar on the phone. He's beat up, and even though I tell him it's all my fault, he assures me it isn't. He tells me we all got lazy and that we need to be more careful. When I ask him about football, he shuts down. He didn't go to the hospital like he should've, and when I ask him about it, he says, "How will I pay for that, Kyla?" I told him I'd give him the money, but he doesn't want to hear it. He knows what I have that money saved up for, so I'm not surprised. In the end, it's more about getting all of us out of here than what's happening right this moment.

He ends the call by saying Johnny is on the other line, which only spikes my anxiety. He's probably calling about the file he stole from Dunnegan's office, which means they already know what we found out.

I really fucking hate being left in the dark.

An hour later, after I'm trying to drown myself in Netflix, there's a knock on the door. I practically skip to it, hoping it's someone who's going to tell me something. I yank the door open to find Magnum standing there. "Hey," I say.

"Hey." He steps forward, and I let him in. He looks the same as he always does. The same as when he picked Oscar off the floor last night. The same when he's driving me places. The only time his guard comes down is when we're completely alone. "You're attending the dinner as planned," Magnum says.

"Okay…" I thought I was, so I don't know why he had to come over to tell me.

His jaw hardens. "I'm sorry about last night. Have you heard from Oscar?"

"I talked to him," I say, realizing that maybe what he just said was his excuse to come over. "He's okay. Still in pain though."

"He'll be at the dinner, too, so—" He gives me a warning look. "—behave yourself."

I wish I could act affronted at that, but I can't. Having Oscar come into my apartment last night was fucking dumb. We should've finished talking in the car and then he could have been on his merry way instead of injured during the most important time of the year for him.

Magnum looks me up and down, but eventually concentrates on my face.

"What?"

"Did he hurt you?"

I shake my head. "He didn't touch me at all." I tug my hand through my hair, pulling at the roots. "He was just furious over Oscar."

Magnum swallows. His prominent Adam's apple gets lost in his copper scruff but then drops down again. "I don't know how long you're going to be able to keep this up," he says. I slice him a look, and he continues. "I know you care for all of them, so what are you going to do?"

I shrug. It's not as if this question hasn't plagued me, and I'm still one hundred percent riding on the hope that I can mold Johnny into a better person. Maybe even open him up to the idea of having others he can count on. Brawler and Oscar are good people, and they would be so good for Johnny. I can't like them all for nothing, right? What if it could be just us? All of us, there for each other?

I know we aren't used to getting everything we want—or at all—but this is one dream I'm going to hold close to my heart.

"I don't really have a plan," I admit, casting a wary gaze at Magnum.

"I just don't want to see any of you get hurt, and in my experience, that's where this is headed. All of you are heading down a one-way street that ends badly."

I shrug again. "This may seem like the most selfish thing to say, but I'm not giving any of them up right now. Hopefully, ever. My heart can't take more loss."

Magnum's gaze cuts to me, and for some reason, it slices right down to the bone this time. "You deserve to have everything, and anyone, you want."

My emotions stir. My body remembers the way he massaged me yesterday. The moments we've had getting to know one another. It's easy to try to shut that shit down, but I can't help the way Magnum looks at me, as if he might feel the same way too. Maybe there's a reason he's asking all these questions.

"Magnum." I take a step toward him.

He takes a step back. "You need to focus on you right now." He licks his lips, gaze dropping to take me in. "I have a feeling this dinner won't be pleasant."

"Fuck the dinner."

He shakes his head. "Not this one." He breathes out, watching my every move to make sure I don't get close again, as if he wouldn't be able to stop himself if I did. "I just needed to make sure you were okay. I'll come get you in an hour to take you up to the dinner."

He retreats, and when I say retreat, I mean it. He turns around and strides from the room without giving me a second glance. My heart is in my throat.

Fuck me. There's something in the water in the Heights. Or I'm just attracted to people who are just as fucked up as I am.

32

When Magnum comes back to get me, I'm perfectly put together. Because this has been hailed as a business meeting, I have a very reserved, knee-length dark blue dress on with my hair in waves down my back. My makeup is muted and tasteful, but with hopefully a hint of 'take me fucking seriously'. I was even able to cover the scratches up on my forehead. I don't know what's going to go down. The meeting isn't what it was going to be originally with all the big businessmen in the Crew getting together with their wives, but I'm steeling myself for anything.

"I'll be by your side the whole time," Magnum says when we're in the elevator.

I turn toward him. There's just something about the way

he's said that that reminds me of the shootout. "If you're holding something back from me—."

He shakes his head quickly. "No. For fuck's sake, no. I'm just telling you I'm there."

I eye him, but he seems sincere. If something big goes down that I wasn't let in on again, I'm going to really make them pay this time.

The elevator dings, and I step outside. There's a gentleman in the doorway of Big Daddy K's suite who's looking inside but turns when he hears the elevator. He's the same age as Johnny, or at least he looks to be.

I stand in front of the two guards, spreading my legs and holding my arms out as they check me quickly before moving me forward. I walk toward the door, but the man doesn't budge. He has dark brown hair with red tints. A dazzling smile that looks as if he's gotten it bleached within the last couple of days. "You must be Johnny's girl. I've heard so much about you." He reaches for my hand to pull it to his lips, but I yank it back. He chuckles loudly and calls back into the suite. "Your girl has spunk."

Johnny arrives, edging his way around the guy who's blocking the entrance. I eye the guy warily as Johnny holds me to him. "There you are, babe. I see you've met Jiko."

"Not really," he muses. "She pulled her hand from mine."

Johnny laughs, throwing his head back in a carefree way. I can tell he and this Jiko guy are somewhat close. "Can't say that I blame her." He throws his arm around me, and Jiko, whoever the fuck he is, moves out of our way as we walk into the room.

The elongated glass table that's always been tucked into the corner takes a more prominent place in the room today. Plates are already set around it along with a handful of guests already sitting at different places. Big Daddy K has his back to me, but my hackles immediately go up. Johnny looks at me, and I wonder if he felt me stiffen. He rubs up and down my back, trying to calm me. "It's going to be okay."

I look over to him, hoping he'll open up even more than that, but he doesn't.

A few more men arrive. Everyone seems to be congregating around the table. Jiko and Johnny talk while I'm huddled into his side. I should be listening to what they're saying, but I peek at Magnum instead. I already know before I look at him that he's staring at me. He has been since we came into the room. Doing his job, as usual. While we watch one another, someone else moves into the room. Magnum's gaze flicks over to the newcomer which is why I look, too.

I stiffen. Oscar limps inside. My heart tries to catapult from my chest. He's in better shape than yesterday because there's no blood dripping from anywhere, but his right eye is shut entirely. Nasty purple bruising mars his face, and he has his hand still wrapped protectively around his midsection. He gives me a small smile, like it doesn't bother him in the least to be back here after getting his ass beat.

Johnny notices my attention has wavered and looks over his shoulder. If he's sorry for doing that to Oscar, he doesn't show it. He calls him over. Jiko looks him up and down, a smirk coming to his face that I want to punch right the fuck off. "Damn, brother. What happened to you?"

"You know," Oscar says, joking his way through this like he's joked his way through everything. "It's the life I chose."

He's being cagey for a reason, making me wonder if Johnny's even confessed to kicking Oscar's ass. Not that he'd get in trouble for it. His father would probably praise him.

Because I don't want Johnny to get suspicious, I don't acknowledge Oscar at all, and he does the same to me. For now, we're just casual and indifferent acquaintances. Which sucks because I really want to wrap him up in a hug, tell him how sorry I am for dragging him into this mess. He would tell me he was in this shit before I even got here, but still. He wouldn't have gotten beaten up if it weren't for me. He can't try to talk his way out of that one.

Oscar was the last guest we were waiting for, so Big Daddy K calls everyone to the table. Help emerges from rooms in the back, carrying trays of steaming food. My stomach growls. I've been too nervous to eat, and it's catching up to me now.

"Sounds like your girl has an appetite," Jiko says. He's sitting across from Johnny and me.

Asshole. Doesn't he know it's impolite to comment on how much a girl eats? "His girl has a name," I bite out.

Jiko's lips curve into a cool smirk. "I assumed she did, but she wouldn't let me introduce myself properly before."

"You don't have to touch people to be introduced to them."

Johnny smirks. He places his hand on my thigh and squeezes. I don't know if he dislikes this guy or likes this guy, but either way, he's taking pleasure in watching me eviscerate him.

"Touché," Jiko says. "I'm Jiko Cardinale. And you are?" I arch a brow at him, and he bursts out laughing. "I see why you like her so much."

Johnny kisses my temple. "He's a friend, babe. You can trust him."

I'm not sure I take much stock into who Johnny thinks we can trust, but for now, I'll play along. "Kyla Samson."

"Johnny tells me you're a fighter."

"Our best one," Big Daddy K says.

A pool of dread fills my stomach. I didn't even know he'd been listening. Even though the server is now placing a bowl of hot soup in front of me and I was hungry just a moment ago, his voice did something to my appetite.

"Kyla's single-handedly making money hand over fist with our fighting ring. They can't get enough of her."

I smile politely, then widen it when I meet Big Daddy K's gaze for the first time. I have a part to play. When he's around, it's that much clearer why I'm here. Play the part. Get this done. Leave.

"As always, I'm so fortunate for the opportunity," I say, pretending to be flattered by him.

Johnny squeezes my thigh again. The smile on his face is so genuine that it almost kills me he doesn't understand that I'm saying it because I have to. Like anyone, he wants his significant other and his parent to get along, but that will never happen. Never, never, never. Over my goddamn dead body.

Or better yet. Over K's.

Other men in the room open up, talking about the underground fighting business. Big Daddy K reveals they've purchased a bigger arena for us. I don't know how they expect to keep this from the cops now, but they have their ways. If you can get away with murder, no doubt you can get away with gambling and fighting. Those businesses are definitely the lesser of the evils Big Daddy K displays on a daily basis.

The topic moves on. I find out that Jiko and his father are both in the room. They're the reason why Johnny and his father went to Chicago for the last few days. They call whatever happened "the trouble" but don't elaborate on it further.

While I'm looking around, trying to pick up on anything, I glance down the table at an empty chair pulled up to a fresh place setting. I frown at it. It doesn't seem like the kind of thing Big Daddy K would miss. No one brings it up, but the thought nags at me all through dinner and dessert. I manage to get more than a few mouthfuls down, which is good because at the end of dinner, everyone is brought out a glass of whiskey.

Big Daddy K gets to his feet. My heart kicks up, but I tell myself this is probably what happens at every meal. I have no idea because I've never been to one before, but it sounds like something a gang boss would do. Get up and say a few words just for the pleasure of hearing himself talk.

"Initially," he begins. "I wanted to hold this meeting to solidify our relationship with our Chicago friends and share my intent of moving my son up the ranks, however, a new reason has emerged that I want to toast to today." Big Daddy K swings his gaze toward me.

I gulp. *What the fuck?* He's smiling, but to me, his smile isn't happy at all. The lilt of his lips pulls at my nerves.

"I'd like to officially announce my son's plans to bring Kyla Samson into the Marx and Heights Crew family."

Johnny turns toward me. It's obvious he knew about this. He's beaming, and his steady hand on my thigh tells me he's so proud in this moment. It's hard not to let a little of that show through because the feelings I have for Johnny are genuine. As genuine as any feelings I've ever had. He cups my face, bringing me forward to press a chaste kiss to my lips. I close my eyes, savoring it.

Then I remember Oscar's in the room, and my cheeks blaze.

"I think she endeared herself pretty quickly to my son," he jokes, and the rest of the table laughs.

"It was her right hook," Johnny says, joining in on the joke.

"No, uppercut," Oscar says.

I swallow, turning toward his voice. Everyone in the room is laughing at the light-hearted banter, and according to Oscar's face, you'd think the same too, but I see the determination underneath. The hurt that's probably ripping him at the seams right now. The guy who just kicked his ass last night is now kissing his girl. But let's be clear, I think I can say with resounding authority now that women are not any guy's property. I'm my own person, and I decide who gets to have me and in what ways. I get the look in Oscar's gaze though. Betrayal.

"I couldn't be happier to have my son find someone he connects with who also cares just as much about the Crew as he does." He snaps his fingers. "Trey."

The guard who got in trouble because of me leaves the room. My stomach twists, but Johnny leans into me. "This is a good thing."

There's a glint in every man's eye around the room, which only heightens my fears.

Out from a side door, Trey pushes Dunnegan into the room.

I squelch the gasp that threatens to burst from my lips. If I thought Oscar was worse for wear, I was wrong. Dunnegan's lip is split. He can barely open either eye, and there isn't a spot on his face that isn't marred by a bruise. His shirt is caked in dried blood, like they only managed to wipe his face off before bringing him in here.

"Sit," K orders.

The seat I knew was there for a reason is dragged out and Dunnegan is forced down into it. His hands are bound at his front, but it doesn't look like he has much fight in him, anyway.

Big Daddy K beams. "For those of you who don't know, this is Joe Dunnegan. He runs my strip club-slash-nightclub. Yesterday, our dear Kyla was there and came back to alert us about something she found."

The men in the room glance at me like I'm on their side. My stomach wants to expel. The delight in their eyes coats my stomach in acid.

"I have to be honest," K says, moving around the room to stand behind Dunnegan. "When I first heard her version of events, I immediately dismissed them, but Johnny was right in sticking up for his chosen. Turns out, we have a no-good, degenerate thief in our mix." Big Daddy throws Dunnegan's head forward. The strip club owner doesn't have enough strength to stop himself, so his head crashes against the table in front of him. The plate and silverware settings shake, and Dunnegan emits a low moan.

I chance a glance at Oscar, but he's not looking at me right now. His eyes are glued in Dunnegan's direction. Big Daddy K said thief. He must've been skimming money away from the Crew.

"I don't want to turn your stomach with the particulars," Big Daddy K says, "But suffice it to say that the Heights Crew will not fucking allow anyone to steal our money or threaten the innocent in the Heights. Is that clear?"

Everyone around the room audibly gives a positive response to that. I get why Big Daddy K does everything with witnesses now. It's a way of pissing on his territory. These guys will tell others what happened here, and then everyone will be so fucking scared of the Crew that they won't dare cross them.

"It wasn't me," Dunnegan finally gurgles out. His voice seems to wake him up that much more. "I told you I had nothing to do with it. I would never do that to you. It was Gregory."

"And as soon as I can find Gregory, he's as dead as you."

Dunnegan looks up to meet my gaze. I try to be strong, stay here and look at him like I'm glad I sentenced this guy to death, but I also know what death can do to people. Dunnegan shared with me that he has a wife. What if it was just Gregory? Gregory was the one we saw in the room with Oscar's mom.

"What did I tell you earlier?" Big Daddy K asks.

The guy breathes in and coughs. Blood spittle dots the

plates in front of him. "You told me there are no second chances."

"And?" Big Daddy K goads.

"And that even if I didn't do it, it was my job to keep tabs on my people."

"Exactly."

Big Daddy K pulls a gun out of the back of his pants. He holds it to Dunnegan's temple. He leaves enough time so Dunnegan understands what's about to happen before he pulls the trigger.

My ears ring. I make myself watch. Bits of flesh and blood spatter upward. Smoke curls around the barrel as Dunnegan falls head first into the table again. Dead eyes stare nowhere as the hole in his head leaks blood onto the table. The river of blood turns the white tablecloth a deep crimson and spreads outward.

Big Daddy K turns on his heel and returns to his drink. He holds it in the air. "You did a good thing for us, Kyla, and I won't forget it."

Vomit lurches up my throat. In that moment, I can't decide if I hate myself or loathe myself. Maybe Johnny sees it because he makes me look away from the gruesome scene and into his icy blue eyes. "You just saved a bunch of girls."

God, I fucking hope so. I hold on to that thought. I hold on to it so tightly along with the remaining shreds of my humanity.

33

Over the next few days, the Crew unravels what's been going on at Candy's while simultaneously trying to find Gregory. It turns out Dunnegan was, in essence, a figurehead. All he could do was talk a big game, but Gregory pulled the strings when it came to Candy's. That's not to say Dunnegan didn't know about it. As soon as word gets around that Big Daddy K took out Dunnegan, women come out, mainly prostitutes and druggies, wanting an audience with K so they can tell him the depraved shit they went through at the hands of both Gregory and Dunnegan.

I don't know what the women are hoping to accomplish, other than getting ten minutes in Big Daddy K's presence and an apology, but that's all they'll get.

Johnny has me on lockdown again. I can't say I blame

him this time. He doesn't want me to go anywhere until Gregory is found. Word spreads, and Big Daddy K makes it a big deal that I was the one who unraveled the shit that went down at Candy's. Everyone in the Heights has a new respect for me. Roses are sent to me daily from people who are just names on a card. Some of them thank me for saving their young girls, and I find some pride in that. I don't know about the other stuff though. That's two murders I've witnessed in the span of about a month. Two more murders than I've ever wanted to witness. It's hard to take solace in the kind words when all I see is Dunnegan's life draining from his face, witnessing the moment it went dark for him.

The only thing I'm allowed out of my apartment for is fights. Johnny even brings Jax and Finn to my place to train. Brawler and Oscar are allowed as well, and I'd like to think it's because of the conversations I keep having with Johnny about needing and wanting friends. He even stays sometimes. Those moments are ten times more tense than my usual training days, but I enjoy them, hoping that the spark of the idea is in his head. The more people around you that you can count on, the better life is.

He gets that because of the Crew, but I'm talking about the *right* kind of people.

Jax and Finn talk strategy in the background. It's T minus two hours before I have a fight at the new underground fights' location. We're getting in some last-minute training as tonight I'll fight my first male in the ring. Well, official ring. They wanted the first fight card to be exciting, introducing everyone to the new digs, hoping they'll spend money like crazy. According to Brawler, they had to hire more people. He tells me he gave Natalia a job, and I'm over the moon. Brawler will make sure nothing shady goes down there. Plus, he'll watch over her like a hawk. She has no idea the amount of heart she has on her side now.

Finn claps me in the upper arms. "You good?"

"Fucking perfect," I reply.

He and Jax gather their stuff. They're going to meet us at The Ring. Apt name for what it is, but like most of the Crew's businesses, it has a front. A sports bar will be on the top story, gathering the legal crowd. However, if you gain entrance into a side door, that's where the real Ring opens up. They've kept me from looking at it, and I can't lie and say I'm not excited to see how it turned out. There's supposed to be legit locker rooms this time around, and I have my own personal ready room.

"See you soon," Jax says.

I nod at him, and the two brothers leave. Johnny and Brawler are already at the venue, which leaves me with Oscar and Magnum. Oscar played in his final game as Rawley Heights quarterback, but it wasn't pretty. Not that I was permitted to leave the tower to see it, but Oscar told me every last detail, right to the point where he had to pull himself out of the game because of a nasty tackle that injured his ribs even more. Apparently, he has an old injury there that Johnny made worse.

I'll never forgive myself for taking that game away from him.

"Ready?" Magnum asks.

I blow out a breath, zipping up my thin sweatshirt and grabbing my bag with my fight clothes in it. Oscar takes it from me. His hands linger on mine before he finally takes the bag away. His face is mostly healed except for some prominent yellow bruising around his eye sockets. His ribs are still injured though. The game he played in didn't help any, but the more he stays away from violence, the quicker he'll heal.

We take the elevator to the basement parking, and Magnum and I get in the car. Oscar takes his motorcycle because even though Johnny is getting better about having others around me, he still isn't keen on me being alone with any of them.

Magnum keeps the partition open. "Nervous?" he asks as soon as we roll past security.

"Hell yes," I groan. It's not really about the fight, it's about all the hype surrounding it. It'll be my biggest fight yet with the biggest stage. All I want to do is give the crowd the fight they want. At the same time, I can't forget that my place in the Crew hinges on the fact that I need to keep showing them I'm useful. I'm useful in this. I'm useful in bringing them intel now, too. I can't step a toe out of line.

Johnny wouldn't care, but his father would.

"I bet." Magnum smiles at me in the mirror, but then the light dies from his eyes. "The fuck?"

He's glaring past me out the rearview window, so I turn, expecting to find Oscar on his bike following us. Instead, there's a nondescript black car on our ass, much like the one we're riding in now. The car hits us from behind, and we lurch forward.

"Fuck," Magnum growls. "Hold on."

He speeds up, and I grab the door. I hadn't put my seatbelt on, so my knuckles turn white fighting to hold steady as Magnum accelerates.

"Move, move!" he yells. In front of us, cars crowd an intersection, but the tires screech beneath us as he maneuvers around them. He yanks out his cell phone. "We're being followed. Corner of—"

We're hit from behind again. I slide across the seat and fall into the area reserved usually for feet.

"Corner of ninth and Hemlock!" Magnum yells. The screech of other tires underlie Magnum stringing curses together. "Brace," he yells.

I barely have time to move before I'm thrown into the seats ahead of me. My head whips to the side and then back until we come to a startling halt among the scream of metal against metal.

I blink. It takes a moment for my vision to clear. My

body is sore. My neck hurts like a bitch. I groan. "Fuck, fuck," I seethe. "Magnum?"

No answer.

I try to pull myself onto the seat, but every time I move, my body protests with sharp, excruciating pain. My side, my neck.

The door behind me opens.

Despite my body resisting, I try to move, but rough hands grab my shoulders and heave me backwards. I want to fight back, but my arm might be broken because it doesn't react the way I want it to, and the pulsing pain in my neck is no fucking joke.

"Magnum!"

A groan sounds from inside the car as I'm being hauled away.

No way. No fucking way. I can't believe this is happening. Johnny warned that people could come for me, but I thought he was being paranoid. At the same time, I'm wondering who this is. Is it Fonz's men, finally enacting their revenge? Or is it Gregory?

Why do I have so many enemies now? Oh right, because I came to the Heights.

"Get her in the car," a voice says.

"Magnum!" I call out again. I have no idea if I'm even yelling that loud. It sounds like it to my own ears, but there's a whooshing there, too.

Shots ring out, and I fall to the pavement.

"Fuck, I've been hit."

A body falls behind me. I try to get up, to move back toward the car. I end up dragging myself with my hands. Magnum comes out from around our car that's sandwiched between two others, a gun outstretched in his hands. He looks murderous. Blood trickles into his eyes, and he pulls the trigger again. The look on his face sheer fury. Shots ring out over my head, the unmistakable almost whistling sound as they pass just over me. He pulls the trigger several more times before a car screeches away behind me.

He spins in a circle, casing the area. When he turns back to me, he lowers the gun, running up beside me. "I'm here, I'm here," he says. "Lay back. They'll be here."

Sirens surround us, and I close my eyes as the pain surges.

Magnum gets to his feet. His voice splits the air. "Who are you?" I don't hear a response, but then the guy groans long and hard. "Who the fuck do you work for? If you tell me, I'll spare your life, but talk soon because I have zero fucking patience." The gun clicks, and I know Magnum's ready to shoot again.

"Gregory. Gregory!" the guy chokes out. "Fuck. You shot me."

"What do you want her for?"

He breathes in through his teeth. "Payback."

I try to tilt my head back, but I can't. I still get a good

view of Magnum pulling his foot back to kick the guy in the ribs though.

The sirens get louder. Magnum tucks his gun in the back of his pants. "Someone must've called the accident in. They're coming, Kyla."

I try to stay as still as a statue as I look into Magnum's gaze. Terror stares back at me. I make my fingers move, and he slips his hand into mine.

"I got you."

Magnum looks up briefly. Tires come to a screeching stop somewhere near us. "Get down on the ground!" a voice yells.

Magnum lets my hand go.

"Show me your hands!"

A spotlight washes out Magnum's face. When I look up, a helicopter hovers over us. Police continue to bark orders out at Magnum, and he follows their every command. He's on the ground, stomach down, face turned toward me. Feet impede my view and then someone kneels beside me. "I've got an injury here," a female voice shouts.

More people crowd me. Somewhere far away, I'm pretty sure I hear Johnny yelling and then more police yelling. "What's going on?" I ask, my body starting to shake uncontrollably.

The woman gets in my face. "You're my only concern. Hold still. Relax."

They get a board and move me onto it. It's stiff and

uncomfortable. They put a brace on my neck, and I whimper as pain slices down my spine.

"I know it hurts. We're going to get you in the ambulance, and I'll be giving you something to take the edge off, okay?"

"Kyla!" a dark voice yells. The whooshing in my ear isn't helping my hearing, but I think it's Johnny. Now that the brace is on my neck, there's no way I can look though. All I can do is stare straight up at the night sky.

"Christ," the lady mutters as they load me into the ambulance. Lights flash off of street signs and houses. "What the fuck is going on?"

"Gang shit," the other paramedic says.

The girl leers down at me, and that's the last thing I remember.

34

I'm in and out of consciousness. I don't know how long I was like that, but I've been fully conscious for a couple of days now, being fed pain medicine to keep the surging pain at bay. My arm's broken, so I'm in a cast, and I haven't been able to take my neck brace off, but the other injuries are subsiding quickly.

Detective Reynolds has been hiding out outside my room. He hasn't come in yet, but it's only a matter of time. I've asked the hospital personnel if anyone's tried to visit me, but they won't say. They also won't let me use the phone or answer any of my other questions about what happened to the guy I was with. Or about the guy on the bike who'd been following us. I'm almost positive now that I heard Johnny at the scene when I was being carted away, but he hasn't shown up yet, and that must mean one thing. He can't. He would be here if he could. They all would.

A nurse comes in to check my vitals. Detective Reynolds is outside again. His boisterous drivel wafts into the room, making me leery. "Are they ever going to let him in?" I ask the nurse as she puts the blood pressure cuff away.

She smiles at me. "I think they're talking about that now." She leans over. "I have a message for you," she whispers. Her body is taut, and I'm instantly on alert. "From Rocket."

I relax, but she doesn't. Someone put some real fear into her to deliver this. "What is it?" I ask, looking up at her.

"He says not to say anything, and that he'll take care of it."

When she returns to a standing position, she doesn't meet my eyes.

Heavy footsteps enter the room at last. The anticipation of having to talk to the detective did worse things to me than just getting it done and over with. Of course, I wouldn't say anything. I wondered why Johnny even bothered with the message.

The detective smiles at the young nurse as she leaves and then he leans against the wall at the foot of my bed. "We keep finding each other."

"More like you keep finding me," I say. "Can detectives also be stalkers?"

"If they have to be."

"Creepy," I mutter, shifting on the bed. I haven't been able to find many comfortable positions to lay in. They say my neck will heal, but I might have to go through a bit of therapy. The brace I'm still wearing is just so I don't do any further damage to it.

"You ready to talk to me now?"

"About?" I ask coyly.

He smiles back, but he's a lot less humorous than he has been. "Who made you and Jacob Cotton crash?"

"Jacob Cotton?"

Detective Reynolds folds his arms over his chest. "You know him as Magnum, I presume."

Huh. It's odd to unravel another layer. "Is he okay?"

"Who made you crash?"

I let out a huff. "I have no idea."

Detective Reynolds clucks his tongue. "He's fine. See? We can have a conversation about this."

I want to haul off and punch him, but my fucking hand is broken. I grit my teeth. I'm so pissed. I should've worn a fucking seatbelt. I don't know what the fuck I was thinking. Tears sting the corner of my eyes. My hand will heal, but I won't be able to fight for a while.

"How did the guy on the scene get shot?"

"Ask him."

Reynolds smiles, but there's no amusement there. He runs a hand through his thick hair. "I don't think you under-stand the gravity of the situation you're in, Ms. Samson."

I dart my eyes to my surroundings. "I think I do."

He shakes his head and an ominous feeling starts in my toes. "No, unfortunately, you don't. Let me enlighten you. Your fingerprints showed up on a weapon used to murder a young girl. How do you suppose that happened?"

The bed may as well have fallen out from underneath me. "What?"

"She was just a teenager. On her way home from school." He pulls out a picture from the file he's holding and turns it toward me. It's a school photo of a young black girl who couldn't be more than fourteen. "Now I know you've bitten off more than you can chew with the Heights Crew. I tried to warn you," he says. "Now you've gone and ruined your life."

I'm aching at the seams to tell him I didn't kill this girl. It's threatening to burst out of me, but I press my lips together and close my eyes. This must have been the reason for Johnny's message. *Don't say anything. He'll take care of it.*

"Not talking to me anymore?"

I keep my eyes closed.

He moves around the room, and when he talks again, I almost jump because he's right beside me. "It's sad what happens when young girls like you get involved with the type of men who are in these gangs. I tried to help you."

The picture of the young girl won't leave my head, and a single tear runs down my cheek. No, of course I didn't kill her, but I think I know what happened to the gun that was in my room now. And yes, my fingerprints were all over it.

The detective sighs. "When you're released from the hospital, you'll be booked into Rawley Police station for first degree murder of a child. I hope you contemplate on that, Ms. Samson."

His footsteps lead him away from the room, and when the door clicks shut behind him, my heart opens up for the first time in a long time. All the grief I've been holding back. All the stress and pressure, all the fucking pain I've had to endure comes out in a flood of emotions that wrack my body with sobs. The expression of my pain hurts, but it would hurt even worse to keep it inside. To hold it back.

I came to the Heights to make my life better, not worse, and now I may have just ruined mine. For wanting something more. Hell, even just wanting the life I should have had.

My heart splinters open when I realize that little girl died because of me. Because someone wanted to frame me for this. To make the Heights Crew pay.

Everywhere I look, innocent people are getting hurt, and I'm at the center.

This wasn't what this was supposed to be at all.

And now if I have any chance of getting out of this, I have to rely on Big Daddy K. The one who gets around the police all the time. The person I hate most in the world.

Isn't life ironic?

E. M. Moore is a USA Today Bestselling author of Contemporary and Paranormal Romance. She's drawn to write within the teen and college-aged years where her characters get knocked on their asses, torn inside out, and put back together again by their first loves. Whether it's in a fantastical setting where human guards protect the creatures of the night or a realistic high school backdrop where social cliques rule the halls, the emotions are the same. Dark. Twisty. Angsty. Raw.

When Erin's not writing, you can find her dreaming up vacations for her family, watching murder mystery shows, or dancing in her kitchen while she pretends to cook.